THE NEXT GENERATION

STAR TREK:
THE NEXT GENERATION NOVELS

0: ENCOUNTER AT FARPOINT

1: GHOST SHIP

2: THE PEACEKEEPERS

3: THE CHILDREN OF HAMLIN

4: SURVIVORS

5: STRIKE ZONE

6: POWER HUNGRY

7: MASKS

8: THE CAPTAINS' HONOUR

9: A CALL TO DARKNESS

10: A ROCK AND A HARD PLACE

11: GULLIVER'S FUGITIVES

12: DOOMSDAY WORLD

13: THE EYES OF THE BEHOLDERS

14: EXILES

15: FORTUNE'S LIGHT

16: CONTAMINATION

17: BOOGEYMEN

18: Q IN LAW

19: PERCHANCE TO DREAM

20: SPARTACUS

Coming soon:

21: CHAINS OF COMMAND

STAR TREK:
THE NEXT GENERATION GIANT NOVELS

METAMORPHOSIS

VENDETTA

STAR TREK®
THE NEXT GENERATION

DOOMSDAY WORLD

**CARMEN CARTER, PETER DAVID,
MICHAEL JAN FRIEDMAN &
ROBERT GREENBERGER**

TITAN BOOKS
LONDON

STAR TREK **THE NEXT GENERATION 12:**
DOOMSDAY WORLD
ISBN 1 85286 318 8

Published by
Titan Books Ltd
19 Valentine Place
London SE1 8QH

First Titan Edition July 1990
10 9 8 7 6 5 4 3

British edition by arrangement with Pocket Books, a division of Simon
and Schuster, Inc., Under Exclusive Licence from Paramount Pictures
Corporation, The Trademark Owner.

Printed and bound in Great Britain by Cox and Wyman Ltd, Reading,
Berkshire.

To the DSPSG's of Section 2. —Carmen

To all the usual suspects. —Peter

For Joan—more than ever my heart's friend.
—Michael

To Deb for being behind me all the way. And to
Katie and Robbie for the sheer joy of it all! —Bob

And to the cooks and delivery people at Mariella
Pizza, midtown New York City, our eternal thanks.
Without you this book would not have been
possible.
—The Authors

Author's Notes

This book began as a result of a party on February 18, 1988, one of Pocket Books's all-too-rare social hours for the *Star Trek* authors. The Pocket Books *Star Trek* publishing program has been in existence for over ten years now and regular readers will no doubt recognize a recurring list of authors. It made great sense to Pocket's editor, David Stern, that the authors in the New York area get together to swap stories, lives and other esoterica on a regular basis.

This particular party, if memory serves, had in attendance Michael Jan Friedman, Allan Asherman and his soon-to-be wife Arlene Lo, Carmen Carter, Margaret Wander Bonnano, and David Stern. During the course of conversation, which centered a lot on the first season of *Star Trek: The Next Generation,* David let it be known that he was then seeking help on getting the *ST:TNG* publishing program rolling a bit faster. Anything that could be done would be appreciated, he assured us in that laid-back, it's-going-to-be-okay style that has lulled many an unsuspecting author into a sense (false or otherwise) of security.

As ideas flew out, someone suggested picking up from the burgeoning sub-genre of the shared universe. These are worlds created by one or more authors and then opened up to many authors writing in the same universe, sharing characters and the like. Perhaps the best-known world is *Thieves' World,* but there are others such as *Heroes from Hell, Liavek, The Blood of Ten Chiefs* and *Wild Cards.* Many of us shared admiration for how George R.R. Martin seamlessly weaved multiple authors' works into one mosaic novel, especially in volume three of *Wild Cards.* It became obvious that the most successful shared universe of all has been, and probably always will be, *Star Trek.*

Ever since Gene Roddenberry created the series in 1964, people have been working with his dream, optimism and characters. First there were the writers for the seventy-nine television episodes, and then he let James Blish handle the first ever *Star Trek* novel. Since then, there have been scores of novels, short stories and comic books all sharing in the same world. There have been some bumps and bruises along the way, but these days most everyone likes to share the universe and keep it as tightly knit as possible. Perhaps now, we thought, was the time to come up with a novel idea that could involve a group of writers.

Though everyone nodded and walked away feeling really good about the idea, no one wrote an outline. This became increasingly obvious as winter turned to spring and spring rapidly gave way to summer. With the Mets rallying for a repeat of 1986, I decided that if no one else was going to try to write the outline, I would.

I prepared an outline and David liked it. He sent copies out to a number of the people who'd expressed interest in the shared novel and said we'd all discuss it at the first annual *Star Trek* authors' picnic. That August saw everyone gather at a park in Manhasset, New York, and this time we lost Margaret, Allan and Arlene, but gained Brad Ferguson and Howard Weinstein. David never showed up. He claimed he was sick. We think he can't be seen in sunlight.

The authors discussed the outline in depth and agreed that something usable was here and that we should all get to work on it. Michael and Bob were set on participating, but Carmen was waffling. She wasn't sure if this was something that could play to her strengths as a writer. Carmen wanted to see more.

Thus were born the semi-frequent writers' meetings. By late 1988, David had hired Kevin Ryan as an assistant editor and they hosted meetings to discuss the book outline. Based on feedback from others, I had revised the story repeatedly. Peter David had already sold Pocket one novel and had established his credentials on the *Star Trek* comic for DC Comics. He readily agreed to be the third member of the writing team (after all, at Peter's speed this would be easily a two-, maybe three-hour job).

Somewhere during all this, DC Comics reacquired the rights to *Star Trek* comics, and it was no surprise that Peter went right back to work on the *Star Trek* title while Michael accepted the challenge of producing a monthly *Next Generation* comic, concurrent with the TV series. This, of course, meant more expensive lunches and dinners to talk about *Star Trek,* which is as fine a pastime as any.

The novel, finally dubbed *Doomsday World,* continued to evolve, and Carmen found herself enjoying the give and take that happened during these meetings and agreed to be our fourth author. I also think she liked the rotating appetizer idea, which featured everything from small breads to cookies to rugelah, followed by pizzas galore.

We finally had an outline we liked and that Paramount Pictures then approved. From there, I broke the story down into thirty-eight elements and we assigned character points of view. We divided the thirty-eight sections among ourselves, swapping a few here and there for balance, and then we worked on a character bible. We also agreed that since I wrote the basic outline, Michael would get the dubious honor of melding four distinctive styles into a final polish. So, finally, by July 1989 we were ready to begin simultaneous writing.

Everyone wrote diligently (although Peter managed to squeeze in *A Rock and a Hard Place* prior to starting his section) and Mike, Carmen and I met at the 1989 World Con in Boston to compare notes. In September we had a meeting to make sure we all felt comfortable, and it was surprising how comfortable we felt about the work done to date. Most everyone was nearing the homestretch, and we liked what was happening as characters and incidents blended together with little trouble.

By mid-October all the work had been done. Nearly three hundred manuscript pages had been produced, and Kevin (for whom the K'Vin are duly named in this story) read through it and pronounced it good. He sent copies to everyone involved and we held the final pizza meeting. It was a grand affair as both Mike and Bob brought munchies, Peter brought some video entertainment and Kevin sprang for the pizzas, while Carmen brought her new kitten.

The five of us went through the book section by section, making notes and discussing complicated details like exactly which way Stephaleh's name was to be spelled. Hours later we were tired, bloated and satisfied. The book was indeed good and we were all very, very surprised that it had worked so well and so smoothly. After going through it, Michael had his notes and went home and in about two more weeks had a polish that Kevin also deemed wonderful (a.k.a. "thank God, it's here!"). Once Kevin finished editing it, the manuscript went to the copy editor and then back to us for one more go-round. And then it went off to Paramount for their blessing and then to type and galley and bound book, which should be flying off shelves even as you read this long, tedious section.

At that meeting we all declared that it was Carmen's turn to do the next story for the four of us. She hemmed and hawed a bit and said that *if* she did choose to write a framework story, she would also reserve the right to final polish. We all nodded yes. Carmen, to this day, swears that the second shared book will have to wait until you, the reader, have judged this effort.

Which leads us to the next step. Feedback. We love commentary, and over at DC Comics I have been spoiled by the monthly feedback from the general readership. We are all available in care of Pocket Books and look forward to hearing from you.

This has been a labor of love and, in my case, since conceiving this story some two years ago, it was more than that. We like what we've done and we hope you do, too. If not, blame Kevin—he's the editor.

Robert Greenberger
Long Island, NY
December 1989

Chapter One

First Officer William Riker sat in the command chair of the *Enterprise* and longed to be the captain of a Galaxy-class starship.

He had spent his childhood reading the history of space exploration and marveling at the exploits of the men and women who had saved their ships from danger or sacrificed their own lives in the attempt. Admirals might plan expeditions into uncharted space, but captains actually made the first contact with alien races and forged new alliances for a growing Federation. Captains were surrounded by an aura of adventure and Riker had never abandoned his dream of someday commanding a starship that would travel to the far-distant reaches of the galaxy.

He had never dreamed of becoming a first officer and dealing with petty-minded bureaucrats.

That was the problem with daydreams: they left out the details. Captains gained all that glory because they assigned boring, mundane duties to someone else. And just now that someone else was him.

"Commander, we are being hailed by the K'Vin embassy."

Riker jerked himself up from a slumped position. Several hours of waiting had gradually eroded his posture, but Lieutenant Worf's announcement recalled the first officer to a sense of official dignity.

"Well, it's about time. Put them through on my signal."

He drummed his fingers impatiently as he waited for certain members of the bridge crew to reassume their positions. Wesley Crusher came down a side ramp from the aft station and scrambled back into the empty Conn station. Lieutenant Solis had remained at Ops, but he arched his back in a bone-cracking stretch. Deanna Troi, who had drifted over to a refreshment dispenser, was slightly less energetic than the ensign in reclaiming her seat in the command area, but she abandoned her unfinished drink without complaint.

After a final visual sweep of the oval bridge to check that everyone was alert and professional in appearance, Riker turned his attention to the viewscreen that covered the curving forward bulkhead.

"Ready, Lieutenant Worf."

A static planetscape gave way to a live transmission from the embassy's administrative assistant. Gezor was of another race entirely from the thickset K'Vin who employed him; he was small-boned and pink-skinned with a mane of curling black hair that crowned his head and ran down his spine.

"Cool days to you and yours, Commander Riker." Despite a rasping accent, Gezor's use of the Federation language was impeccable. "Having completed the examination of your Petition for Territorial Trespass, the K'Vin embassy of Kirlos grants provisional clear-

2

ances to Lieutenant Worf and to Lieutenant Geordi La Forge."

"Provisional?" A prickle of apprehension made the first officer voice this question rather more sharply than he had intended.

"Yes," said Gezor with a lazy blink of his heavy eyelids. "It appears that the clearance form for Lieutenant Commander Data has not been completed satisfactorily. Without a full disclosure of the requested information, he cannot be permitted to enter K'Vin territory."

Assuming a genial expression that was far from sincere, Riker launched into an explanation. "As I indicated on the form, several of the line items are not applicable to Mr. Data. As an android, he does not have a biological mother or father. Nor does he—"

"And I am still waiting for transmission of his medical history," interrupted Gezor. Although delivered in an unruffled monotone, his gruff announcement effectively drowned out the rest of the first officer's words.

"As I said before," Riker's voice increased in volume, "he is an *android*. He does not *have* a medical file."

"Then Lieutenant Commander Data cannot be granted right of trespass by the K'Vin embassy. And his removal from the landing party will, of course, invalidate all related petitions. Provisional clearance for Lieutenant Worf and Lieutenant Commander La Forge is hereby denied."

Riker clenched his jaw until he could trust himself to speak. "But, Gezor, the Federation embassy on Kirlos has already approved—"

"The K'Vin are not responsible for the inadequacies of the resident Federation embassy. Therefore, if at any point the *Enterprise* landing party attempts to cross through K'Vin territory—"

Riker lunged out of the captain's chair to stand, feet astride, in the center of the command deck. He was a big man, and it was difficult for him to resist using his looming height to intimidate others. Perhaps someday he would learn how Captain Picard managed to compel respect without that physical advantage; until then, however, Riker intended to make use of any asset available to him.

"You know very well that they have to cross through K'Vin territory to reach the archaeological site! That's the whole point of their mission!"

Gezor met this statement with a reproving frown. "In that case, Commander Riker, you must fill out the appropriate forms in their entirety for proper clearance of personnel."

Riker moved a finger across his throat.

Lieutenant Worf snapped off the communications link with the embassy. Gezor's face winked away; once again the viewscreen presented an image of the day side of Kirlos, the same view that had been displayed since the ship's arrival in the solar system two days earlier. The planet's surface, unbroken by seas or oceans, was a monotone patchwork of beige and tan.

"Contact is suspended," confirmed Worf.

Taking a deep breath, Riker consciously eased the stiff cast of his shoulders.

"The K'Vin have resisted us at every step of the way in our attempt to put a landing party on Kirlos." He turned to Troi, still seated next to the empty captain's chair. "Why?"

"I'm not familiar with the Sullurh as a race," she said, puzzling over the nuances of the exchange she had just witnessed. "Yet I don't detect any real

4

hostility from Gezor. Rather, he appears to be a loyal employee of the K'Vin and one who interprets their regulations very literally." To Riker's surprise, the counselor then smiled. "If anything, I would say that he is simply bored."

"And I'm providing today's entertainment," he said tightly. "Well, enough of that."

Crossing his arms over his chest, the first officer glared belligerently at the planet Kirlos as he contemplated his next move. The portion of the planet facing them included a round, flat area that researchers had nicknamed the Valley—interesting, but not interesting enough to divert him from his pique. Then a sudden inspiration eased the tight line of his frown into a broad grin. His arms loosened and fell back down to his sides.

"Mr. Worf," Riker called out with obvious relish, "reestablish contact with the K'Vin embassy."

When Gezor reappeared on the viewscreen, his expression was bland and betrayed no reaction to the prolonged break in communications. Nevertheless, Riker prefaced his speech with a conciliatory bow.

"Gezor, there has been a regrettable confusion in the filing of the landing party's Petition for Territorial Trespass. Lieutenant Commander Data should have been included in the accessory requisition section of the petition, since he is part of the research equipment allotment. As a highly advanced technological device, he is essential to the landing party's investigation."

The administrator took his time considering this proposal, time enough for him to blink three times, then finally replied. "Yes, in that case, the appropriate information requirements would be satisfied. Under the circumstances, I will allow a second petition for personnel clearance of Lieutenant Worf and Lieutenant La Forge to be filed along with the amended

5

equipment manifest. Stand by for transmission of the instructions for that procedure."

The planet Kirlos wiped across the viewscreen, signaling an end to the connection with the K'Vin embassy.

"More forms," groaned Riker.

Wesley Crusher swiveled his Conn chair to face the first officer. "I guess this is all part of the burden of command, right, Mr. Riker?" he asked with a grin.

Riker grinned back.

"Ensign Crusher." Stepping closer, Riker clapped a hand on the young man's shoulder. "I've been neglecting your interest in the Kirlos project. How very selfish of me to stand in the way of your educational progress."

"Sir?" Wesley stirred uneasily in the Conn chair.

"This is an excellent opportunity for you to learn, in-depth, another one of the challenges of starship management." Glancing over his shoulder, Riker addressed Lieutenant Worf. "The ensign will be handling all further communications with the embassy."

"Yes, sir." The Klingon checked the flickering lights that chased across his communications board. "Still transmitting. The amount of incoming data appears to be rather large."

"Well, just let the ensign know as soon as it's all in. I'll be in a meeting with the captain, so the bridge is yours." With a final hearty slap to the ensign's shoulder, Riker strode away from the helm to the captain's ready room. Then, while waiting to be allowed through the doors, he turned back to add, "And don't skip any of the line items, Mr. Crusher. The K'Vin are very thorough."

"Yes, sir."

Ensign Crusher was no longer smiling.

* * *

The captain's desk had been cleared of all objects. All objects except for the small statue which Geordi La Forge set down very carefully in the center of the table. Each element of the piece was so perfectly balanced that the carving stayed erect without a base to steady it.

Jean-Luc Picard was jolted out of his normal reticence by its beauty. He eagerly leaned forward in his chair for a closer inspection.

The figurine was of a member of an unfamiliar humanoid race. Its compact, muscled body had been caught in motion, leaping up from a crouch. The skirts of its tunic and its long bushy tail floated in air. Picard had assumed the subject was a dancer until he saw the bared teeth set in a snarl. Its eyes were closed to narrow slits, and it had the cold look of a predator about to kill its prey.

The predominant color of the statue was a rich orange, but it was shot through with delicate veins of green and white. The surface was so highly polished that it gleamed even in the subdued light of the ready room.

"What is it made of?"

"A rare form of marble called arizite," said Geordi.

"Yes, I've heard of it. But I've never seen it before." The captain reached out to touch the statue, then caught himself. "May I?"

"Be my guest," said La Forge with an expansive wave. "When I told Professor Coleridge you were interested in archaeology, she sent it up especially for you to inspect."

Riker strode through the doors of the office in time to hear the engineer's last comment. "Yes, but she left the paperwork for the transfer to me."

Picard was too absorbed in examining the statue to spare any attention to Riker's entrance. The marble

7

weighed heavily in his palm and was cool to the touch. It was also flawless. No nick or scratch marred its surface.

"You say the ruins are full of such remains of the Ariantu culture?"

"Oh, yes. And evidently this is just one of the minor pieces." Geordi stepped aside to let Riker view the object in the captain's hands. "According to Nassa . . . I mean Professor Coleridge, the gamma level of Kirlos was evacuated in a very short period of time, though we are not sure why. The result is that the resident Ariantu abandoned almost all of their possessions. In time, the excavation team should be able to re-create an incredibly detailed portrait of their day-to-day life."

"Ah!" sighed Picard with an envious gleam in his eyes. "I would very much like the opportunity to—"

"Don't even think it, Captain," cut in Riker. "Under no circumstances are you to set foot on Kirlos."

Picard's head snapped up. The blank look he gave his first officer was a sure sign of his suppressed irritation. "Really, Number One. This is carrying your concern for my safety too far. You can't convince me that I would face the slightest danger on Kirlos."

"Who said anything about danger? I'm tired of filling out forms!" Riker swung one leg over the back of a chair and settled down at the desk across from the captain. "If we try to petition for the inclusion of a starship captain in the landing party, the K'Vin will want to know how many hairs there are on your head and what your mother had for breakfast the day you were born."

"Yes, I see," said Picard, with a return to his previous good humor. "Well, it was but a passing thought." However, he continued to gaze at the statue, and all that it stood for, with obvious longing. A hail

8

from the ship's intercom scarcely touched his thoughts.

"Lieutenant La Forge and Lieutenant Worf, please report to sickbay for landing party physicals."

"On my way, Doctor," said Geordi after a tap to his insignia. He and Riker exchanged commiserating looks, but the chief engineer had already passed beyond the threshold of the room before Picard realized he was leaving.

"Damn. I meant to thank him for this." Picard restored the Ariantu artifact to its place of honor on the desk, but it still held his attention. Riker rocked back in his chair, arms folded across his chest. Since he made no attempt to break the captain's concentration, the two officers shared a companionable silence.

With a sidelong glance at his first officer, Picard finally said, "You know, Number One, that I have full confidence in your choice of landing party members."

"Certainly, Captain."

"But you must admit," continued Picard with studied disinterest, "that the composition of the landing party to Kirlos is a little . . . unusual."

The first officer nodded solemnly. "Well, that's true. Usually the chief engineer stays aboard the ship."

"Granted. But in this case, Nassa Coleridge specifically requested Geordi. From what he's told me, she was a sort of mentor to him before he decided to enter Starfleet Academy, and his VISOR will be an enormous aid to their search through the ruins. And there's no question that Data is well suited for this type of scientific research." Picard failed to suppress the faint trace of a smile. "But why Worf? I thought Lieutenant Keenan was scheduled for the next planet security assignment."

"Worf volunteered." When Picard met this explanation with a raised eyebrow, Riker added, "Why wouldn't a Klingon want to beam down into the middle of disputed space?"

"Hardly disputed!" scoffed the captain. He leaned back in his chair, not quite matching Riker's level of informality but relaxing all the same. "The K'Vin and the Federation have been camped out on Kirlos for more than thirty years without exchanging a single shot. In fact, I've heard that Ambassador Stephaleh and Ambassador Gregach have a standing arrangement to play dyson every week."

"Isn't that a coincidence," said Riker without any further elaboration.

"I begin to understand." Picard shook his head in mock disapproval. "The wages of sin. Perhaps now the lieutenant will be more careful about what games he plays with the members of his security force. And the stakes involved."

Riker covered his grin by absently stroking his beard. "You can bet on it, Captain."

Dr. Beverly Crusher placed the tip of a hypo against the side of Worf's neck and listened for the telltale hiss of the injection. Almost immediately, Worf started to get up from the diagnostic table, but she hauled him back in place. It was harder to do than she'd expected. Not a reassuring discovery.

"I'll let you know when I'm done, Lieutenant Worf." The doctor calmly dialed another medication setting even though a sound like distant thunder reverberated from deep in the Klingon's chest.

Geordi waited patiently for his fellow officer. "Why all the inoculations?"

"Just a precaution," said Crusher, triggering another injection. "A large number of alien races are crowded together down in the tunnels of Kirlos.

Biofilters may keep existing strains of contaminants from reaching the settlement, but there's always a chance you could pick up a newly mutated virus. This will give you a broader base of immunity."

Then, most unfortunately, she added, "Actually, my best advice is for you both to stay well hydrated and to stay cool. According to the Federation embassy's medical records, most of the fatalities on the planet are from heat exhaustion."

"That is the death of a beast of burden!" cried out Worf, speaking for the first time since entering sickbay.

The ominous rumbling sound rose up from his chest to his throat. Crusher could feel the vibrations in her fingers when she touched the metal cylinder to his neck a third time. In a well-meaning attempt to distract him from the final injection, the doctor asked, "I thought Keenan was scheduled for this assignment."

The Klingon snarled, flashing a large white incisor from beneath a curled lip.

Crusher stepped back from her patient, nearly dropping the empty hypo to the floor of sickbay, but she still managed to say with some dignity, "You can go now, Lieutenant."

Chief O'Brien clung to the controls of the transporter with the white-knuckled desperation of a drowning man. Like most transporter operators who had grown accustomed to the job, he liked a steady ebb and flow of traffic through his domain. There was a certain vulnerability to his position, tied as he was to a duty post in a small room, that made him wary of prolonged interactions with the crew. On this particular occasion, however, Lieutenant Commander Data had arrived well in advance of the other members of the landing party, and he displayed no inclination to wait for his companions in silence.

"And what is even more interesting," continued Data, warming to the subject he had introduced soon after his entrance to the transporter room, "is that when these magnetic and rotational characteristics are considered in the light of recent spectrographic examinations of the substratum formations, the congruences indicate that Kirlos is an artificially constructed planet. Unfortunately, this still does not explain . . ."

Data halted his narrative in midstream. There was something very familiar about the look in Chief O'Brien's eyes. Captain Picard often developed a similar expression just prior to requesting that Data cease speaking.

"Do you perhaps wish to say something at this point?" asked the android.

O'Brien started, as if waking from a dazed sleep. "No, *sir,*" he said, with what Data considered a rather odd emphasis on the disparity in their rank. "I can't think of anything that would be appropriate to say at this time."

Data was still puzzling over the somewhat ambiguous wording of this response when the doors to the transporter room hissed apart.

"I envy you, Data," said Geordi as he and Worf walked inside. "You don't need to stop by sickbay before going on an away mission."

"That is correct," acknowledged Data, turning his attention away from O'Brien's comment with some reluctance. "However, I have undergone minor adjustments to my thermostatic controls. According to my research on Kirlos, even in the tunnels we will be exposed to daytime temperatures of . . ."

He stopped talking. His head swung back and forth as he tracked Geordi's waving hand. "What is the significance of that gesture?"

"It means 'not now,' Data." Geordi broke into a friendly grin. "Don't worry. I'll explain later."

"Ah. Thank you." Satisfied with this promise of future enlightenment, Data followed Worf.

"Transporter coordinates laid in," announced O'Brien as he scanned the control panel readings. His fingers tapped out the first steps of the molecular transfer process. "By the way, I thought Keenan was scheduled for this assignment."

The small chamber seemed to amplify Worf's growl. He glared at O'Brien as Geordi took his place on the platform.

The transporter chief triggered the beam-down process. "Good-bye, gentlemen."

The landing party faded away in a glittering cloud of yellow light. Then, and only then, did O'Brien smile.

Chapter Two

"IT'S YOUR MOVE, GREGACH," Stephaleh said softly. She always sai things softly; it was her way, and had been for all of her fifty-three years. A soft voice— backed by a will of iron.

It had been a full life for Stephaleh, one that was quietly winding down with this assignment as ambassador to Kirlos. Her time on the man-made world passed pleasantly these days, highlighted by evenings like this one, spent playing games of skill with her K'Vin counterpart, the gruff Ambassador Gregach.

She looked across the table at her opponent. Gregach sat slumped in his seat, both hands gripping the armrests.

He was typical of the K'Vin, a large, slow-moving people with thick, gray skin. Of course, Gregach was a little heavier than the average K'Vin, but he was also leading a rather sedentary life. His extra weight made his small green eyes appear even smaller than they actually were.

Stephaleh had always been fascinated by the pair of small tusks that jutted out from Gregach's jawbones —also typical of his race, a reminder of the K'Vin's predatory nature, a caution that they were a people to be reckoned with.

Nearly a hundred years ago, the K'Vin had joined the United Federation of Planets. But it had never been a match made in heaven. The K'Vin were too fierce, with too great an appetite for interfering in the affairs of other worlds—including those protected by the Prime Directive.

Unable to see eye to eye with the rest of the Federation, the K'Vin had severed all official ties with that august body and gone their own way. But they had left one bridge unburned—the embassy they maintained on the divided world of Kirlos.

"Gregach?"

"Mm?"

"It's your turn, Ambassador. Again."

"So it is."

He always brooded over the game of dyson, and she had often suggested that they strike it from their evenings together. But he always waved away the suggestion and insisted that they play.

Gregach shook his head. It wasn't necessarily a difficult game, he told himself, just one that required a great deal of thought. All he had to do was pick a length of tubing, straight or curved, from the box before him and place it in his construct, which was distinguished by his usual deep purple, in contrast to Stephaleh's pale yellow. The idea was to complete a sphere before one's adversary. However, each player was allowed to usurp the other's construct, at which time the tubing would shift in hue to that of its new owner.

15

Taking a nearly finished sphere away from Stephaleh, he snorted in triumph. However, as he watched, she countered with a maneuver that spoiled his other sphere. Seeing his limited possibilities, he sulked as he perused the playing area in a new and dimmer light. It was becoming obvious that she was going to win . . . again.

Gregach looked at Stephaleh and wondered what it was about the Andorian that made him feel so comfortable with her—comfortable enough to suffer defeat after defeat in this game and still maintain his good humor. Certainly it was not a rapport based on similarities.

While his race, the K'Vin, were short and heavyset, Stephaleh was an Andorian—therefore tall and graceful. Even in her advanced years, Stephaleh seemed perfectly poised and able to manage even the most strenuous of gymnastic moves while her lined light-blue visage showed few wrinkles.

On the other hand, age *was* beginning to exercise its claim to her. Her antennae had begun to droop the slightest bit, and the white hair atop her head was thinning somewhat, although it took someone who knew her well to notice the change.

When she had arrived on Kirlos some three years ago, Stephaleh had made the first overture by inviting Gregach for a meal. To his surprise, she had researched his people and served an excellent dinner featuring grilled inlati, a spicy fish native to the K'Vin homeworld. That very night, she had suggested they play a game. One game had become another, and then another. After three years, their games had provided countless hours of entertainment for them both.

Gregach didn't fool himself. She was here for her last assignment before retirement—or death—and didn't want trouble. Winning him over quickly was a masterful stroke and one he didn't mind a bit. His own career might have been stalled by this posting, but he was determined to enjoy it as best he could.

Besides, Stephaleh was far more stimulating company than the fellow soldiers he had brought with him—disappointed men, for the most part, who merely wanted to drink each night into oblivion. If he'd had to depend on them for interesting conversation or witty jokes, his existence on Kirlos would have been a good deal grimmer.

Tonight it was his turn to dine at the Federation embassy. It was a taller building than the one that housed the K'Vin embassy—fine for his Andorian friend, but Gregach preferred being low to the ground. At least the dining room was on the ground floor, and the dusk meal was always hot and ready when he arrived.

He never brought a retinue, preferring candid conversation and gossip with Stephaleh. She was an excellent hostess, always anticipating her guest's needs. She seemed to know when he was suffering from a cold or exhaustion and planned the evening accordingly.

"Gregach?"

He roused himself from his reverie. "Yes, yes, I know."

He selected a curved piece and placed it in his third construct, completing one hemisphere. It looked odd in the light, coming up from the round table they used. The edges of the construct twinkled, and the rest seemed to just absorb the illumination.

"There," he said at last.

"Thank you. I was beginning to drop off," she jested. In turn, she considered the constructs before

17

her. One, the sphere stolen from Gregach, was the most promising. It needed a completed main axis before the circle could be closed.

Removing a straight piece from her box, she studied it. It was starting to show wear from so much use, she noted. Then she placed it inside the sphere, finishing the axis.

"I will have you in one move, Ambassador," she announced with a smile.

Gregach made a sound of annoyance, low and throaty. He closed his box, conceding the game.

"No use," he said, "in prolonging the agony."

They took the spheres apart in silence, taking their time, in no hurry to bring the evening to an end. Gregach idly wondered how his predecessors had tolerated Kirlos without evenings like these.

It was a forbidding world where people lived entirely underground, among and on top of the ruins of a race long gone and still not entirely understood. A place of excessive heat—especially for a K'Vin—without any hope of a cooling breeze.

And yet, for thirty-five years now, the K'Vin had shared it with the Federation—not because it had any great value. But it was a way for both parties to keep track of each other. And perhaps keep alive the hope, among individuals on both sides, that the two powers might become allies again.

As he dismantled a partially completed construct, Gregach couldn't help but compare it to his own unfinished career. His superiors had made Kirlos sound like an important place when they'd first described it to him—but he had known better, even then. The rest of the Hegemony regarded it as a backwater, a shelf on which to place a military hero of the previous regime.

But even after years on Kirlos, he still dreamed of a

transfer to the frontier—to a place like Slurin or Lethrak, where truly important events were taking place.

"Thank you," said Stephaleh, "for approving the forms for the Federation officers and equipment."

Gregach dismissed her gratitude with a gesture. "It was nothing. My assistant attended to it." He put away the last bit of tubing. "They'll be arriving shortly, then?"

Stephaleh nodded and leaned back in her chair. Her back was tired, and the cushions didn't really help. Rather than prolong a conversation, even with a friend, Stephaleh found herself longing for a soak in a tub of scented water. "Yes, very shortly. It appears that our archaeologist knows one of them—their chief engineer."

"The one with the eyes?"

"They all have eyes, my friend. But yes, the one with the VISOR, which should aid in the work." She flexed her fingers to prevent them from cramping again, as they had during dinner.

"Imagine spending your entire life looking at everything through filters, never seeing what things really look like," he continued.

She moved in her seat, adjusting a cushion. "He sees far more than you or I do. In fact, his vision may be the most sophisticated in the galaxy. But even so, there are limitations. And I'm told the device is painful."

"My people are still leery of letting Starfleet personnel anywhere near Kirlos. It's seen as an escalation of hostilities between our peoples," he said.

They both softly laughed at the thought of hostilities here on this dry, hot world with no valuable resources.

"They are here at Professor Coleridge's request, not

19

mine," Stephaleh reminded him. "And your people have approved the visit. They will come and look at the dirt, find some artifacts that may tell us something about the Ariantu, and go away. What harm can they do?"

"Hmmph," responded Gregach. "Starfleet is merely acting on orders to check up on the K'Vin, or so my people say. *I* think the same as *you*, but their very presence has people back home up in arms. Couldn't they have come by shuttle?"

"You know the shuttlecraft have limited range, Gregach. Besides, I wouldn't mind a look at the new Galaxy-class cruiser. This is the first one in the area. Quite impressive vessels, I'm told."

"And powerful enough to lay waste to Kirlos."

"Perhaps they've come to do something about the traders you allow on your side of the world," she jested. "Really, Gregach, must you allow those Ferengi merchants stall space in the market? We both know they carry stolen merchandise—everything from Romulan ale to iridium."

"And what about the Federation allowing Rhadamanthan ships to transport bogus entertainment packages?" Gregach shot back, rising to the challenge. "My government cannot protect the rights of creative work if the Federation allows just any race to duplicate the material and sell it for hundreds of credits below our cost."

"The Federation trade commissioner has already begun investigating the Rhadamanthans and the Ferengi and the Ditelans. We're making efforts, Gregach, but I'm told the K'Vin government has not looked into a single Federation charge."

Gregach snorted and rubbed a finger over one short tusk, inspecting it for flaws. It was an unconscious action of which Gregach was never fully aware. "Now,

now, Stephaleh, let's put away the posturing. Don't look for a second victory tonight. After all, neither of us can control the actions of our duly respected governments."

Stephaleh nodded in agreement and picked up her drink. Like her people, it was tall and thin and a light shade of blue.

They were interrupted by the appearance of Zamorh, Stephaleh's aide. He came into the room in great haste and looked a little silly, huffing and puffing. Even to the Sullurh, Gregach reminded himself, this world's heat could be debilitating at times—and they had settled here long before any of the other races.

"Ambassador," said Zamorh, "word has arrived from the *Enterprise*. The officers are beaming down now." His speech was punctuated by gasps for breath.

"Thank you, Zamorh. We will greet them in the transporter chamber," said Stephaleh, rising from her chair. The movement, she told herself, would do her some good, and the change from the ordinary would be most welcome.

"Remember what we agreed to, Ambassador," Gregach said as they moved through the building.

This caused the Andorian to slow down and look at her colleague. "Of course, but I don't agree with your position, and therefore you will outline it to all of them, including the professor. She will not like it, either."

"She will live with it, as will the Federation. I personally don't care one whit what happens. But I am speaking for the K'Vin government, and their word will not be ignored."

"That is never my intention, as you well know." Stephaleh did not appreciate his constant passing of responsibility from his office to his government, but

21

she supposed most of the decisions were dictated from high enough up the chain of command that he had little choice but to accept them.

Moving down a corridor, the ambassadors and Zamorh passed the few people left working on the evening shift. The Federation embassy was rarely busy until the early hours of the morning, when people wanted to complain of the poor deals made the night before. The Sullurh led the way, conducting them past works of art Stephaleh had chosen to bring from the art museums on Andor. The pictures depicted great sieges from her planet's past. Gregach liked the fact that her race was a savage one, although somewhat less so than his own.

He pondered the number of races that had started off violently and changed over time. He could think of few that started off benevolently and reached high levels of technology. *The killer instinct,* he mused. There was much to be said for it. Filing that thought away, he walked into the transporter room, where gleaming metal coexisted with the rough-hewn walls of the original Ariantu structure.

A human technician stood behind the console awaiting the teleportation of personnel. Also present was the embassy's security chief, a human named Powell, burly and dark-haired. Stephaleh had picked him from a number of officers looking for planetside postings through Starfleet. He served her well, though he was less experienced than she would have liked.

Stephaleh looked up as her sensitive antennae detected the transporter effect before anyone else in the room noticed it. The sparkling columns manifested themselves; three shapes became distinct. To her surprise, the android named Data was a good deal more human-looking than she had imagined possible. Of course, she had heard of the remarkable machine that had been found on a distant world some twenty-eight years ago. But in person, he was quite something to marvel at.

The black-skinned man with the VISOR stepped forward first and broke into a broad, natural grin. "Hi. I'm Geordi La Forge. This is Security Chief Worf and Lieutenant Commander Data," he said, gesturing to the two behind him. Data nodded, expressionless. Worf, the dark, menacing-looking Klingon, just stared. All three moved off the platform before anyone could respond.

"I am Ambassador Stephaleh n'Ehliarch. And I would like to present Ambassador Gregach, who represents the K'Vin Hegemony." The Andorian bowed slightly from the hips while Gregach, emulating humans, reached out to shake hands—not so much in deference to another race's customs, Stephaleh knew, as to get a feel for each visitor's strength. She watched with a slight smile as he winced after shaking hands with the Klingon.

"Let me take you to a room where we can talk and get comfortable," she suggested. "Drinks?"

In the grand reception room, Zamorh went to an ornate carved cabinet and opened it, revealing a refrigeration unit. He poured out a variety of brews—juices and synthehol drinks—which he arranged artfully on a tray and offered to each guest. Data abstained, as did Worf, but Geordi helped himself to a fruit juice. Gregach chose synthehol, complaining under his breath about the lack of a decent beer on the Federation side of Kirlos. Stephaleh also had a juice and stood in the center of the room.

"I welcome you all to Kirlos, may your stay be a pleasant one," she said, holding her glass high. The others returned her salute and sipped their drinks.

With the one formality out of the way, she sat in a large chair stuffed with cushions. Zamorh had placed it in the position of authority, so all eyes would have to turn to Stephaleh.

"I hope we don't have to be overly formal, Lieutenant Commander La Forge," she began. She smiled warmly at him.

"Of course not, Ambassador. We're just a bunch of people who are needed to help dig up the countryside," he replied with a grin. "In fact, I was wondering where Professor Coleridge is."

"Zamorh, my aide, has already sent for her. To be honest, we did not expect you to receive approval to beam down until tomorrow."

"Ah . . . yes, well, our Commander Riker found a way to expedite matters with your aide . . . Gezor, isn't it? Very efficient staff." He directed this remark to Gregach, who sat in a straight high-backed chair. "Your people are most thorough."

Gregach nodded and returned to his drink. He wanted to watch the conversation, measure each Starfleet officer. La Forge seemed to be the natural leader, easygoing and pleasant. The VISOR was off-putting to Gregach, but he realized that the thought was silly. The android, with its sallow skin, appeared to be functional and useful but not a real soldier. On the other hand, the Klingon was fierce and appeared menacing, even sitting and looking at ease. Gregach longed for the days when he was a youth on border patrol, occasionally skirmishing with Klingon craft far from home. At least they were a people to fire the blood and make life a challenge. He hoped to talk with Worf before the *Enterprise* left orbit.

The group made small talk for a bit about where the *Enterprise* had last been and some of its more notable ports of call. Gregach noticed that Zamorh always seemed to hover in the background with a refill or a fresh napkin to bead up the condensation from the glasses.

Stephaleh found herself growing increasingly tired as the time passed. She was unused to staying up late; except for her sessions with Gregach, she tended to retire early—earlier and earlier, it seemed to her. Now fatigue played around the edges of her mind, and she stifled several yawns. Perhaps a stimulating drink to keep her awake, maybe just a cup of coffee? She could feel her mind wandering, like the underground rivers on her native Andor. . . .

Then Zamorh left the room and came back minutes later with a tall, dark-skinned female right behind him—a human who walked purposefully, letting each step carry her forward. She wore a simple dark blue jumpsuit that needed cleaning and a cap of some indeterminate style. Beneath the cap, long straight black hair framed a familiar round face with almond-shaped eyes, high cheekbones, and a wide, expressive mouth.

A Sullurh walked in her wake, striving to keep up with her long strides. If Stephaleh hadn't expected him to be trailing behind, she might not have noticed him at all.

Before the ambassador could make introductions, La Forge was on his feet, his smile threatening to split his face. "Professor Coleridge!" he cried. La Forge looked surprised when she swiftly crossed the room and embraced him in a huge hug that would have knocked the breath out of a smaller man.

"You look good, Geordi. Very good. A commander now, I see. Excellent."

Geordi's fingers brushed the pips on his collar and he shrugged. His smile had not yet faded, and he wanted to ask her a million questions. Instead, re-

25

membering the surroundings, he chose to get business out of the way first. He introduced the other officers and then announced with a wave of his hand, "And this is Nassa Coleridge, the greatest archaeologist of them all!"

"I am pleased to meet you both," said Coleridge. "This is my helper, Thul. He was assigned to me when I arrived here, and thank goodness for him." Thul, small and not very imposing, nodded briefly and then stood off to one side.

"And now, Geordi La Forge, let's sit down and see if we can't put you to work," Coleridge continued. She took a seat herself, between Gregach and Data. Though it was getting late, she appeared ready to wrap up the details of the dig.

Stephaleh noted this. "As I said earlier, I was not expecting to conduct this session until tomorrow," she began, massaging her left leg, trying to ease a cramp that had only just dug its claws into her. She cleared her throat. "First, some background. Ambassador Gregach and I agreed two years ago to open Kirlos to widespread archaeological exploration, since we are all curious about the Ariantu. It is of scientific importance that as many of the artifacts be preserved as possible, since they may be our only clues to a lost civilization. To that end, we have mutually agreed to allow a Federation-sponsored dig, which happens to be on the K'Vin side of the world. Ambassador?"

Gregach roused himself and sat up a bit straighter before beginning. "Professor Coleridge has requested your assistance, Lieutenant Commander La Forge, because of your unique VISOR. However, it must be stressed"—and he looked meaningfully at Worf—"that no military presence is to disturb the populace. On either side."

Worf grunted. "I am a member of Starfleet, and

26

Starfleet is not a military organization. We just acknowledge that at times, when dealing with the unknown, security is . . . prudent."

"Quite so," Gregach agreed, turning to Stephaleh. "The amount of time we have agreed on is one week, no more."

Coleridge let this sink in for several seconds before she spoke up. "Ambassadors, when I made my appeal, I clearly indicated that I needed help for *two* weeks. I spent hours working on Gezor's silly forms." She waved her arms to punctuate her point. "You have halved my request with no notice."

"I'm sorry, Professor," Stephaleh began. "Politics may not interest you, but Ambassador Gregach and I have our instructions and priorities. We decided that having a Starfleet vessel in orbit for two weeks would be unnecessarily distracting for the citizenry. A starship in orbit fuels fears."

Once again, Coleridge thought about the words before replying. "I just don't agree, Ambassador. I need Geordi, and he tells me I need Data. I was counting on two weeks."

"You will have to content yourself with one week, Professor," Stephaleh said as pleasantly as possible. "Look at it this way: at least you can begin tomorrow, one day early."

"That may be. What about transportation of our findings?"

"I have decided to establish a weight limit on how many artifacts can be removed from the K'Vin side for study by the Federation," Gregach said. "If you exceed the limit, we will ask for compensation from the Federation, and our negotiations will begin anew. Instead, I would ask you, Professor Coleridge, to limit yourself to one metric ton of material."

"That's most generous, Ambassador," she replied,

truly surprised. She'd thought he was talking in the dozen-kilo range. "Well, as Sarek once said, 'It is always best to accept what one does not expect.'"

"Surak, Professor," countered Data.

"What was that?" Coleridge looked surprised.

"Your quote. It was from the earliest writings of Surak. Sarek is an ambassador."

"Of course. Silly of me," she said with a smile.

Worf took in the conversation. His original assessment of the political climate on Kirlos had apparently been right on target.

The warrior K'Vin had allowed themselves to be domesticated by Federation diplomacy. There didn't seem to be much in the way of action to look forward to.

Then he noticed Zamorh and Thul, talking in a corner away from everyone else. Neither seemed at ease; their remarks were brief.

An odd race, the Sullurh, he thought.

If there was anything he had learned as security chief on the *Enterprise*, it was to be suspicious of all strangers until they proved themselves worthy of trust. He even had his doubts about some members of the *Enterprise* crew, never having served alongside them.

"Then it's agreed," said Coleridge. "We can begin in the morning. I'll first transport back to the *Enterprise* some of my findings, so they can be relayed to the institute."

A not-so-fake yawn allowed Stephaleh to call an end to the evening's meeting. "You gentlemen have rooms waiting," she told the *Enterprise* officers. "And *I* must bid you all a good night." With that, she rose.

Zamorh recognized his cue. He held the door open for her as she slowly strode from the room.

Gregach stood, too. He looked at the *Enterprise* trio

and added, "You and Professor Coleridge will be my guests for a meal sometime during your stay here. We'll show you why the Federation yearns to have us as allies again—for our cooking. And, Lieutenant Worf, I suspect *we* will have some things to discuss as well. Good nighttime to you all."

Chapter Three

Captain's Log, stardate 43197.5: A priority message from Starbase 105 has informed us of an unwarranted attack on a Federation outpost in an adjoining sector. The situation on Tehuán is critical, with high casualties and widespread damage to the settlement. As the *Enterprise* is the nearest available starship, we have been ordered to provide immediate assistance.

PICARD ENDED his log entry with a deliberate depression of the padd controls. He didn't welcome the destruction of Tehuán, but he couldn't deny that the call to action was welcome. Kirlos offered neither the scientific interest of unexplored territory nor, due to the K'Vin restriction on Starfleet personnel, the distractions of a shore-leave facility. With the exception of the three members of the away team down on the planet, no one on the starship would regret leaving this place. The captain thought of Worf and revised that number to two.

"Captain to the bridge."

Riker's hail pulled Picard out of his reverie. "On my way, Number One," he said, rising quickly from his desk. As he made his way to the bridge, the captain impatiently dismissed his philosophical contemplation of the Tehuán tragedy and turned his attention to more practical concerns.

"Status report?"

Riker jumped up from the captain's chair. "Ready to break orbit as soon as the away team has been recovered."

"What?" Picard, who had been heading for the vacated chair, came to an abrupt halt in the command center. He noted the high color creeping up his first officer's neck, a sure sign that Riker was fighting to control his temper. "Why aren't they aboard yet?"

"Following planetary regulations, I informed the Federation embassy that I was recalling the away team. Somehow this news reached the K'Vin embassy as well, and Gezor has objected to their unscheduled departure."

"So?" Picard glanced impatiently at the main viewscreen. Time was of the essence in a medical assist mission, and he wanted to see deep space, not Kirlos, on that wall.

"The K'Vin have threatened that such an unwarranted action will result in a nullification of the away team's existing petitions and will very likely result in *Enterprise* personnel being barred from K'Vin territory."

"Is that all? Well, I can certainly think of worse fates," said Picard. "Contact the transporter room and have O'Brien stand by to beam up the away team at my signal."

"Yes, sir!"

Riker quickly lifted a hand to his communicator,

but the motion was arrested by a high-pitched squeal. Everyone on the bridge winced as communications speakers crackled with a sudden burst of static; the view of Kirlos scrambled into electronic snow.

"Captain." The tactical officer at the aft station looked up in alarm. "I'm receiving a priority intercept from—"

A pale blue Andorian appeared on the main viewscreen.

"Ambassador Stephaleh," said Picard. His eyes widened with surprise. Until now his interactions with the Federation diplomat had been brief but informal; this interview was obviously going to be different. He knew enough about Andorians to interpret the cast of her antennae: her good humor was conspicuously absent.

"Captain Picard, I will not delay your urgent mission with social amenities; I'll come right to the point. I would prefer that the *Enterprise* away team remain on Kirlos."

Picard answered with equal directness. "I regret the inconvenience to Professor Coleridge, but I'm afraid she will just have to find another—"

"Professor Coleridge is not my concern," said the Andorian with a twitch of her jointed antennae. "This is strictly a diplomatic matter. The K'Vin embassy has been following the progress of the archaeological excavations with great interest, and any disruption of that project will annoy their staff. I have no desire to annoy the K'Vin."

Riker stepped up to stand by the captain. "But as far as I can tell," he said, "the only person who seems likely to be annoyed is the administrative assistant, Gezor."

"You are more politically naive than I realized,

32

Commander Riker. What bothers Gezor bothers the K'Vin ambassador."

"But these aren't just ordinary crewmen," objected Picard. "We're talking about key starship personnel: my chief engineer, my chief of security, and my third-in-command."

"And you have no relief crew for them? I hadn't realized the *Enterprise* was so badly understaffed, Captain Picard. How very awkward for you."

The ambassador's whispery voice was capable of carrying considerable sarcasm. Picard was forcibly reminded of Stephaleh's reputation as a tough negotiator.

"Well, of course I have a full crew complement, but I—"

"Captain, I can't order you to leave the landing party on Kirlos. I can only stress that the *de facto* peace which has existed between the Federation and the K'Vin Hegemony has been maintained by a careful avoidance of conflict. I have no desire to test the strength of that relationship; it is in the best interests of galactic diplomacy that the away team remain on Kirlos."

"My apologies, Ambassador Stephaleh." Picard capitulated with a nod of his head. "Considering the circumstances, I will allow my people to remain on Kirlos until our return."

Her image began to fade away immediately.

"Thank you for your cooperation, Captain."

And she was gone.

The genial expression on Picard's face was gone as well. He turned to his first officer. "Number One, contact the away team and inform them of our departure."

Dropping down into his command chair, Picard

issued a terse set of orders to the helm for a departure from Kirlos. Once the starship had swung free of its orbit around the planet, he designated a high warp speed and ended with a flatly uttered "Engage."

The *Enterprise* shot forward into warp space. Pinpoint stars on the viewscreen were transformed into streaks of light.

Picard turned to his first officer and said, "Galactic diplomacy indeed. I wouldn't put it past Stephaleh to be more concerned about her weekly game of dyson with Gregach. Of course, one can't take the chance she's telling the truth."

Riker opened his mouth to reply, but Picard rushed on before the first officer could utter a word. "No one on board this ship, myself included, is indispensable. We can function perfectly well without the landing party. It's the principle of the thing. I do not like abandoning members of my crew on a remote and backward planet to fend for themselves without the resources of a starship."

This time, when the captain paused for breath, Riker was quicker to take advantage. Mischief gleamed in his eyes when he said, "I'm worried about them, too, sir. I only hope they're still alive when we return."

A long silence stretched out between the two officers as Picard struggled to maintain his bad humor. "Your concern is duly noted, Number One." Picard smiled despite himself. The sting of Stephaleh's victory was not so sharp as to obscure his reason.

After all, what could possibly go wrong on Kirlos?

It was only on very rare occasions that Geordi La Forge wondered what it would be like to be sighted. Indeed, his blindness was a part of him, and the concept of seeing as most humans did was so alien to him that he had not even been able to seize the opportunity to attain "normal" vision.

Still, every so often, when someone commented on a particular texture or hue, or when a low whistle from a crewman indicated appreciation of the curve of a woman's hips—a curve not readily apparent in the heat-emitting images that fed Geordi's brain—the *Enterprise* engineer wondered what it would be like to have normal vision.

Rarely, though, was he glad that he was blind.

This was one such occasion.

He clung desperately to the back of the speeder sled, which was racing through the streets of Kirlosia at a horrifying speed. The air whipped past him, and random profanities were shouted at him. There was nothing he could do about it—Nassa Coleridge was at the stick of the high-speed antigrav sled.

For what seemed the hundredth time, Geordi checked the strap that kept him belted in. "Professor!" he shouted. "We could slow down, you know!"

"What?"

"I said we could—forget it," and he gave up as his words were blown back in his face.

Strapped onto the back of the sled was a case containing a vast array of archaeological equipment. When Geordi glanced back to make sure it was still in place, he saw the other speeder sled directly behind them.

Worf was piloting it, and although Worf never smiled, Geordi could tell from the pulsing of heat through the Klingon's body that the security chief was enjoying himself immensely.

Behind Worf, holding on securely, was Data. Geordi was quite certain that Worf was hoping to test the android's mettle and nerve. He needn't have bothered. Data was absolutely unflappable.

"Would you care to take the scenic route, Geordi?" the professor had asked. She had sounded ever so pleasant, ever so sweet. Geordi should have known instantly that she had something up her sleeve. But this insanity would never have occurred to him.

They shot down the Strip, inhabitants scattering. Over the rush of the air Geordi could have sworn he heard Worf actually emit a sound of amusement. Geordi had often wondered just what a Klingon might consider amusing. Now he knew.

Suddenly the sled veered off the main drag and began to dart through side streets. The streets of Kirlosia seemed mazelike to outsiders, but Nassa Coleridge navigated them with practiced ease. Geordi was grateful for all the training he had gone through in Starfleet—training that enabled him to cope with such trivialities as vertigo. Otherwise Coleridge's zigzags would have induced a wave of nausea.

Coleridge had powered down slightly, for if she had maintained her previous speed she would no doubt have lost Worf and Data. Even so, they were just able to keep up. The decrease in speed also made conversation a bit more feasible.

"You okay, Geordi?" Coleridge called back to him.

Drawing as much air as he could into his lungs, he shouted back, "Fine, Professor!"

"Geordi, college was a long time ago," she said. "You can call me Nassa."

Coleridge had pulled her hair back into a chignon before mounting the sled, but several strands had come loose. As a result, when Geordi tried to reply, he got a mouthful of hair.

"Just up ahead!" she called out and pointed.

36

From behind them on the second scooter, Worf saw signs in several languages, all of which said the same thing: this was a K'Vin exploration area, and only authorized individuals were permitted.

Geordi looked forward to a reduction in speed, for he assumed that this was where they would be disembarking.

He thought wrong.

"There it is," she called out with an inclination of her head. "Hole sweet hole."

The sled suddenly angled upward sharply and Geordi gasped. "Aren't we getting off here?"

"Gamma level is five miles down," she replied. "I didn't think you'd want to walk it."

The sled dropped down like a stone, and Geordi saw a brief flash of a large hole in the ground, about a hundred feet in diameter. And then, as fast as he saw it, he was inside it.

The sides were constructed of transparent aluminum supports. Lanterns lined the walls, providing light—not that Geordi needed very much, thanks to his VISOR. Their path went down at a dizzying angle, and Geordi reflexively gripped the sides of the sled. Of course the sheer speed of the vehicle was keeping him locked in place anyway, not to mention the straps. But it was nevertheless a disconcerting experience.

Geordi felt pressure inside his ears and made rapid chewing motions to counter it.

"You're looking at months and months of field work," Coleridge shouted. "Impressive, isn't it? And all along the way, we found bits and pieces of Ariantu culture. Here a cup, there a fragment of a statue. Like putting together a jigsaw puzzle that, when complete, will give us a picture of a long-gone civilization."

"And . . . and what is that picture?" shouted

Geordi, trying to concentrate on something besides the idea that they might wind up smeared along the insides of the tunnel.

"Mostly a verification of what the K'Vin culture remembers about the Ariantu," she replied. "They— Hold on."

She banked around a sharp curve and Geordi gasped.

As if it hadn't been close at all, Nassa continued calmly, "The Ariantu were a predatory race, very aggressive. The current anthropological theory holds that they might be distantly related to the Om'raii."

"Oh?"

"In many respects, yes. Much more warlike than the Om'raii, though. K'Vin legend makes reference to groups of Ariantu known as paacs." She spelled the word.

"Not p-a-x," Geordi observed, clutching the sides of the sled. Was it only wishful thinking, or were they beginning to slow down?

"Latin for 'peace'? No, definitely not that. Most of the shards we found were either from statues of warriors or from weapons. Hold on."

"I've *been* holding on."

"Good. We're coming in for a landing."

The tunnel opened up, and the sled veered gracefully to the right. Moments ago they had been surrounded by tunnel, and Geordi was stunned by the change.

All around them were catwalks and cross corridors, stretching to the left and right as far as the eye—or the VISOR—could see. Also Geordi could now sense a slow, steady pulsing. All around him were huge banks of complicated machinery. He gasped, for the engine area appeared to be miles long, and the technological devices were sophisticated far beyond anything he had ever seen before. At a glance he was able to guess the basic functions of some of the machines, but he realized that he could easily spend years down here and barely begin to understand all of the equipment.

"Impressive, isn't it?" Coleridge asked. The sled was barely moving now as she cruised slowly toward a large ramp.

"To say the least," Geordi said in awe. "Where is this place?"

"This is the gamma level."

"Surface is alpha, Kirlosia is beta, this is gamma. I'm starting to detect a pattern."

"Good lad."

The sled moved onto the ramp, and after gunning the engine one more time—for effect, Geordi suspected—Coleridge shut it off. As she walked around back to unstrap the equipment, Geordi heard the soft thrumming of the other sled's engine. Worf confidently maneuvered it along the ramp and brought it to a stop next to Coleridge's.

"Any problem keeping up, Lieutenant?" Coleridge said teasingly.

"None" was Worf's stiff response. "Although your leadership was somewhat . . . aggressive."

"'A leader has to lead,'" said Coleridge, slinging the equipment onto her back. She didn't ask for help, nor did she seem remotely interested in acquiring it, so Geordi didn't offer. "John F. Kennedy said that," the professor added.

"Harry S Truman," replied Data, stepping off the sled.

She eyed him askance. "I was pretty certain it was President Kennedy."

"'A leader has to lead, or otherwise he has no business in politics.' Harry Truman, born 1884, died 1972. He ascended to the presidency on April—"

39

"Fine," said Coleridge, smiling and putting up her hands. "You win." And out of the side of her mouth she said to Geordi, "Is he like this all the time?"

"Yes."

"How do you stand it?"

"Patience. A lot of patience."

"Uh-huh." She gestured. "We are now five miles below Kirlosia. This entire area is an engineer's dream. You're looking at the guts of Kirlos—as near as we can tell, at any rate."

"This is the equipment that keeps Kirlos going."

She nodded. "We didn't find it any too soon, either. Much of it was running down. Air filtration, gravity— everything that you take for granted in a natural world but you have to create for an artificial one—comes from here. It's been in operation for who knows how long. We did the maintenance that was required and basically saved Kirlos."

"So now what? This is where you're digging?"

"No. I'll show you where. Come on."

She started down a ramp, walking so briskly that Geordi had to run to keep up with her. He was amazed. The woman had to be twenty years his senior. "You're keeping yourself fit, Nassa," he huffed.

"Zan says I'm obsessive about it," she replied without turning.

"Zan"—he paused—"was your husband, right?"

"Right."

"But you spoke of him in the present tense. Pardon for asking, but isn't he—"

"Dead, yes. That's right."

Their booted feet clacked on the metal ramp. From all around them Geordi got a growing sense of the power needed to run the planet. Everything seemed to be throbbing with energy.

From behind them Data said, "I do not understand

40

why you would speak of your deceased husband in the present tense. That shows an alarming misperception of reality."

"Data!" said Geordi sharply.

But Nassa Coleridge laughed that pleasant, deep laugh of hers. "I perceive reality just fine, Mr. Data. I like to speak of Zan that way. It makes me feel closer to him. But believe me, I know he's gone. Stupid accident." She shook her head. "You change your life for someone, and then he goes and dies."

"How did you change your life?" Data asked.

Geordi stopped, turned, and said in a low voice, "Data, I really don't think that's any of our business. Do you?"

Data was about to respond, but Coleridge, who was still proceeding at a brisk clip, called back, "Honestly, Geordi, you don't have to be quite so defensive of me. I don't mind answering Data's endless questions.

"I started out as a field worker in archaeology, Data," she continued as they hurried to keep up with her. Even Worf was impressed by the speed of the cocoa-skinned woman. "I was plain old Nassa Gant when I met Zan Coleridge, a scholarly and loving man who had no interest in field work at all. University life, that was for him. And I loved him enough to convince myself that I could be happy teaching. So I married him and spent ten years of my life training others to do what I loved."

She paused, turned, and Geordi stopped in surprise as she patted him on the cheek. "That's where I met this young chap. You don't mind if I tell them, do you, Geordi?" Without waiting for him to respond she continued, "Geordi came to the university, unsure of what he wanted to do with his life. He took my course and came that close"—she brought her thumb and forefinger together—"to becoming an archaeologist."

"Can you blame me?" Geordi said with a smile. "You had a knack for making it sound fascinating."

"And so it was, for me," she replied. She started walking again. Geordi fleetingly wondered just how far down they were going.

As if she had read his mind, Nassa said, "We're only going a hundred feet down. It's just that the ramps curve so damned much. Look." She pointed upward, and Geordi looked at the route they had followed. Sure enough, they had spent most of their time going from side to side. The ramps' angle of progression was very slight.

"Anyway," she continued, "the problem is that most of archaeology can be pretty boring. I felt Geordi was a bit too aggressive and exploratory to fully appreciate the joy of finding one pottery shard after thirty days of digging. Starfleet seemed more in keeping with his nature, and I steered him in that direction."

Geordi was inclined to amend that, for a number of people and factors had influenced his choice of Starfleet as a career. Still, Nassa Coleridge had been a major element in the equation, and he saw no reason to contradict her. So he smiled and said, "I always did crave excitement."

"And then, some years back, Zan was killed in that accident."

"What was the nature of it?" asked Data.

She paused and for the first time sounded just a bit melancholy. "Traffic," she said. "I'd really rather not discuss it, if you don't mind."

"Of course," said Data softly. Geordi was mildly surprised. Did Data understand that sometimes grief wasn't easy to get over? It was, after all, a distinctively human attribute. It could be that his android friend was coming along rather nicely in the emotions department.

Nassa reached up and unpinned her chignon. She shook her head, and the black hair tumbled about her shoulders. "With Zan gone, there was nothing left to hold me there. So I left my teaching post to return to field work. Ah, here we are."

She had arrived at a low doorway, which she had to duck to get under. Geordi did not, reminding him once again of the woman's not inconsiderable height. Data didn't have to duck, either, but Worf most certainly did.

They went through a darkened passageway that was only a few yards long, and then Coleridge vanished through the other end. Just before Geordi got there he heard her say, "Here we are," and her voice seemed to echo slightly, as if she had spoken from a much larger room.

He stepped out right behind her and stopped, amazed. "Much larger" was hardly the phrase for it. The area was vast—miles long, miles high.

And it was empty.

Completely, utterly empty, except for the spots where digs were in progress.

"Welcome to delta," Coleridge said expansively.

Geordi looked down, his VISOR scanning the makeup of the floor. "Some sort of porous rocky material," he said.

"In old Earth language, it would be called tarmac," Coleridge said, "although it does, of course, contain elements that are not found on Earth."

And then a voice came softly from Geordi's right, so unexpected that he almost jumped: "I'm glad you're finally here, Doctor."

He spun and there was Thul. It was only then that

Geordi realized that he had totally forgotten about Coleridge's Sullurh assistant.

It was clear from Worf's tone that he had also forgotten, and there was a distinctly annoyed edge in his voice. "Where did you come from?"

Thul pointed over to one side, and the away team saw a transmat booth identical to the ones that studded the streets of Kirlosia. "That is how," he said politely. "I hope that does not upset you."

"You . . . There's a booth set up here?" said Geordi incredulously.

"Of course," replied Nassa.

"Well, then, why didn't you have us transported," demanded Geordi, "instead of making us risk that crazy ride on the speeder sleds?"

"Because," Coleridge said patiently as if addressing a child, "you crave excitement. Remember? And you must admit that my way was much more exciting."

Geordi sighed and started to walk slowly toward the digs. Coleridge was saying, "We're all set up over there," and Thul was now just behind her and to the right. Worf took the opportunity to hang back and speak in a low voice to Data.

"Thul," Worf said in distinct irritation, "is annoyingly easy to lose track of."

"He is very unassuming," said Data thoughtfully. "Some might consider that a positive character trait."

"I do not," Worf replied.

"What would you suggest we do?" asked Data.

Worf pondered that a moment. "Perhaps I should shoot him," he said, engaging in his own unique brand of Klingon humor.

Data's eyebrows went up. "That seems a bit extreme."

"That was not my extreme plan. I suspect you would not want to hear my extreme plan."

"I suspect you are correct," said Data. "I would have to ask you not to take any action against Thul, no matter how irritating you might find his non-offensiveness."

"Is that an order?" was the cold reply.

Data blinked at that. "That would seem the proper word for it. However, I would prefer to think of it as a request—one that I hope you will honor, since the alternative is court-martial."

Geordi, meantime, was talking animatedly with Nassa. "So what kind of a place was this, anyway?"

"What do you think it is?"

"Teacher quizzing the student?"

"Archaeologist asking for the opinion of a learned individual."

Geordi thought about it a moment. "Space port. Only thing that makes sense."

"That's what we thought. There's just one problem."

"That being?"

"No doors."

Geordi stopped and looked at her. "Nothing?"

"Nothing. No bay doors, no false walls, nothing. We're inside solid rock with no way in or out. So if there were ships down here, how did they exit and enter?"

"There are ways," Geordi said slowly. "Local warps, wormholes even."

"Wormholes?"

"Yeah, wormholes. Basically they're like tunnels, warps in the fabric of space. Hole at either end, heavy gravity tunnel in between them. Go in one end, come out the other. But natural wormholes aren't stable, and it would take very sophisticated technology to manipulate such energy. Even we can't do it yet."

"'We' meaning representatives of the pinnacle of

civilization." She smiled, then stopped at the edge of the dig area and slid the equipment off her back. "Here's where I'm going to start digging. We chose this spot carefully, using detailed scientific means."

"Like what?"

"I pointed to a spot on a map and said, 'Right here.' I'm hoping you'll use that VISOR of yours to scan the area and pick out a better spot."

Geordi glanced around. There were a half-dozen other digs already in progress, all manned by members of the K'Vin Hegemony. The diggers afforded the UFP representatives brief annoyed stares before returning to work.

"I'll be more than happy to do whatever I can, Nassa," said Geordi slowly, "as will Worf and Data. But I'll tell you right now, there's not much we can do about the nasty looks we're getting from the others."

"Can you sense looks?"

"I can sense hostility all right," he said. "I admire your sticking to your guns about the dig here, but it looks like we're in the middle of a political mess."

Nassa made a rude noise. "I leave politics to the politicians. It's all background noise to the real work we have to do here. Let drones like Gezor get worked up about it. I have more important things to do."

Chapter Four

GREGACH HAD NOT EXPECTED this conversation to take more than a few minutes. Now he would have to wait just a little longer for his dusk meal.

The ambassador could almost taste his spilat—not a simulation, but an actual fresh-killed spilat slaughtered in the age-old manner, so that its poisons could not back up into its sweet and succulent flesh . . . sliced and spiced and singed just lightly, leaving thick green juices to flow in savory abundance. . . .

"I am surprised," he said, tearing himself away from his anticipation long enough to address his assistant, "that you are opposed to this, Gezor. A major excavation can only mean more work for your people."

The Sullurh hoisted his shoulders up around his ears in a catch-all motion that could signify fascination, confusion, or indifference, depending on the context. In this case, Gregach gathered, the last possibility was the applicable one.

"'Opposed' is too strong a word, Ambassador. A more appropriate word would be 'concerned.'"

The Sullurh was perhaps a third of Gregach's weight and a good head and a half shorter than the ambassador, due only in part to his slight stoop. At times Gezor seemed to disappear into the stonework of the embassy. But when he had something to say, the ambassador had learned, it was in his interest to listen.

Gezor was not remarkably bright—after all, he *was* a Sullurh—but he often displayed an intriguing slant on things. And he made it his business to know what was on people's minds—something Gregach did not always have time for, with his constant politicking for a more prestigious position in the Hegemony.

"I must say," commented the ambassador, "I am a little surprised. Coleridge has created a great deal of employment for your people with her little project."

"My people," said Gezor, "are not my prime concern, as you know. I am a servant of this embassy first and a Sullurh second."

Gregach nodded. "Of course. I did not mean to imply otherwise." Gezor had worked hard to establish a reputation for himself in the embassy. It was not fair to impugn his character by ascribing to him a kinship with the common Sullurh. "But what, *exactly,* is your objection to her?"

The Sullurh screwed up his face, making his large pinkish eyes appear even larger. "There is something about her that seems . . . inappropriate. She is . . . too extroverted," he decided at last. "Too given to humor. Archaeologists are not noted for such qualities, no matter what their race."

True, conceded Gregach. But that sort of deviation was hardly cause for alarm. "What are you saying? That she is a spy of some sort?"

48

The Sullurh stared at him for a moment. "Perhaps." A pause. "And then," Gezor continued, "there is the matter of the Starfleet officers."

This, Gregach noted with some satisfaction, was something that had made *him* think twice as well. But Stephaleh had quelled his suspicions with her openness on the subject.

And of course each of the officers had a practical reason for being here. But if this archaeological project *was* a ruse, would not such reasons have been conveniently provided? And would it not have been Stephaleh's duty to support the deception *despite* their relationship? And . . .

He stopped himself. What was he *thinking?* The Federation had nothing to gain through such elaborate duplicity. No military intelligence, certainly. Nothing at all, in fact, that could improve their position vis-à-vis the K'Vin.

There were no secrets here on Kirlos, he mused, no inclination to be secretive and nothing to be secretive about.

So try as he might, he could not get overly excited about Gezor's suspicions. Like most things in life, the Federation project was probably just what it seemed to be. Subterfuge was by far the exception, not the rule—a lesson that had stood him in good stead throughout his military career.

"I appreciate your warning," he told Gezor finally. "I will have the excavation site watched closely. But I will not prohibit either the woman or the Federation officers from taking part."

If his aide was disappointed with Gregach's decision, he gave no sign of it. But then, Gezor was very perceptive; he would know that he had nothing to gain from further argument.

49

The Sullurh again hunched his shoulders up around his head. "As you wish, Ambassador."

Gezor was the perfect assistant, Gregach reflected. Loyal, insightful . . . and he had an acute sense of when to let a matter drop.

The K'Vin swiveled his chair toward the viewscreen on the north wall and placed a call to Stephaleh. As always, it took time for his communication to be cleared through Federation embassy protocols.

He barely noticed as Gezor exited from the room. His thoughts, as he waited for Stephaleh to appear on the screen, had already returned to the promise of the succulent, recently slaughtered spilat.

Worf scanned the building—its sparkling concave walls, its haphazard placement of whimsically shaped windows. Four stories high, it dominated this part of town, contrasting severely with the featureless gray shell of beta level's "sky."

He grunted.

"So this is it," said Geordi.

"Yes," said Coleridge. "The new Commercial Trading Hall." She laughed that deep, throaty laugh of hers—a sound which, Worf decided, was not completely unpleasant. "The emptiest building in town, gentlemen. If there are twenty people in it at any given time, I'll eat my tricorder on the spot."

Data looked at the archaeologist, and Geordi caught the look. "That's only a figure of speech, Data. She doesn't really intend to eat it."

The android nodded. "I am familiar with the expression, Geordi. Commander Riker has employed variations of it." He turned back to Coleridge. "My question, Professor, concerns your estimate of the building's occupancy level. One would think that with

50

space at such a premium in Kirlosia, no edifice would remain vacant for very long."

"Indeed," said Coleridge, "one would think so." She seemed to measure her words—not unlike a Klingon, Worf noted. "And had this place been built to serve any other purpose, it would probably be packed to the rafters. But commerce is something the Kirlosians prefer to carry on in less public venues."

Judging from Data's expression, he hadn't quite caught her meaning. Worf tried to couch it in blunter terms, even though Klingons did not pride themselves on their merchanting expertise.

"No witnesses, no taxation," he said.

"That's right," agreed the archaeologist, casting Worf a grateful look. After all, she was not used to dealing with an android; she had not known at which level of complexity to pitch her explanation. "These merchants are supposed to pay taxes on their profits, Data, not only to the Federation, through Kirlos, but also to their home-system governments. What's more, they may be dealing in goods that are deemed tradable commodities by the Federation but are considered contraband elsewhere. So, for a number of reasons, most business transactions are kept out of the public eye."

"I see," said the android. "But if the merchants' requirements are in opposition to the use of such a facility, then why was it built?"

Geordi chuckled. "That, Data, is one of the great mysteries of life. It's called bureaucracy."

The Klingons had a name for it, too. *"Crakh-makh borguh,"* muttered Worf. Literally translated, it meant "an infestation of carrion-eaters."

Coleridge turned to him and smiled. *"Crakh-makh togh-uruk selah,"* she intoned.

"May the carrion-eaters choke on our flesh."

Worf looked at the human female in a new light. She had put an awkward spin on the words, but at least she had made the attempt. For most non-Klingons, the Klingon language was impossible even to listen to, much less speak.

He *knew* he had liked something about Coleridge. With a curt nod, he acknowledged her effort. *"Mughdar kocghlat,"* he told her.

"And drown in our blood."

The archaeologist's smile widened.

"What the devil are you two talking about?" asked Geordi.

Coleridge shrugged her wide shoulders. "Bureaucracies, of course. Isn't that the subject before us, Mr. La Forge?"

Geordi frowned. Worf knew he hated being left out of things, especially jokes. Then again, he had once likened Klingonese to gargling with metal filings—so Worf had no sympathy for him in this case.

"Great," said the chief engineer of the *Enterprise*. "I hope you're having a good time. Wait till I start telling quantum mechanics jokes to Data. See how you like . . ."

He never finished his gibe. It was drowned out by a ground-shuddering roar and a sudden blossom of flame from the roof of the trading hall tower. The blossom collapsed in on itself almost immediately, giving way to smaller tongues of red fire that lapped at the building's exterior through every window on the top two floors.

"My God," said Coleridge.

But it wasn't over. It had only begun.

A moment later a second explosion tore the entire crown off the building, sending streams of deadly fire onto the rooftops of the smaller structures around it.

Suddenly the streets were full of people, screaming, running, knocking others down in their haste.

For Worf, the sight was like a blow between the eyes, for it brought back memories he had been trying all his life to put aside—memories of the conflagration on Khitomer, starting with the Romulan fire from the sky and ending with a single Klingon youth scrabbling for life in the choking, crushing rubble.

And here he was, just as helpless as before. Just as confused, with no enemy in sight. No one to fight back at.

Suddenly someone gripped his arm. He whirled, his phaser in his hand before he knew he had even drawn it.

But it was no enemy who had confronted him. It was Geordi.

"Worf," he cried over the din, "we've got to help evacuate these buildings, get these people out of the area!"

Gradually the Klingon steadied himself, took a deep breath, exhaled it through clenched teeth. The smell of smoke was thick in the air.

"Worf, are you all right?"

Calmer now, he was able to see that the chaos in the streets was the worst of it. If that could be controlled, fatalities could be kept to a minimum.

Data and Coleridge were already on their way to the ravaged trading hall, making headway as best they could against the tide of those who were fleeing the vicinity. If there were survivors trapped in the ruins of the tower, Data was best equipped to free them.

"Worf?"

With a glance, he assured Geordi that he was all right—indeed, denied that he had ever been anything else.

"Orders, sir?"

"What? *Me* order *you*—in *this* mess? *You're* the security officer—start securing!"

It was all the Klingon had to hear. Wading through the ragged mob, he fired his phaser in the air. It had the desired effect.

"That way," he bellowed, pointing to the west where none of the buildings had been affected. One by one, the Kirlosians started to get the message.

From the vantage of her office window, Stephaleh looked out on the flames and black smoke that crowned the ruined trading hall. The smoke was gradually starting to spread over the rest of the Federation sector.

"Then everything is under control now?" she asked.

From behind her came Zamorh's somewhat breathless response. "Yes, Ambassador. The area has been evacuated and the nearby buildings have been foamed —apparently in time to prevent any real damage. The trading hall, however, cannot be saved."

"And those removed from the hall?"

"Two of the three should live," stated the Sullurh. "One, I am told, will not—a Maratekkan named Rammis."

Stephaleh acknowledged the information with a soft hiss between her teeth. "Had it not been for that android left here by the *Enterprise,* all three would likely still be in that inferno." She paused as one of those painful lower-leg cramps came and went. How she hated such small reminders of her mortality. "What about the cause of the explosions? Any word on *that* yet?"

"None," said Zamorh. "Although it is obvious that this was done on purpose. An accident is out of the question. There were no systems in the building capable of blowing up."

The ambassador's antennae twitched impatiently, but she otherwise kept her annoyance to herself. After all, no one had worked harder than Zamorh to mobilize the embassy rescue teams and have them sent to the site. Without him she would have had to do it all herself, and though that would normally have been her preference, she was no longer physically capable of enduring prolonged stress. Damn this growing-old business. . . .

"Ambassador?"

"I am aware that this was not an accident," she said. "I meant to ask if any instruments of destruction had been found or any evidence of who planted them. That sort of thing."

"Your pardon, Ambassador. I should have understood." The Sullurh's feet scraped on the smooth floor. "But to answer your question—no. There have been no significant discoveries—at least, not yet." More scraping, a sound that would have been indiscernible to most species of sentient beings, but not to an Andorian. "On the other hand, one may draw conclusions."

She turned to look at him, putting the flames and smoke behind her. "Conclusions?" she prodded.

Zamorh was not a tall individual, even for a Sullurh. And the spaciousness of her office made him appear even smaller, even more fragile. In prehistoric times, the Andorians' main food staple had been a creature about his size—though of course, Stephaleh's people had come a long way from their predatory beginnings.

"Yes, Ambassador. However, you may not be pleased when you hear them."

That piqued her interest. "Not pleased? By the deities, why not?"

"Because I believe," said the Sullurh, "that the K'Vin are responsible for this."

Stephaleh skewered him on her gaze. That possibility had not really occurred to her. "Your reasoning?"

"It is simple, Ambassador. They are resentful."

She smiled a thin-lipped smile. "Of what, Zamorh? Of an empty building, a waste of well-meant Federation funds? The trading hall was the worst idea I've had to tolerate in thirty-five years of diplomatic service. How could the K'Vin be resentful of *that?*"

The Sullurh seemed undaunted. But then, he seldom shied away from a confrontation with his superior. "They do not see it as a failure, Ambassador; they see it as yet another reminder of our intention to stay on Kirlos indefinitely. Of our insistent claim to a world that they covet—and have coveted since the day they achieved interstellar flight."

Stephaleh folded her arms across her narrow chest and peered at Zamorh from beneath her fringe of white hair. "You are talking about the distant past," she said. "It has been some time since the Federation and the K'Vin Hegemony have actually exchanged hostilities. And nowhere is that more true than on Kirlos. For the deities' sake, Zamorh, would Ambassador Gregach engage me in games of skill if he really considered me his enemy?"

Again Zamorh brought his shoulders up around his triangular ears. "Why not? Is it not wise to test an opponent's proclivities before initiating a bigger game?"

The ambassador began to pace. "Why have you not mentioned this before?"

The Sullurh met her gaze, his large pinkish eyes seeming not to blink. "We have never seen a building destroyed before." And then, since that explanation seemed insufficient, "I know how you enjoy your contests with Ambassador Gregach. I did not wish to sow dissent for no reason." He glanced at the window. "Though now I wish I had said something before this disaster took place."

She frowned. "Why would Gregach have agreed to the archaeological project? Why offer cooperation with one hand and enmity with the other?"

The Sullurh stared at her for a moment as he pondered the question. "Perhaps," he decided, "to put us off balance. And remember, Ambassador, the excavation has not begun yet. All the K'Vin have given us is their word."

Stephaleh continued to pace, mulling over her assistant's theory. Of course, she told herself, the K'Vin were only one possibility. There were any number of other groups and individuals in Kirlosia who might have seen fit to destroy the trading hall, and for any number of reasons. Non-Federation merchants, for the control that the building represented. Kirlosian establishments that currently hosted trader meetings and stood to lose if those meetings gravitated someday to the trading hall. Even vandals, just for the hell of it.

But the K'Vin . . . the more she thought about the idea, the more difficult it was to dismiss it. And it brought her pain, like the stiffness in her back that seemed to victimize her every morning now. For if Gregach *had* been deceiving her, *had* been playing her for a fool . . .

No.

She could not allow herself to get carried away like this. It was too early to start tossing blame around indiscriminately.

Besides, in her long career as a diplomat she had come to trust completely in her ability to judge character. Never once had she been wrong. And her

instincts told her that Gregach was what he seemed—
no more, no less. Certainly he was capable of
deception—but he was incapable of deceiving *her*.

She stopped pacing, turned to Zamorh. All this time
he had remained in one place, awaiting her decision.
He would not be pleased with it.

"As much as I value your opinion," Stephaleh told
him, "I must disagree with you in this instance. At any
rate, I cannot take action until our investigation is
complete." She looked at him. "I would like you to
oversee it personally from this point on."

The Sullurh bent his head slightly. "Of course,
Ambassador."

There was a certain stiffness in him; Zamorh did
not like to be disagreed with. He took it personally.

But then, that was one of the qualities she valued in
him. He was not afraid to stand up for what he
believed in. And more than anything else, he believed
in the Federation's right to be on Kirlos.

"Thank you," said Stephaleh. "You may go."

The Sullurh left.

Chapter Five

Captain's Personal Log: Starfleet's description of the attack on Tehuán had not prepared us for the devastation we found upon arrival at the outpost. But then, words are never equal to the reality.

A THICK LAYER of black dust had settled over the surface of the Tehuán valley. It blanketed the broken rubble of the settlement buildings, covering the raw scars of newly shattered stone; it buried scorched grass and colored the uprooted trees an ash gray. The slightest breeze sent the fine powder swirling back into the air, obscuring the light of the sun, turning day into twilight.

"Dammit, it's everywhere," said Beverly Crusher.

She could already feel pinpricks of grit edging beneath her uniform collar and trickling down her back, but she dismissed the discomfort just as she dismissed the acrid stench of smoke and the oppressive heat. With a practiced eye the doctor scanned the colonists grouped around her, automatically catalog-

59

ing the severity of their injuries. Then her attention focused on a still figure huddled on a blanket. A quick inspection revealed dust under a bloodstained bandage, dust that had worked its way into the oozing wound on the woman's leg.

"We gave up changing bandages," said a man who knelt by the doctor's side. "It only made things worse." Like all the colonists, he was covered with the black powder, but a thin trickle of sweat running down his cheek revealed pale skin and the white stubble of a beard beneath the grime.

The makeshift hospital had no ceiling, only a few high walls that cast a protective shadow over the injured. Despite the shade, however, this woman's skin was hot and dry to the touch. A quick pass of Crusher's med scanner confirmed the severity of the infection in her blood system.

"Dr. Stoller, this one should have gone up sooner." Crusher reached for her communicator. *"Enterprise,* beam this patient directly to sickbay."

The man watched in bewilderment as a glittering cloud enveloped the woman, carrying her away. "I'm sorry . . . I didn't think she was that badly injured." He lurched to his feet, but swayed in the effort. "I'm the wrong kind of doctor for this work. Better with plants than people . . ."

Crusher jumped to her feet and reached out an arm to steady him. She resisted the impulse to send Stoller up next; his injuries were minor and sickbay was already flooded with colonists, some near death. Despite his protests, she led the botanist over to a low-lying wall where he could sit.

"Wait here. You'll be treated soon."

Looking across the ruins, Crusher checked the progress of the personnel from her department. Paramedics advanced behind her like a blue wave washing over a dusty plain. They moved quickly, following the path of triage tags that she had laid down.

One person detached herself from the main group and approached the chief medical officer. As Edwards drew closer, Crusher noted the puzzled look on the woman's face.

"Dr. Crusher, I've found something very odd."

Before the doctor could hear an explanation, her communicator trilled, closely followed by Riker's voice: "Recovery teams have located another survivor under a collapsed building. Serious internal injuries. You'll be needed in surgery."

"Acknowledged." Crusher had already arranged for transport back to the ship before she remembered the paramedic who was still waiting patiently to one side; Crusher also remembered what responsibilities had been assigned to this particular paramedic. Her curiosity about the woman's errand faded, overshadowed by the more immediate demands of the upcoming surgery.

"Whatever you found will have to wait until later, Edwards."

Then Crusher felt the grip of the transport beam. The ruins of Tehuán dissolved away.

Riker stumbled over a fallen beam and cursed at the swiftly setting sun. He had headed back for the main camp when there was still enough light to pick his way through the rubble, but shadows were growing longer and darker.

"Will?" Deanna Troi's voice came out of the darkness ahead.

He moved toward the sound, carefully skirting a wall of crumbling stone. The counselor was waiting on the other side. Farther on, a half-dozen people were gathered around the glow of a field lantern. Riker was

61

too far away to feel its warmth, but the light was reassuring.

"Are these the ones?" he asked. Over fifty colonists had insisted on staying on the surface to help with the rescue efforts, but few of those volunteers had the information he needed.

"Yes, they were all witnesses."

He stepped forward, but Troi grasped his arm and held him back.

"Colonists, by the very nature of their undertaking, are strong and very resilient. But this unexplained attack has shaken them deeply, even those who escaped uninjured. Try not to pressure them for details."

The first officer shook his head. "Deanna, it's the details that I *need*. We still don't know who raided the colony."

His answer brought a frown to Troi's face, but she released her hold and walked with him to the clear space amid the rubble. The circle of people widened to allow Riker to sit down. He studied the drawn faces one by one as the counselor introduced the colonists to him.

"I need an explanation of what happened here," said the first officer.

A young man named Shaun shuddered and glanced nervously up at the sky. The others drew closer to the lantern's glow. Gathering up a fistful of the black dust from the ground, the farmer let the dirt sift through his fingers. He began to talk in a hoarse and halting voice.

"This was some of the finest loam on the planet. Now it's baked into dry dust, along with the crops. We grow . . . we *grew* an exotic fungus, what you would probably call a mushroom. Good for eating, but with some additional medicinal—"

"Shaun," interrupted Riker softly. Despite Troi's warning, he trusted their courage. Any one of them could have been safe aboard the *Enterprise* by now, but they had chosen to stay instead. "About the *attack?*"

Shaun didn't answer, but the woman sitting by his side responded. Clark took a deep breath, as if to brace herself for the memories.

"They came at night, when I was out in the fields gathering specimens for study. At first I thought I was seeing a cluster of meteors, but they grew brighter and moved like a storm of comets flaming through the air. Then they changed direction and I knew they were nothing natural. But I still wasn't afraid."

"How many ships were there?" prompted Riker.

"I counted at least eight," said a botanist named Delia. "Possibly ten." The others nodded their agreement.

"What did the ships look like?" But no one answered.

"I couldn't see them," said Delia finally, with a weary shrug. "All I could see was the bright flash when they fired their weapons. And they shot at anything . . . at everything. Houses, maintenance stations, fields, roads." She pointed to the high, jagged peak of a mountain overlooking the valley. "They even fired at Cahuapetl, triggering a rock slide that damaged the eastern part of the settlement. I heard the hiss of rising steam when they fired on the Río Pequeño."

Riker frowned when the narrative stopped. "But where did they center their fire?"

"That's just it!" cried a biochemist named Delaplace. "There was no focus. It was like . . . like target practice. Without meaning, without sense. They destroyed the valley and then left." Her hands began to tremble.

"We didn't have a chance," said the last of the colonists to speak. Blanc's mouth twisted into a bitter grimace. "No defense system, no weapons. Next time we could be wiped out entirely. Next time—"

"Hopefully, there won't be a next time," said Riker, cutting into the flow of words. He didn't need Troi's empathic powers to recognize their escalating fear. "The *Enterprise* will stay here to protect this settlement until the danger is gone. You have my word on it."

The expression of relief on Troi's face confirmed that his words had curbed their panic, but young Shaun still jerked his head up to check the night sky. It was an automatic action by now. His fear was too deeply rooted to be allayed easily.

Riker's resolve to protect the Tehuán colonists hardened into a personal vow.

Wesley Crusher heard the word "come," took a deep breath, then stepped through the opening doors of the ready room. This wasn't the first time he had paid a visit to the captain's private realm uninvited, but the decision to face Picard in his lair still required courage. And a certain amount of desperation.

Once inside the room, the young ensign found himself facing still more obstacles. Picard was staring out the star window, his back to the door. He did not appear to have noticed Wesley's entrance.

"Captain?" Wesley winced at the unexpected break in his voice.

After a long silence, Picard swiveled his chair around. He fixed Wesley with a stern gaze. "The Borg would have stripped the settlement of its technology, not simply destroyed it."

"Sir?"

"And the Ferengi wouldn't have wasted their energy

64

reserves by firing on fields and rivers. Don't you agree?"

"Yes, sir," said Wesley, nodding. "That would seem—"

"Ten ships, all using standard phaser weaponry." This statement brought a frown to the captain's face. "At least that's the report from the away team's preliminary damage survey."

"About the away team, sir?" Wesley saw a chance to voice his own concerns and was anxious to take advantage of it before Picard continued. "Request permission to volunteer for—"

"Permission denied, Ensign."

"But—"

Picard's frown deepened. "Ensign Crusher, you were not chosen for a landing party assignment. Your unscheduled arrival would only distract Commander Riker from his duties. If he requires more help and requests additional personnel, you can volunteer for planet duty."

"Yes, sir," said Wesley, fighting to keep the disappointment out of his voice. He took a small step backwards, wondering how he could best retreat from the captain's presence.

"I suppose it's only natural for you to be drawn to the activity on the planet." Picard's frown faded away, but unfortunately his interest in the ensign did not go with it. "It takes a certain maturity of perspective to see that there is as much challenge on the bridge as on the away team."

"Yes, sir."

"I can see you're not convinced." With a wave of his hand, Picard motioned the ensign to take a seat by the desk. "Tell me, what are Tehuán's principal commercial activities?"

"They've only got one," said Wesley as he sat down

across from the captain. By this time, he sincerely regretted the impulse that had brought him here. "Agriculture."

"And what is their annual income from exports of their produce?"

He had only skimmed the planet brief on Tehuán, but Wesley was relieved that he remembered the second answer as well. "They're operating at a loss. This is a newly established colony that hasn't reached operational levels yet."

Picard nodded. "So the settlement's commercial properties are of little value, and the colonists have accumulated no wealth." He paused as if waiting for Wesley to make a comment, then fired out another question. "What about the planet's strategic importance?"

"It hasn't got any. It's not even near the major trading routes." Wesley sat up in the chair and cried out, "But, sir. This doesn't make any sense!"

"Exactly my point," said Picard. "Why attack Tehuán?"

The captain swiveled back to the star window with its view of the planet. "It's my job to find that answer."

Lost in thought, he didn't notice Wesley's quiet departure.

The second day on Tehuán was the worst for Riker.

Starting at dawn, he directed the search teams in the gruesome task of searching for the dead. Even with the use of antigrav lifts and earth-movers, he was soon covered with dirt and his muscles were aching from the strain of scrambling over the rough terrain. And this time there were no rewards for all their effort. No voices cried out for release from beneath the debris.

The breezes that had cooled the valley died out by afternoon. Sweating heavily in the still air, the first officer watched as yet another body was pulled out from under the rubble of a collapsed building. The attending paramedic ran a scanner over the remains, then shook his head. Despite the technician's attention to detail, he knew the examination was merely a formality, since sensors had already probed the ruins for signs of survivors the day before.

"That reminds me," said Ravitch as he began to cover the body. "Lieutenant Edwards was looking for you earlier."

Riker acknowledged the comment with a grunt of resignation, then worked his way through the ruins to an area he usually tried to avoid. A dozen neatly wrapped bundles were stacked side by side along a crumbling wall. Only their size gave a clue as to what lay inside.

Edwards was in charge of the morgue.

"Are you squeamish?" she asked, looking up at the first officer.

"Not particularly," he said.

"Good. Then come look at this."

Edwards was kneeling on the ground beside the corpse of a colonist, but her body was shielding the upper torso from his view. With an involuntary grimace, Riker stepped closer and to one side and looked down. The sight brought an uprush of bile to the back of his throat. After he had absorbed the shock of seeing the disfigured face, he tried to catch up to what Edwards was saying about the body.

". . . was recovered near a rock slide. An autopsy will determine the specific cause of death."

"That's fairly obvious, isn't it?" After a moment's hesitation, Riker crouched down beside Edwards for a closer examination of the blackened marks on the head and neck. "Those are phaser burns. He must have been caught in a pass from an attacking ship."

"But they're *not* phaser burns," said the medic. "The appearance is similar, but there's a mottled skin pattern beneath the carbonization that I'm not familiar with. And this is the third corpse I've found with those marks."

To Riker's relief, she pulled a blanket up over the charred head. Rocking back on his heels, the first officer puzzled over this information. "This could mean the attackers used a new weapon."

"Forensics isn't my specialty. I can't explain the marks."

"Then beam this body up to the ship for immediate examination."

"Commander Riker," said Edwards. "Speaking from personal experience, I would guess that autopsies aren't exactly a priority with Dr. Crusher right now."

Riker smiled grimly. "They are if the captain requests them."

Chapter Six

GEORDI LOOKED OUT the window of the quarters that the United Federation of Planets had provided for them as he pulled on his right boot, and he smiled. He called behind him, "Ready to sample the nightlife of Kirlosia, Data?"

Data, sitting patiently in a chair nearby, tilted his head slightly. "It would be odd if nocturnal activity differed appreciably from that of the daytime," he said thoughtfully, "especially since day-night differentiation on Kirlos is an arbitrary matter."

Geordi sighed. He knew that huge lights lined the upper reaches of Kirlosia, and their dimming at a set time was the sole reason for nightfall in the outpost city. Nevertheless, having Data remind him of the fact took the enjoyment out of it. Telling the android that, though, would doubtless be a waste of time. "Right, Data," he said. "But tell you what . . . let's try to enjoy it anyway. Okay?"

Endeavoring to match Geordi's waning enthusiasm, Data simply said, "Okay."

Moments later they met Worf and Coleridge down in the lobby. Data could not help but observe that Thul was not present. It was just as well. Klingons were noted for being irrational about some things, and certainly Worf's immediate dislike for the harmless Sullurh assistant was one of those things.

Geordi, for his part, was startled by Coleridge's appearance. Earlier she had been wearing a simple jumpsuit. Now she was clothed in a caped purple ensemble that swept low to the floor but was slit provocatively high up one thigh. She did a turn in place. "You like?"

Geordi felt distinctly uncomfortable seeing his former mentor dressed this way. Still, he couldn't help smiling. "I like fine," he said.

They exited the building and turned to the right. Coleridge was busy trying to uphold her self-proclaimed responsibility as guide.

"This is Embassy Run," she was saying. "It leads directly from the UFP embassy, there"—she pointed behind them—"to the K'Vin embassy." She pointed ahead of them into the growing darkness. The K'Vin embassy was too far off for them to see—even for Geordi's VISOR—but he nodded cordially as if it were in plain sight. "Embassy Run," she continued, "is one of only two straight, normal streets in the whole damned city. The other is the Strip, which we buzzed down earlier; it slices diagonally across from the southwest to the northeast corner of the city. It crosses Embassy Run, and that intersection is pretty much the hottest spot in the city."

"That's the place for us, then, right, guys?" said Geordi brightly.

Data nodded politely and Worf grunted, which was about as much enthusiasm as he could be expected to show.

"Stick with me," said Coleridge, "and remember, no wandering off into the back streets. You could get seriously lost. And don't count on a transmat booth to save your hide. In the back streets they can be few and far between."

"You getting all this, Data?" Geordi asked.

Data blinked in surprise. "Of course. Would you like it repeated verbatim or simply condensed?"

"Just save it for later."

"All right."

They stopped at the intersection of Embassy Run and the Strip and took it all in.

To Geordi it appeared to be a massive, dazzling display of lights. The street was crammed with sign after flashing sign, some with burned-out lettering, others in full glory lighting up the night.

Data, for his part, studied the many varieties of beings who crammed the streets. Randrisians, Andorians, Tellarites . . .

A soft hand touched his arm. He turned and saw an exotically dressed female of the Thialtan race.

In a low voice she said, "Looking for some fun?"

"I believe that is the general concept," said Data affably.

"I can show you some," she said. "Once you've had a Thialtan, there's no going back."

Before Data could respond, Worf was standing in between him and the Thialtan. Worf looked down at her and rumbled, "He's with me."

The Thialtan regarded him coolly. "Kinky," she said.

Data frowned.

"Don't ask," Worf warned him and turned back to the Thialtan. "It's for his own protection. Thialtan sexual prowess is well documented. He is an android. There is a good chance you would blow his circuitry."

71

She smiled. "For starters," she said. Then she shrugged, turned on her heel, and walked away with a provocative switch of her hips.

Data watched her go, certain that there had been some sort of subtext to the conversation that he had missed completely. "She said there would be no going back. Where was I going to?"

"You are going to stay near me," said Worf sternly. "As security chief, it will not reflect well on me if the ranking officer is found disassembled in the morning."

It was an odd situation for Data. Generally he was with Riker or the captain in away-team situations. But being in command? What a curious concept.

"Hey!" Geordi was shouting from a distance. "Come on, you two!"

Geordi was standing just outside the largest establishment in the area. There was a huge flashing sign that read "Busiek's," and from inside the place came loud music, rough laughter, and occasional cheering. An odd odor also seemed to float from Busiek's; after a moment, Data recognized it as the smell of alcohol. This was verified when various sentients staggered out of the place in a diminished capacity.

"This would seem to be the equivalent of the Ten-Forward lounge," Data said as they walked quickly after the chief engineer. Geordi and Coleridge had already vanished into the recesses of the tavern.

"Somewhat rougher, I would think," said Worf. "Watch your step."

Data looked down and trod very carefully as they entered the bar.

The android was promptly assaulted by a barrage of sights, sounds, and aromas, a dazzling texture of sensations that he had never encountered before. He looked around, his yellow eyes wide.

72

A dim haze seemed to hang in the air, and all varieties of Kirlosians were crammed together in the confines of the tavern. Some sat huddled in conversation at small tables in the back. Others crowded around the bar, where there hardly seemed to be any room. Geordi and Coleridge had managed to find some space, though, and were already working on their first drinks.

Unlike the gleaming metallic sheen of the *Enterprise* rooms, the tavern was made of older synthetics with a rough-hewn look to them. The lighting, thanks to the haze, was somewhat dim, but Data's eyes immediately adjusted. As he walked, he looked down and saw that something on the order of sawdust covered the floor.

"Should we sit somewhere?" the android asked.

Worf surveyed the crowd, nodded briskly, and started to pull Data through. He got to an empty table at exactly the same time as two Inanh merchants. They glowered at each other, but to Data's relief, the Inanh backed down and Worf and Data slid behind the table.

A female Zoloch shuffled over and took their drink order. The Zoloch, because of their three-armed maneuverability and three-legged stability, were widely considered to be, among other things, the best waiters in the galaxy.

"I have heard of great hostility between Federation and K'Vin allies," said Data, looking around. "But I perceive a massive blending of all concerned here. Perhaps these racial divisions are exaggerated."

"I think not," Worf said. "Look again. They all stay with their own kind. Even at the crowded bar, notice that none of the Hegemony come into physical contact, even casually, with a Federation member."

Data saw immediately that Worf was quite correct.

73

He also saw that Geordi and Coleridge were into their second drinks and looking very friendly.

"I never knew you were like this," Geordi was saying.

"Like what?" Coleridge smiled.

"Like this . . . warm and approachable. I mean, I had such tremendous respect for you at the university and—"

"And now you have no respect for me?" But she was smiling, her almond eyes sparkling with amusement.

Flustered, Geordi said quickly, "That's not what I meant. I—"

She patted his hand. "I know what you meant, Geordi. You're not in awe of me, and that's as it should be. Differences in years are much larger when teenagers and adults are involved. But we're both adults now."

He grinned lopsidedly. "We sure are. You know . . . you do look really good tonight."

She ran her fingers through her hair coquettishly. "Yes, I know," and they both laughed.

Behind the bar, a large horned creature covered with thick matted hair was mixing drinks as quickly as he could. Nassa pointed him out to Geordi and said, "See him? That's Busiek. He owns the bar and knows everything about everything. Any questions, ask him."

"Everything about everything?" Geordi was feeling exceptionally mellow and he called out, "Hey, Busiek!"

The bartender turned and looked at him inquiringly.

"What's the diameter of this planet?"

"Forty-two hundred miles," Busiek said briskly.

"Average surface temperature?"

74

"Minus sixty-two Celsius."

Geordi paused. "What's the average wing speed of an unladen swallow?"

"European or African?" asked Busiek.

Geordi looked back at Nassa. "Damn, he's good."

Data, still trying to take everything in, noticed Gregach's second-in-command over in a corner. *Gezor.*

The curious thing was, Gezor looked intensely interested in not being noticed. He was wearing a cloak, the hood of which was pulled up, and even Data had not recognized him until the hood fell away briefly while Gezor was drinking. Gezor very quickly pulled it up again and seemed to cast a quick glance around, as if to make sure he had not been noticed.

There were two other Sullurh at the table with him, neither of whom Data knew. They were huddled close together, discussing something in what appeared to be urgent tones.

"Excuse me."

It was a deep, full female voice, and Data turned, wondering if that curious Thialtan woman had returned to resume their conversation.

She was not a Thialtan, and she was definitely not interested in Data.

A green Orion woman, wearing a tiger-cat smile and very little else, had sidled into the seat next to Worf. Worf was regarding her appraisingly.

What was running through his mind was clear. If Thialtan sexual prowess was well documented, that of Orion women was legendary, bordering on mythic. And they were nearly as durable as their Klingon counterparts.

Worf never took his eyes off her, partly out of fascination, partly out of self-preservation. He was

75

treading on dangerous ground letting her get this close to him. Then again, what good was the life of a warrior if it did not include danger every now and then?

"I haven't seen many Klingons here," she said, every word seeming to drip with sexual tension.

"Kirlosia is for scientists, merchants, and tourists," Worf replied slowly.

"And what are you doing here?" she asked. Her face was very close to Worf's, and Data wondered if that was really very hygienic.

"Talking to you," Worf rumbled.

"Is that all you do? Talk?" She ran her tongue along her upper teeth. "Or are you a man of action?"

"It depends on the provocation."

"I can be very provocative."

"No doubt," said Worf.

She sucked air noisily between her lips, and her eyes were smoldering. "Let's leave."

The Klingon regarded her. She was tempting. Quite tempting . . .

Just then, a dagger the length of Worf's forearm embedded itself in the tabletop.

Worf looked up. And up.

A massive Orion pirate was standing there glowering at the two of them. "Drusanne," he said dangerously, "what have I told you about running off?"

"I go where I wish," she said, and gripped Worf's arm. "I'm not your slave. And where I wish to go is with . . . what's your name?"

"His name is mud," said the pirate.

"No, his name is Worf," said Data helpfully.

Without looking at Data, Worf said, "I can handle this, Lieutenant Commander."

"Handle what? Is there going to be a problem?"

"Only if the Klingon doesn't let go of my woman," said the pirate.

Data glanced over and said, "Actually, I believe that *she* is holding on to *him,* not—"

"Commander," said Worf.

"I am my own woman," said Drusanne. "And you can't order me around, Grax. I'm leaving with him."

"You're not leaving with anyone," said Grax, "unless it's me. Must I make examples of these two in order to prove that?"

By way of punctuation, he poked Data in the chest.

"I would not do that, if I were you," said Worf.

"Why not?" laughed Grax.

"Because it gives me an excuse to wipe the walls with you. Or perhaps I should just shoot you. That would simplify matters."

"That will not be necessary, Lieutenant," said the android.

"Not now, Data—"

But Data pressed on. "It would seem to me that you are about to engage in a test of brute strength."

"It won't be a test," said Grax. "It will be a slaughter."

"Perhaps," said Data politely. "However, such an exercise would result in serious property damage, possibly bodily harm, and other consequences definitely in violation of Federation regulations. In that event, I would be forced to arrest Lieutenant Worf for conduct unbecoming an officer, and arrest you as the instigator."

Grax laughed and swung a fast right at Data. Worf lunged to intercept. Data was a hair faster and caught the fist in his hand. Grax gasped as Data held him tightly without the slightest show of strain.

This commotion had caught the attention of others

at the bar, including Geordi and Nassa. "Oh, my God, that Orion is going to kill Data!"

"I wouldn't bet the crystals on that," said Geordi.

Indeed, Grax's arm was quivering under the strain of Data's grip. "This is quite unfair to you, sir," Data was saying politely. "I am an android. Combat with me would be even more futile than combat with Worf."

"I can beat him, damn you!" said Grax, struggling in Data's iron grip. "I can beat anything living, which explains you!"

"Not really, but that would be an irrelevant digression," said Data. "Since the main question seems to be who is stronger, you or Lieutenant Worf, may I suggest a compromise?"

Grax and Worf looked at each other, and then back at Data.

Moments later the table had been cleared and Worf and Grax were opposite each other locked in a furious arm-wrestling contest. All around them people were shouting encouragement or discouragement, and bets were flying.

Data stood nearby, and Geordi said to him in a low voice, "I'm really impressed. You handled that very well."

"I felt it was necessary to take command of the situation," said Data primly. "To be honest, the burden of command is not difficult to bear. Far simpler than I would have thought."

Now others were crowding in, and Data was too polite to shove to maintain his place. As a result he soon found himself on the outer edge of the crowd.

It was of little consequence to him. He had already gauged the Orion's strength when he held the pirate's fist. He knew of Worf's strength and had already calculated to the third decimal point precisely how many minutes it would take Worf to defeat the pirate.

Still, he wanted to hear what was happening, for Worf was muttering some interesting things that might be of use in other situations. So he turned up his hearing a notch—and heard the wrong conversation.

"And that'll be the beginning of the end for the K'Vin embassy."

It was said in hushed, conspiratorial tones.

And it was coming from behind Data.

He turned and saw Gezor still seated at his table with the other two Sullurh. They nodded and then abruptly stopped talking, lifted their drinks, and clinked the glasses together as if in agreement.

Data was absolutely positive that Gezor had said it. But why? What had Gezor been talking about?

Could it be something innocent? Perhaps they were going to remodel the embassy, which would mean an end to the old one.

No, that made no sense. Something in Gezor's tone was wrong. Something about the situation was wrong.

He waited for them to say something else, but they just sat now, as if silently communing. Data wished Counselor Troi had come along.

Then Gezor waved toward the waitress for their check. She ignored them—not unusual treatment for the Sullurh. But it was clear that they intended to leave, and Data suddenly decided they should not be left unattended.

The android quickly made his way through the crowd. His greater strength allowed him to push through easily, and he ignored the epithets that were hurled at him. He found his way to Geordi, who was shouting encouragement to Worf, and spoke quickly into the engineer's ear. Geordi tilted his head and looked with curiosity at Data.

"Are you sure?" he asked.

"Yes," said Data. "We may have to act quickly. And Worf must come with us. He is head of security."

"Worf's in the middle of an arm-wrestling match!"

"No. He is at the end. Three . . . two . . . one!"

At that instant Worf slammed the pirate's arm down, and a cheer roared up from the crowd. The pirate, rubbing his throbbing arm, stood up, kicked his chair away, and stalked off.

Geordi looked in confusion from Worf to Data and back, and then shrugged. "I give up. You do know everything."

As money exchanged hands and the crowd broke up, looking to get back to their abandoned drinks, Data and Geordi went quickly to Worf's side and told him what was happening. His reaction was less than enthusiastic.

"No," said Worf.

Data blinked in surprise. "No?"

"No," said Worf firmly. "First, we cannot simply follow the Sullurh wherever they go. This city is very segmented. Crossing through the wrong section is asking for serious trouble. If you want him questioned, I will do so, but following him is a mistake. Second . . ."

His voice trailed off and he growled in anger. For the Orion woman was walking out of the tavern on the arm of a well-dressed Pandrilite.

Data, ignoring the second half of the statement, said, "If Gezor is planning some sort of subterfuge, he may not admit it under questioning. Following a suspect, however, is the accepted technique in all the best detective literature."

"Oh, God," sighed Geordi. "You're saying 'the game is afoot,' right?"

Data gave a brief nod. Worf scowled.

At that moment Nassa tapped Geordi on the shoulder and said, "Pardon me, but to paraphrase Emerson, all nature seems at work, and I have to answer its call."

"That wasn't Emerson," said Data. "That was Coleridge. Samuel Taylor Coleridge."

She winced. "Coleridge. That hurts." And she walked off.

The moment she was out of earshot Geordi said quickly, "Okay, Sherlock. Where are they?"

Data turned and pointed—at an empty table.

Quickly he crossed the tavern, sliding slightly on the sawdust. Worf was right behind him, and Geordi followed a moment later, after leaving a hasty, apologetic message for Nassa with Busiek.

They ran out the door, looked right and left.

Out of the corner of his eye, Data spotted Gezor. The other two Sullurh had vanished somewhere into the back streets, but Gezor was walking briskly down Embassy Run toward the K'Vin embassy.

"There," he said in a low voice, and they started off after him.

They were fortunate. In any other city a Klingon, a gold-skinned android, and a black human wearing a VISOR, all dressed in Starfleet uniforms and moving surreptitiously, would undoubtedly have attracted attention. In Kirlosia, however, there was such an ethnic mix—not to mention that *everyone* acted as if he or she had something to hide—that the people who passed gave them only the most cursory of glances before going on about their business.

However, the farther they got into K'Vin territory, the more the glances started to linger. Worf stared back, mouth pulled into a snarl, and that discouraged further inquiries. But they were definitely being noticed, if not questioned.

Gezor, for his part, did not seem to have noticed them. He continued on a slow, steady pace, unhurried and unconcerned.

At one point he stopped, as if to consider his course, and the three pursuers, hanging back a safe two blocks, stopped also. They stepped into the shadows of a nearby building and tried to look unobtrusive. Geordi whispered to Data, "Are you sure there's any point to this?"

"No," said Data reasonably. "That is why we are following him. To discover if there is a reason."

Geordi couldn't argue with that sort of logic. Still, as they started to walk again when Gezor did, something bothered him.

Gezor had already passed one transmat booth and was now walking briskly past a second. In the distance was the K'Vin embassy, which more and more seemed to be his destination. But if it was, why hadn't he used the first transmat booth? He voiced his concern to Data.

Data pondered it. "I am not certain. There are several possibilities."

"And they are . . .?"

They were now getting quite close to the K'Vin embassy. The crowds had thinned to almost nothing.

"He *could* simply want to get some exercise," said Data. "Or it is possible that he is supposed to pick something up along the way. Or perhaps he is to meet someone. Or—"

The embassy loomed ahead of them now, its great turrets casting an awesome multi-armed shadow.

And about twenty yards from the embassy, Gezor suddenly veered off. Immediately the *Enterprise* trio picked up speed as Gezor vanished to the right into a side street. By the time they got there, the Sullurh had disappeared, swallowed up by the shadowy maze of the back streets.

"Or what else?" said Geordi, now completely confused.

"Or else," said Data thoughtfully, "he was aware of us and wanted us to follow him close to the embassy."

"But why?"

And at that moment, with a cataclysmic explosion, one of the proud turrets of the embassy blew apart.

The trio ran like hell, Worf shielding the other two with his body. Debris rained down on them, and a fine powder of rubble filled the air, mixing with screams and shouts.

Seconds earlier, there had been no one on the streets. Now suddenly it was surging with life before the echoes of the explosion had even died down.

"We have to see if we can help!" shouted Geordi. "There may be people trapped in there!"

"No," said Worf firmly. Khitomer flashed through his mind. "There may be further explosions. Running into one will do no one any good. Wait to make sure all is secure."

But Data was already off and running. He was heading toward the embassy at full speed.

"Data!" shouted Geordi. He knew damned well that Data could hear him, but the android didn't even slow down. "Worf, I'm not letting Data go in there by himself!" And he started off after his friend. Worf, clearly fed up, nevertheless followed them.

As they got to the embassy, there were shouts all around them. "Look! Federation men! What are they doing here!"

"Perhaps they're responsible!"

"I'll bet they are!"

Geordi did not like the sound of that at all.

Data, for his part, didn't seem to notice. He was searching desperately through the rubble. "Clues," he said. "There have to be clues."

"Data!" said Geordi desperately. "This is not Sherlock Holmes time! Do you understand? We are seriously outnumbered, and I think we'd better get the hell out of here!"

Data looked at Geordi in puzzlement. "Outnumbered? Certainly we are not being held responsible for this?"

Geordi sighed in exasperation even as he scanned the ruins with his VISOR. There were no signs of body heat, and no one seemed to be trapped beneath the rubble. It appeared that the offices of that turret had been empty when it blew.

At that moment, Gregach stumbled out the front door, coughing and hacking. He was gripping something in his hand; it appeared to be a bone with meat on it. Worf immediately went to him and prevented him from falling, slapping him on his broad back to stop the choking. Four guards, covered with bits of debris, came running up and helped steady Gregach. The ambassador was staring forlornly at the meat, grumbling, "A K'Vin can't even enjoy a decent spilat anymore."

Then he stopped, pulled himself together, and tried to focus on what was happening. He stood, looking Worf in the eye. "What are you doing here?" he said. There was just an edge of danger to his voice. And then, just as quickly, he said, "No. Don't answer that. If you say the wrong words, they'll tear you apart."

He inclined his head slightly toward the mob that was coming toward them, shouting angry epithets and insults about the Federation, about Klingons, about anything that came to mind.

They were in seriously hostile territory.

Quickly Gregach slapped a hand on Worf's shoulder and said in a loud voice, "You three are being held for questioning!"

"What?" said Geordi.

A roar went up from the crowd, now about sixty strong and growing. The guards formed a tight circle around the away team.

Data looked up from the rubble and addressed the ambassador. "Sir," he said politely, "you seem to be under the impression that—"

"I'm under the impression," said Gregach quickly, "that you are deep in an area you shouldn't be in at all, near an event that shouldn't have happened. Either I bring you in *there* for questioning or I leave you *here* with the crowd. *Your* decision."

"Yes," said Worf testily. *"Your* decision, *Lieutenant Commander."*

Data's mouth moved. But for the first time in memory, nothing came out.

It had all seemed like a game, like a holodeck scenario come to life. Data had ignored Worf's warnings about hostile territory. He had not considered the motives that might be pushing Gezor. Instead, he had blundered in, been led around, and suddenly jeopardized the well-being of the away team, not to mention diplomatic relations between the K'Vin and the Federation.

His command was not off to an auspicious start.

Chapter Seven

IN HER THREE YEARS on Kirlos, Stephaleh had never been wakened during the night. She always took that as the sign of a good posting. But tonight her dreams were shattered when Zamorh woke her with a shake and spoke in an urgent voice.

"Ambassador!" he called, hoping to bring her awake fast. "The K'Vin embassy—there was an explosion!"

Alert, although racked with spasms and aches, Stephaleh sat up in her round bed. "Gregach, is he alive?"

"Yes, Ambassador. In fact, he's standing by, waiting to speak with you."

She struggled to her feet, wrapping herself in a down-filled robe, one of the few Andorian artifacts to be found in her room. It was brightly colored, bearing a pattern from an ancient clan that Stephaleh had always suspected she belonged to. She slipped her feet into comfortable shoes and blinked several times.

Summoning her will, she made her body move without showing signs of age.

It took her a few minutes to negotiate her way from the bedroom to the office, where she preferred to hold her conversations on the screen. Zamorh kept pace, bringing her up to date. "It seems, Ambassador, that the Starfleet officers were in K'Vin territory at the time of the explosion. As soon as it happened, Lieutenant Worf signaled Security Chief Powell. They have some information for you and are on their way."

"Why didn't they beam over?"

"It seems that transmission lines were disrupted abruptly, by order of Ambassador Gregach."

Now that was an odd wrinkle, she thought. Gregach had never before suspended the transmat net linking the two sides of Kirlos. This was indeed a serious problem and one that required a great deal of thought. Tensions between the two governments had never before affected her dealings with Gregach, but they were nonetheless duty-bound to their respective governments.

Finally, she arrived at her office. Zamorh had turned on the lights and was busying himself in a corner, preparing some tea for her, just as he did every morning. What would she do without him when her assignment here was over and she had to return to Andor?

"Put Gregach on line, please," she said, lowering herself gently into her chair. It brought some comfort; she smiled. For now, however, it was time to be an ambassador, so she put the smile on hold.

The screen flickered once, and then Ambassador Gregach, smoke-streaked and haggard, filled the image area. "Stephaleh, has anything happened at your building?"

"No, nothing. Are you all right, Gregach? What happened over there?"

"An explosion. No one knows what caused it." He shook his head. "The fires have been put out, and the doctors are tending to the injured. None have died—yet. But something is happening on Kirlos and it is not to my liking."

She looked at him. "Then you believe they are linked, these events?"

"Two explosions: first in a Federation building and now in my embassy. It is too much to be coincidence. No, my friend, this is something insidious."

A Sullurh brought him a report, and he stopped to glance at it. Stephaleh's attention was drawn momentarily to the Sullurh. It was not Gezor, she noticed. She wondered where Gregach's assistant was. No doubt tending to the repair of the embassy. Or perhaps initiating an investigation.

"We *do* have deaths," Gregach noted. "Some maintenance functionaries overcome by smoke when they tried to quench the fires." He looked up from the report. "Now this has become murder, Stephaleh. Something must be *done.*"

She stopped and thought. Why would people want to cause destruction on both sides? Who could be responsible? And was Zamorh right—did enough people dislike the Starfleet personnel to want them gone from Kirlos? Enough to cause death and destruction? He had voiced those thoughts yesterday, and she had shrugged them off as idle speculation. Now she had to stop and reconstruct the conversation, recalling his words to see if he did, indeed, have a point.

"Gregach, who do you suppose caused this, if it was indeed an act of sabotage?"

"Oh, it was sabotage all right, Stephaleh. I wish I

could say who—because if I knew, I would have them killed. But I do not know. Perhaps when we examine the explosion site in the dawn light."

"Of course. Now please tell me, why was the transporter net disrupted?"

"Ah, well, you see, we did not want whoever was responsible for this to make an easy escape by transmat. Our security forces are tracking down several possibilities. Did you know your own Starfleet officers were in the area?" He leaned forward to watch her reaction.

"Yes, I did," she said. She had learned it only moments ago, but at least it had not come as a surprise. Her face remained calm, and as always, she kept her voice down. The Andorian welcomed her cup of tea just as Gezor appeared on the edge of the screen and summoned Gregach's attention. He whispered furiously in the ambassador's ear and she watched with interest as Gregach's head bobbed up and down.

"Ambassador, the *Enterprise* officers are here," Zamorh said quietly.

She nodded and with a low hand gesture asked for them to be brought in. With Gregach distracted, she lowered the audio pickup—usually set high to indulge Gregach, who always good-naturedly complained about Stephaleh's whisper. The door swung open and Data walked into the room, followed by Worf and Geordi. This was the first time Data had walked in the lead, and she watched with interest. They looked tired and dirty—the result, no doubt, of the explosion. At least they were alive.

"Ambassador, we have just come from the K'Vin territory. There was an explosion at the embassy," Data began.

She shushed him and pointed to the monitor.

Gregach remained in consultation with Gezor, who was now gesturing with both hands. He seemed agitated to Stephaleh.

"Ambassador Gregach," she said.

The thickset K'Vin looked up and noticed that the link was still open. And to his surprise, Data was visible on his screen behind Stephaleh.

"The *Enterprise* officers have just arrived," said the Andorian. "Once we have debriefed them, I am sure they will be most happy to tell your people exactly what they saw. Should they contact Ilugh?" Ilugh was the head of Gregach's personal guard, a soldier who had served under him in more than one military campaign.

"No need, Ambassador. I have already spoken to them personally," he replied. "And released them." He paused, composing his thoughts and looking again at Gezor, who had not moved out of screen range, as he usually did. Stephaleh suppressed a surprised reaction; it hadn't occurred to her that Gregach would question them before contacting her. Something seemed different about Gregach, as if he had wakened from a long nap.

"These circumstances have been tragic, what with destruction and death," Gregach said. "I do not see any other course, at present, but to suspend the archaeological dig and order—no, make that *request* —that all United Federation of Planets personnel remain on their side of Kirlosia."

"You're cutting us off, just like that? Would you like us to stop breathing the air pumped from your circulators?" Stephaleh's anger showed in her sarcasm, and Geordi watched, amazed. He knew then that she was not someone he wanted to cross.

"I do not see another choice. Until I know who or

what caused the explosion, I must restrict the number of people with access to official K'Vin buildings."

"And what of the destruction of a Federation building? That came first and we cast no suspicions on you and your people. Why accuse us so readily? Have you some proof—or just fear?"

Gregach was taken aback by her words and her anger. He seemed genuinely ashamed of the situation, but also gave no sign of backing down. He couldn't. A battle was brewing and he wanted to remain sharp. "I am sorry you feel that way, Ambassador, but I must do as I see fit. We will speak again when I have news." And the screen went dark.

Stephaleh leaned back in her chair. She considered the three *Enterprise* officers across the expanse of her imported Andorian desk.

"And so," she said, "you believe that Gregach's assistant knew about the incident in advance?"

Data nodded. "Precisely, Ambassador. Even if I had not overheard his conversation, his choice of routes would have suggested a certain foreknowledge."

"And if he knew about it," said La Forge, "it's not so improbable that he helped cause it."

"Or," said Worf, "that he and his accomplices had a hand in the trading hall incident."

The ambassador kneaded one hand with the other. It helped relieve the stiffness. "You're suggesting treachery," she said, "that extends into the ranks of the K'Vin embassy." She turned to Zamorh, who sat to one side of her. "Can you shed any light on this?" she asked him.

The Sullurh stared at her as he gathered his thoughts. "Precious little," he said finally. "I do not know this Gezor very well, nor do I know his family. Therefore, I cannot vouch for his intentions. However, I *do* know this: he has served Ambassador Gregach for some years now, and Gregach's predecessor for some years before that. Moreover, I cannot think why he would want to turn traitor. Where is the profit for him—the advantage?"

"A good question," said Stephaleh. She turned back to the officers. "Care to take a stab at it?"

The android suddenly looked perplexed.

"The ambassador means," explained La Forge, "that she wants us to provide an answer—if we can."

"Ah," said Data. "Of course."

"Unfortunately," said Worf, "we can provide no answer." He scowled—a typical Klingon, noted Stephaleh—and glanced at Zamorh. "Not without better knowledge of what motivates the Sullurh."

The ambassador could almost see Zamorh's hackles rise. Yet he remained still and expressionless in his chair.

An Andorian would never have received the implication so calmly. But then, Zamorh was no Andorian.

She addressed all three officers, but the Klingon in particular. "Let me assure you," she said, "that the Sullurh are a simple, straightforward people. They are not easily swayed from their loyalties. That is why we—both the Federation and the K'Vin—have drawn upon them in staffing our embassies. Believe me, they would not be tempted by either financial gain or the promise of power, even if such things were offered to them." She sighed, sat back in her chair. "Now, it may be that this Gezor has violated the trust that Gregach placed in him. But if he has, it is a very un-Sullurh-like trait that has caused him to do so."

"All right," said La Forge. "Maybe trying to figure

out Gezor is the wrong approach. Maybe we try to figure out his allies."

Stephaleh kneaded her hands some more. "Allies," she echoed.

"He would *have* to have had allies," said Worf. "It is highly unlikely that, with a profile as high as his, he could have procured the explosives on his own."

The ambassador nodded. "Yes, I suppose it is."

"Is there any group," asked Data, "that has expressed disaffection for the K'Vin? Or for the embassy in particular?"

Stephaleh shrugged. "Not openly." She turned to Zamorh. "To *your* knowledge?"

He shook his head. "As you say, not openly. However, there *is* a contingent of Xanthricite traders who have had numerous disagreements with the K'Vin embassy of late—if only in matters of commerce."

"What about the Randrisians?" asked Worf. "Are they not present on the K'Vin side? And have they not had a history of confrontations with the K'Vin?"

"Good point," said Stephaleh. "Though the confrontations you speak of are generally considered ancient history, both by the K'Vin and by the Randrisians."

The Klingon grunted. "Never underestimate the power of ancient history," he maintained.

"No," said La Forge. "It's got to be bigger than that. Don't forget—the trading hall was destroyed, too. What would the Randrisians and the Xanthricites have against the trading hall? Or against the Federation?"

The ambassador looked at him. "A conspiracy that transcends the K'Vin-Federation division?"

"That's right," said La Forge. "A group with reasons to undermine *both* embassies."

"That," observed Stephaleh, *"would* be big."

"Unless," Worf interjected, "the destruction of the Commercial Trading Hall was just a ploy, so that when the K'Vin embassy was victimized, suspicion would naturally come down on the Federation."

"Intriguing," said Data. "The Federation would be suspected of seeking revenge, though in actuality it would be a victim. Just as the K'Vin are victims."

"Yes," said Stephaleh. "Intriguing indeed. But we have no proof of any of this. No evidence that a conspiracy even exists."

"But neither can we rule it out," insisted Worf.

"One must remember," said Data, moderating, "that it is the nature of a conspiracy to be secret. Our inability to readily identify its members is an indication neither that it exists nor that it does not. Both are equally valid propositions."

"Which brings us back to Gezor," noted La Forge. "He's still our only lead."

"I believe," said the ambassador, "that a reference to square one would be appropriate here."

"We must do *something,"* growled the Klingon. "Whoever is behind these two incidents will continue to create havoc until we stop him. Or *them."*

"It appears that Lieutenant Worf is right," said Data.

Stephaleh spread her hands. "What would you have us *do?"*

"How about contacting Gregach?" asked La Forge, "and telling him what we know about Gezor?"

The ambassador weighed the option—and rejected it. "He will not listen," she concluded. "He has already shut his ears to us. And he will be *particularly* disinclined to consider something like treachery on the part of his first assistant." She frowned. "Not that I blame him. Why accept advice from someone you no longer trust—when it impugns the reputation of someone you still believe in? Perhaps if I had some proof of . . ."

Her thought was cut off by the appearance of Ekrut, another of her Sullurh assistants. "Your pardon," he said, "but there is someone downstairs to see you, Ambassador. His name is Thul, and he seems to have urgent news."

"Thul," repeated Data. "Doctor Coleridge's assistant?"

All three of the officers were on their feet in an instant. Negotiating a course around her desk, Stephaleh followed.

Worf was the first to reach Ekrut. *"What* news?" he thundered.

Dismayed, Ekrut backed off a step. "The . . . the museum," he said in a small voice.

"What about it?" prodded the ambassador.

"He—Thul says there was an explosion."

"Damn," barked Geordi. "The *professor* was supposed to be at the museum today." He touched Ekrut on the shoulder to reassure him. "Did he say anything about Professor Coleridge?"

The Sullurh shrugged, glancing uncomfortably at the ambassador. "I am not certain," he confessed. "He spoke of *many* things—and all at once. It was difficult to sort them all out."

"Come on," said Worf. He plunged ahead, pressed the heat-sensitive plate that summoned the turbolift. The lift was waiting, and the doors opened instantly.

All six of them entered, Ekrut last of all. "First floor," commanded Stephaleh. The atmosphere in the cubicle was so thick that one could have choked on it.

Then they were at ground level, the doors were opening, and there was Thul seated on a chair in the lobby, his head cradled in his hands.

Again the Klingon charged ahead, followed by La Forge and Data. Stephaleh couldn't keep up; her legs had cramped.

When Thul saw them all coming, he looked up. But he didn't cringe as Ekrut had. He simply stared, his large eyes glistening with reflected light.

Worf stopped short of the Sullurh, his question already answered. His hands balling into fists, he snarled like a beast at bay.

"Oh, my God," said Geordi. Apparently he had his own way of gauging the situation; he didn't need to actually see the tears.

"Has something happened to Professor Coleridge?" asked Data—somewhat innocently, Stephaleh thought.

Drawing a ragged breath, Thul regarded the android. He nodded.

The museum had been one of the more popular tourist attractions—the operative words being "had been."

Now the small structure, which had been so carefully stocked with the treasures of the Ariantu race that digs had produced, was little more than an archaeological memory itself.

Geordi was the first one out of the transmat booth, which quickly discharged Stephaleh, Worf, Data, and Thul. They almost crashed into Geordi, for the chief engineer had come to a dead halt a mere couple of yards in front of the booth.

A huge hole had been blown in the side of the two-story building, and the roof had collapsed. The explosion had been so powerful that windows in the neighboring buildings for two blocks around had been blown out. Even though the calamity had occurred some minutes before, a fine mist of debris still hung in the air.

Crowds of people were milling around in confusion as a rescue crew sifted through the rubble.

And a body lay off to the side, covered by a blanket.

Geordi ran toward it even as he heard Thul muttering behind him, "The museum wasn't open yet. She was the only one there! I should have been helping her. It should have been *me*."

Geordi skidded to a halt. He dropped to his knees and hesitated over the blanket, not wanting to pull it back. Knowing what he would find. . . .

He wasn't sure what happened next. All he knew was that he had turned away without removing the blanket. He was sitting there, his knees drawn up to his chin, slowly shaking his head. Data was standing in front of him, Worf off to the side. Thul looked grief-stricken.

"She was kind to me," Thul was saying. "She never condescended. She treated me as an equal. She treated everybody that way."

"It's *her* under there," said Geordi. "Isn't it, Data?" It wasn't really a question.

Data nodded.

Slowly Geordi turned and brought himself to lift away the blanket. He "saw" the object under there, but that's all it was. An object. Not a human being, not someone filled with life and hope and enthusiasm. Just a lifeless sack of flesh.

He ran his fingers over her face.

Once that had been the only way a blind man could discern features. Now Geordi's VISOR provided him with other means, but they were mechanical. Distant. Cold.

Cold, like her skin. He traced the gentle lines of her

face . . . and then gasped at the indentation he discovered, where a falling piece of the building must have crushed her temple. Her cheek was sticky, and he realized that it was dried blood that made it so.

He pulled away, holding his hand away from him as if it were a separate piece that he could remove. "Thul," he said softly, "was it quick? Did Nassa . . . suffer?"

Slowly Thul came toward him. "She was still alive when I found her," he said. "I pulled her from the rubble. But she died right afterward."

"She never regained consciousness?"

"For a moment," said Thul softly. He paused. "She said something just before she died. She said, 'Maud Muller.' "

Geordi sat there, uncomprehending. "What? Who is that?"

"I don't know."

"Maybe," Geordi said quickly, "maybe this Maud Muller is the one who blew up the building. Or maybe—"

But Data was shaking his head. "No, Geordi."

"What? Well, then, who—"

" 'Maud Muller,' " said Data, "is a poem, by John Greenleaf Whittier. A couplet from it is very well known. It is 'For of all sad words of tongue or pen, The saddest are these: "It might have been!" ' I believe that is what she was referring to." He paused thoughtfully. "Of course, sometimes she tended to misattribute her sources. So it is possible that—"

"Shut up!" It was a cry of agony from Geordi. "Just shut up, Data! You think you know every damned thing in the world. You don't know anything! She was talking about all the things she could have accomplished. Maybe she was even talking about her and me and—and you're going on about sources! Who gives two credits, huh? She's dead! Can't you understand that?"

Data stood there for a long moment, and then he bent down and placed a hand on the shoulder of his grieving friend.

"No," he said.

Geordi looked up at him.

"I comprehend," said Data slowly. "I can even attempt to approximate mourning. But I do not *understand.*"

In a sense, Data envied Geordi his grief. When Tasha Yar died, he had felt an emptiness, as if something had been removed. But no genuine grief. Perhaps that emotion was something that had been deliberately left out of his makeup in order to spare him unnecessary difficulty.

And why should he be spared something that all sentient beings had to suffer in one way or another? He knew the answer even before he had completed the question in his mind: because he would have to experience so much more of it for so much longer. He did not know the limitations of his durability, but there was a good chance that he was immortal by human standards.

Geordi, Worf . . . they would live their allotted spans, mourn those they lost, then die and be mourned in turn. But Data would lose *everyone*—and still go on, remaining untouched by each loss.

Decades from this place, this time, young Wesley Crusher would die, perhaps in the android's arms. And they would be the same arms, the same Data that stood now on Kirlos in the ruins of the museum building.

Others would come, people who had not yet been born, and their lives, too, would pass before his eyes. He would cross the decades, the centuries, with the gift of immortality, which so many had sought—and he would lament it. Unable to die, unable simply to shut himself off, since his inexorable desire for knowledge would compel him to continue.

Friends and grandchildren of friends will die, he thought, *and I will mourn them all, as best I can. But no one will ever mourn me.*

Geordi was silent for a long moment. "I'm sorry I snapped at you, Data," he said softly.

"It was very human of you," said Data.

Geordi reached under the blanket, took the cold hand in his. "She meant so much to me, I can't even begin to tell you. When you're blind, you need someone to help put the world in focus. That's what she did. I was very different in those days, Data. Very inwardly directed. She helped me to look outward and love the world . . . and myself. And I thought I knew her so well. Then we came here, and I realized there was so much *more* about her. You don't think of teachers as people, y'know? You think of them as . . . teachers. These separate beings that exist only in classrooms. So to encounter her now, so different—it was exhilarating. It made me feel so young again, like it was in the old days when everything, absolutely everything, was a mystery."

He shook his head and frowned. "We've got to find the ones who did this, Data. We've got to find the ones responsible. They can't get away with this."

"They will not, Geordi."

All this time Worf had been silent, as if considering something. And suddenly he tilted back his head and roared, an earsplitting bellow that started in a low register and grew higher and louder. Geordi flinched, and Data actually clapped his hands over his ears. Thul ran back about ten yards and Stephaleh turned her antennae away to spare herself the sound.

Worf stopped after about ten seconds and looked down at Nassa again. "She knew the language of the Klingon," he said, "and she had the heart of a warrior. It was appropriate to honor her with the Klingon death scream."

Geordi said simply, "I'm sure she would have appreciated it, Worf."

He stood. Stephaleh walked over to him and said softly, "I shall arrange for the body to be returned. In the meantime I suggest you go back to the embassy immediately. With this newest attack, relations will deteriorate even further, and I would prefer to have everyone safe when that happens."

"Right. Right, okay." Geordi looked down at Coleridge one more time and then, without a word, headed back for the transmat booth. Data and Worf fell into step behind him.

The ambassador's antennae twitched in sympathy. She had known Coleridge for only a relatively brief time. And besides, Andorians did not permit themselves to become too emotional about such matters as death.

She bent over to cover the body and felt a twinge in her lower back. At first she started to curse the unrelenting pains of age, and then she stopped. The alternative to pain and old age, she realized, was death. Nassa Coleridge would never feel pain again, but that was hardly beneficial.

At least the aches, the pains, the twinges, were reminders that she, Stephaleh, was still alive. Perhaps she should be grateful for them.

She rose, and her right thigh cramped up completely. She started to massage the muscles and thought, *Yes. Perhaps.*

Chapter Eight

STATIC SHOTS of the surface of Tehuán flickered rapidly across the main viewscreen of the *Enterprise*. Too rapidly. Captain Picard shut his eyes and rubbed at the bridge of his nose. The stream of sensor images was giving him eyestrain. Or perhaps, he thought glumly, he was giving way to the frustration of trying to uncover a reason for the attack on Tehuán. Perhaps he was trying too hard, thus losing sight of an essential detail that would become obvious once he simply relaxed.

After a moment's repose, he felt the throbbing in his temples ease. Picard opened his eyes again. Pain slammed back into place, and the mystery of Tehuán remained as impenetrable as ever.

Damn.

He missed Data. He needed Data. Not only did the android possess a certain rapport with the computers that facilitated research, but he also acted as a sounding board for Picard's own thoughts. Data might not always provide the solution to a problem, but his comments often inspired a new perspective that led to that solution. At the moment Picard was definitely lacking inspiration.

He turned at the sound of footsteps coming from the aft deck and was relieved to see Lieutenant Dean approaching the captain's chair. The science officer was a spare man with a wiry build. He worked quietly and efficiently, but at the pace of a human being. Picard pushed aside the unfair comparison with Data. What mattered was that the report was finished at last; now they could make some progress.

But Dean shook his head in bewilderment. "Computer analysis hasn't revealed any distinctive features of this settlement. The five other colonies in this sector are also basically agricultural and equally vulnerable to attack. None of them is especially prosperous yet, but Devlin Four has a large reserve of trade goods. It will probably be the next target."

"I disagree," said Ensign Burke, leaning over the railing of the upper deck to join the discussion. He lacked the imposing bulk of the Klingon security chief, but he spoke with the typically emphatic manner of a security officer. "Sensor scans from all alerted outposts are negative. There are still no signs of an alien fleet in the sector, and a dozen ships couldn't travel from Tehuán to Devlin without being detected."

"So," Picard sighed. "They have been 'Swallowed up and lost in the wide womb of uncreated night.'"

"Is that Shakespeare, sir?" asked Wesley Crusher, looking up from the Conn console.

"Milton. I gather you haven't read *Paradise Lost.*"

"Uh, no, sir." The ensign hurriedly returned to his sensor readings. He tapped the control panel, and the viewscreen froze on a single aerial view of land cradled between two mountain ranges. "Surface scan completed, Captain. No indications of damage to any other areas. The settlement valley seems to be the only site that was attacked."

Picard had expected as much, so the confirmation provided little useful knowledge; but at least the parade of images was over. How ironic that from this distance the devastation of the colony appeared as nothing more than scattered black smudges on a swatch of green. In a few seasons, once rain had washed away the dust and new growth had covered the scorched ground, even those signs would be erased.

Yet there were older, deeper scars that the vegetation had not completely masked out.

"Ensign, increase magnification by ten." The ground sprang closer, but the outlines were still faint. "There's something very familiar about—"

Picard was cut off by an intercom announcement: "Crusher to captain. I have the report you ordered."

"I'm on my way, Doctor." Even as he answered the call, he was springing out of his chair. Since he had demanded the information over the strenuous objections of his chief medical officer, there was no excuse for delay. Nevertheless, when the doors to the forward turbolift opened, the captain hesitated before stepping inside the compartment. He allowed himself one final lingering look at Tehuán.

"Ensign Crusher, call a geologist to the bridge to inspect that view. I have some questions about the terrain."

Beverly Crusher was waiting in her office; her temper had not improved since their last encounter. As soon as he crossed the threshold of the room, she slammed a data padd down on her desk.

"We're still treating casualties, and I have to take

time away from the living to deal with those who are beyond help."

Since he'd heard this argument before and it hadn't swayed him then, Picard made no comment. Crusher jammed her fists into the pockets of her lab coat and glared at him, but he could tell her anger was nearly spent.

"Besides, I hate autopsies."

"What did you find?" asked Picard, suddenly certain the doctor had discovered something worth reporting.

Her description was crisp and to the point. "Three bodies with similar markings—a radial pattern of subcutaneous hemorrhaging—were recovered in the vicinity of the rock slide. But they weren't killed by debris and they weren't killed by a ship's phaser barrage."

"So the attackers were using a new weapon."

She shook her head. "Quite the contrary. I'll skip the forensic details, but physical evidence indicates the colonists were killed at short range by the blast from a hand-held disrupter."

"A disrupter?" He hadn't expected that old-fashioned twist. "That means at least a few of the raiders actually beamed down to the planet surface."

"Yes, but they were careful not to leave any witnesses."

At last Picard began to sense some meaning in the events that had puzzled him. That meaning was still hidden, but eventually it could be teased out into the open.

"So the attack wasn't simply vandalism or terrorism. They, whoever they are, wanted something on the surface. But what? Not mushrooms—the landslide site is at the foot of the mountains, far distant from the fields. Something else. And the answers are on Tehuán. . . ." He trailed off, distracted by the memory of his last view of the valley. What possible connection could there be . . .

"Are you beaming down there?" asked Crusher, jarring him out of reverie.

"I'd have a difficult time justifying that action," he said with a hint of embarrassment. "Not very long ago I subjected your son to a lecture on why my place is on the bridge."

"Captains have the prerogative of changing their minds."

"I'm tempted. But, no, I can't leave the ship. Not with so many of my bridge officers down on Kirlos and a hostile fleet hiding somewhere in the sector. Commander Riker is a perfectly capable away-team leader; my duty is here on board the *Enterprise*."

She tried to hide a smile and failed. "But you don't have to like it?"

"No," he admitted, smiling back. "I don't have to like it. Just don't tell that to Ensign Crusher."

Riker scrambled over loose rocks, fighting to climb higher up the slope of the mountain, but he made little progress on the shifting layer of stone, and his movements raised a billowing cloud of dust. Between fits of coughing, he swept his tricorder in a wide arc around him. The readings were unchanged and unremarkable.

He slipped the instrument back into his pocket and searched for another path upward.

"Will, if you're not more careful you'll end up in sickbay," Troi called out from below.

"I know what I'm doing," he said through clenched teeth, even though she was too far away to hear him.

She was an empath; perhaps she would sense his irritation and leave him to his work. Shifting his weight from one foot to the other, Riker reached out and groped for a new handhold. The rock underneath his boot wobbled, then gave way entirely and sent him tumbling down the slope to level ground.

When he opened his eyes, Troi was standing over him, blocking out the light of the noonday sun.

"Just what were you trying to prove?" she asked.

Sitting up made his head spin, but otherwise he seemed to be all right. Which probably accounted for Troi's lack of sympathy. "The captain asked for a thorough examination of the area around the rock slide."

"What did you find?"

"Rocks," he said, struggling to his feet. He checked his tricorder for signs of damage, but it had also survived the fall intact. "Instrument readings don't show anything underneath the slide, in the slide, or on top of the slide."

Yet Picard had sounded so certain that this site held the key to the attack on Tehuán. Given that conviction, Riker knew that if he didn't find any evidence, the captain would insist on looking for it himself. No matter that neither of them had any idea just what it was they were searching for.

"Three people died here." He kicked up a shower of reddish orange gravel with his boot. "I want to know why."

The ground absorbed his abuse without yielding up any secrets.

"Will, not all puzzles can be solved."

"Tell that to our captain."

Troi's silence was all too expressive of Picard's frame of mind on this issue. Beyond a doubt, he would be dissatisfied with the preliminary tricorder report, but Riker still had another six hours of daylight in which to sift through the area.

Squinting against the sky's glare, he looked up at the crumbling ridge that had defeated his attempts to climb the side of Mount Cahuapetl. The skin on his hands had been rubbed raw. Blisters were forming on his feet. He was hot and tired and thirsty. And he had no idea what to do next.

At times like these, Riker envied the captain sitting in comfort on the bridge.

Chapter Nine

ZAMORH WALKED INTO Stephaleh's office bearing data
padds with information, which she barely looked at.
Quickly she affixed her signature and let Zamorh
leave. She stared at a report on her computer screen
and snapped it off. Nothing seemed to satisfy her and
she knew why. In a very short amount of time
everything she liked about her job had fallen apart.
There was death, destruction, mutual suspicion, and a
manifestation of the cold war between the Federation
and the K'Vin Hegemony right here on Kirlos, in her
home. And her leg still bothered her.

She had let Zamorh inform Gregach about
Coleridge's death. She wanted the time to compose
herself and her thoughts. First, the interrupted night's
sleep had made her irritable, and now Coleridge's
death had made the problems personal. Given her
office, the death of *any* Federation member should be
personal—but this was someone she had known and
respected.

Already, complaints were coming in from civilians and merchants about being denied access to the K'Vin markets. Trading had come to a standstill, and trading was this planet's lifeblood. She had no undersecretaries to whom she could delegate responsibility; Kirlos was not considered big enough to warrant such help. Instead, she fielded the complaints when she could and let Zamorh handle the rest.

Most of all, Stephaleh wanted to talk with Gregach, have him come for a meal and a game. She wanted to be alone with Gregach, to hold an intelligent conversation without suspicion. But Gregach seemed changed by the events—the old warrior in him struggling to make a last stand. She couldn't deny him his nationalism, but deep down she hoped that he really didn't suspect Federation personnel of causing the mishaps. If only she could get him alone, without Zamorh or Gezor nearby. Lately it seemed the Sullurh aides were always there.

Zamorh just then walked back into the office. He stood silent, waiting for his superior to speak.

"So, Zamorh, I have been handed a problem. And now people expect a response. Any word from the UFP Council?"

"None yet, Ambassador. And nothing from the *Enterprise,* either."

Stephaleh would have been satisfied to talk directly with Captain Picard, since he was an experienced officer and that meant being a diplomat at times. His counsel would have been helpful. But he had problems of his own aboard the *Enterprise*—in fact, she had given little thought to the reason the starship had left orbit. A world ravaged by something unknown. Could it come to Kirlos, too? It would certainly be the last thing she needed at present.

She flipped a switch on her desk console and spoke

clearly, with not a hint of strain. "Communications, get me a direct line to Ambassador Gregach. And do not let them stall us."

In a few moments, Gregach was on the screen. He had apparently been eating, and some juice remained on his chin. So like Gregach, she thought fondly. Then, pushing fondness behind her, she spoke. "Ambassador Gregach, I regret the events that have taken place in the last few hours. Our planet was peaceful and our relations pleasant," she began. Gregach just watched. "After you closed your border to us, an incident occurred that cost the life of a member of the Federation. Until this is cleared up and the culprit found, I am afraid I have no choice but to close our border to K'Vin personnel until further notice. I invoke this right by virtue of the treaty between our people."

Gregach took this in and nodded. "I expected martial law, Ambassador. I regret Coleridge's death and my condolences are already on file. Our police force is investigating, and we think some suspects will turn up within a day."

"True suspects?" she asked. "Or are you just going through the motions?" She sounded cold, despite herself. Her tone had gotten even softer.

"I do not like the implication, Ambassador. Nor do I like being denied access to free trade markets. And now I will return to other matters—*K'Vin* matters."

As the screen went dark, Stephaleh sighed. It was a *long* sigh. She could feel their friendship dissolving as the formality increased in their conversations. Just days ago Gregach would have damned the rules and beamed over for a private conference. But things had changed, and now each of them had to play the role dictated by politics and events.

"Zamorh," she said, "inform the population that

111

the K'Vin territory is closed to them until further notice. I want it on the data nets first and then posted in all public spots. When that's done, return to your investigation of all that's happened. I want some answers, by the deities, or else I will go mad." An afterthought: "On your way out, please ask the *Enterprise* officers to join me."

The Sullurh nodded and scurried out of the room, leaving Stephaleh alone with her thoughts. She turned to her window and looked out at the gather-swell of people on the streets. Rumors had a way of uniting those that politics could not.

Everyone knew of the incidents and the deaths by now. Many continued to blame the Starfleet presence while others speculated that the Federation personnel had been brought in to stop some underground movement. How odd that a purely scientific mission had turned into something like this. . . .

The crowd flowed and ebbed, lapping at the steps of the Federation embassy. Voices rose and fell in the same rhythm, knife-sharp voices erupting from angry throats.

But each time, the mob was turned back by the presence of the armed guards at the top of the steps. And though their phasers were still on their belts, it was clear that they were there for a reason.

Lars Trimble had never been part of a crowd before. It was a frightening experience.

Nor had he ever *intended* to be part of this surging, seething throng. Far from it. All Trimble meant to do was protest whatever was going on here, whatever was destroying the long peace of Kirlos and, more important, endangering the well-being of his family.

Others here had their businesses foremost in mind

—and surely there was nothing wrong with that. The havoc lately had killed a lot of big deals.

Lars Trimble had no big deals to yell about—though he *might* have, if he hadn't been so damned honest.

There was only one place in the galaxy where a man could lay hands on the mysterious *shrol'dinaggi*—the legendary Torquan remembering-stones. That place, of course, was on Torqua, the seventh planet in the K'Vin home system.

Until just a few months ago, the remembering-stones had been inaccessible to Federation citizens. Then, one night at Busiek's, Trimble had encountered a visiting merchant with a source for the *shrol'dinaggi*. His problem was that he could not deal them in K'Vin territory. It was illegal to own or to sell them—something about side effects and threats to one's mental health—and he did not wish to maintain a high profile in this matter.

Besides, the demand for the stones was much greater on certain Federation worlds—where they were also illegal, though the penalties involved weren't quite as high. Individuals of great wealth would pay dearly to sample the unique experience offered by the *shrol'dinaggi*. To taste century after dark, lusty century of primeval history—even if it was K'Vin history, and not their own. . . .

Arrangements had been made for shipping, receipt, payment—arrangements that called for Trimble to act only as a middleman, never to actually see or handle the merchandise. It was safer that way.

Suddenly Lars Trimble the struggling grain merchant had a chance to become Lars Trimble the *shrol'dinaggi* king—and a very rich man indeed.

In the end, however, he couldn't do it. There was

too much illegality on both sides of the fence. Too much risk—and too little sleep at night.

Maybe he just wasn't greedy enough. Or maybe he didn't want to have to explain to his children how he'd suddenly become so wealthy.

Then this spate of disasters had descended on Kirlosia. The destruction of the Commercial Trading Hall, the incidents of obvious sabotage that had followed—one on the K'Vin side, a second in the Federation sector, each one apparently a retaliation against the one before it.

And the irony was that even if Trimble had sold his soul to get the stones, the deal would never have gone through. With the city truly divided now, he could never have gotten payment to his K'Vin partner. Nor would the *shrol'dinaggi* have been smuggled out of K'Vin space on the basis of good faith alone.

But the fact that these incidents had taken place didn't represent any kind of poetic justice—not to Lars Trimble. Because, thanks to *them,* his honest grain business had gone sour as well.

Did these troubles have anything to do with the Federation ship and the three officers it had left behind? He had heard whispers to that effect, even before the explosion in the museum.

Trimble looked around him at the sea of angry faces. He listened to their shouts. Apparently, *they* believed that the Federation officers had caused this. They weren't sure *how,* but they seemed certain that there was a link.

And more and more, as he pressed toward the tower in the midst of them, so was Trimble. He found himself cursing the Starfleet officers out loud. And the louder he cursed, the more his apprehension seemed to diminish, to be swept aside in the sounds and scents of the mob's mounting fury. The potential for vio-

114

lence hung low in the air, so thick that he could almost reach out and grasp it.

But somehow it no longer frightened Trimble. Now, it seemed almost exhilarating.

Up at the top of the steps, the embassy guards were drawing their phasers.

Data looked out the convex window of the ambassador's office and noted the mood of the crowd at street level. Stephaleh had gone down to quiet them, but she had seemed to doubt her ability to do so.

Beside him, Worf grunted. "I still do not think it was wise for her to go down there alone." His eyes narrowed beneath the bony ridge of his brow. "We should have gone along to protect her."

Data turned toward him. "Perhaps, but she is not exactly alone. There are embassy guards holding the crowd at bay."

The Klingon shook his massive head. "They are no protection. More likely than not, they have never used a phaser in their lives."

The android saw that there was no arguing that point, so he changed tack. "In any case, it was the ambassador's wish that we remain here in her office, since our presence on Kirlos is very much at the heart of the mob's discontent."

"Sure," said Geordi, who had been pacing the room for the last several minutes. The chief engineer had been imbued with a manic energy since the death of his former mentor. "They don't like what's going on, so they find a convenient bunch of scapegoats." He shot a glance in the direction of the window. "Did it ever occur to them that maybe *we're* not too happy either? That . . . ." For a moment, he seemed to have trouble getting the words out. "That maybe *we've* been hurt by all this, too?"

When Data first began his stint on the *Enterprise,* he would have answered those questions. Now—thanks in large part to Geordi's tutelage—he recognized them as rhetorical. As a result, he did not respond to them.

"They are frightened," said Zamorh. Data glanced over his shoulder; he had almost forgotten that the Sullurh was in the room with them.

Apparently Zamorh had not learned to distinguish between a rhetorical question and one that wanted answering.

"When one is frightened," he went on, "one does not think clearly."

Worf grunted again. "All the more reason to provide adequate protection. To shoot first and ask questions later."

Data had the distinct impression that this argument was going around in circles. Rather than contribute to its momentum, he peered down again at the plaza, where the ambassador was just emerging.

Stephaleh had been in the diplomatic service for more years than she cared to count. She had helped negotiate treaties involving entire star systems, even empires.

But she had never faced a mob.

So why, she asked herself as she came out from the shelter of the embassy building, *are you intent on facing one now? You, with your aches and pains, your complaints and your frailties? Should you not have remained behind your desk and allowed others to deal with this situation?*

Perhaps she *would* have deferred to someone else— if there had been someone else to defer to. As it was, she had no choice but to face the mob herself.

The captain of her guards, the human named

116

Powell, glanced at her as she approached the line that he and the others had established. He seemed surprised to see her.

"Put your phaser away," said the ambassador. "And have the others do the same."

With obvious reluctance, Powell complied. A few moments later the rest of the guards followed suit.

Stephaleh had hoped that the gesture would serve to quiet the crowd. To drain off some of the tension from the situation.

However, it had the opposite effect. Emboldened, the crowd grew louder. A couple of the merchants even climbed to the top of the steps, stopping only a couple of meters from where she stood.

But that was *good,* she told herself. It gave her someone through whom she could negotiate—a pair of intermediaries. It was a lot easier, she reflected, than trying to deal with a faceless mob.

Stephaleh acknowledged each of the intermediaries with a glance. Her antennae dipped forward—a reflex left over from the days when Andorians used them to communicate.

"What is the meaning of this?" she asked—with, she hoped, just the right mixture of indignation and curiosity.

"The meaning," said one of the intermediaries, a tall and spindly Rhadamanthan, "is that something is going on here—something that already jeopardizes our livelihoods and that in time may jeopardize our lives."

"That's right," said the other, a remarkably stocky specimen, even considering his Tellarite heritage. "If the Federation and the K'Vin are hatching a war here, we deserve to know why. And to be given some warning, so we can protect ourselves."

The crowd roared its approval of those sentiments.

Stoically, Stephaleh allowed the wave of emotion to crest and break before she responded.

Finally she held up her hands. "Listen to me," she said, again addressing the intermediaries in particular. "There are no secret motives on Kirlos—not on the part of the Federation, at any rate."

"No?" said the Tellarite. "Then it's a coincidence that all of this began with the appearance of the *Enterprise?* And a coincidence also that the Starfleet officers were present when the trading hall fell—and again when the K'Vin embassy was nearly destroyed?"

"Give us credit for some intelligence," said the Rhadamanthan. "It's plain that Kirlos is being used as a pawn by the Federation, whether your superiors have chosen to inform you of it or not."

The ambassador couldn't help but be taken aback at the suggestion. Was it possible? Could the Federation be maneuvering behind her back?

No. She rejected the notion. That was not the way the Federation worked, especially not with one of its most trusted and experienced diplomats. If something was afoot, she would have been told of it.

"You are jumping to conclusions," she told the Rhadamanthan, exhibiting a composure she did not feel. "We had nothing to do with the explosion at the K'Vin embassy. Nor, for that matter, do we have any proof that the attacks on the trading hall and the museum were K'Vin-inspired."

"Of course not," said the Tellarite. "Because those Starfleet spies staged all *three* incidents—to goad the K'Vin into warring with us!"

Another thunderous cheer from the crowd—this one longer than the first. Stephaleh began to feel the situation slipping out of her grasp. She had to find a new approach—and quickly.

"The Federation goads *no one* into war," she rasped —giving her not-altogether-feigned anger free rein. "What could we possibly gain from it?"

"Only the Federation knows that," sneered the Rhadamanthan.

Obviously intimidation wasn't going to work, either. Things had already gone too far for that. Somehow she had to take the initiative.

Suddenly Stephaleh knew what she had to do. Without hesitation she started down the steps, cleaving a path between the Rhadamanthan and the Tellarite. Leaving them behind, open-mouthed, she descended into the roiling mass of the crowd. Powell uttered a protest; she ignored it.

At first, the ambassador had a feeling that the merchants might not yield to her approach. Then, at the very last second, the mob parted—and she made her way through it, slowly and purposefully, until she reached her goal.

He was a human—tall and lanky, with a reddish gold beard and small intensely blue eyes. When he saw the aged Andorian advancing on him, he took an involuntary step back, and would have taken more, apparently, if he'd had room.

Stephaleh didn't stop until she was looking up into his ruddy, open face. His eyes became even smaller as he tried to decide why she was standing in front of him and not up at the top of the steps trying to calm the crowd.

This time she knew she had chosen well.

"I know you," said the ambassador, in a soft voice that only those immediately surrounding her could hear. "You're an honest man, trying to make an honest living. All you want is a peaceful place to do that."

There were sharp complaints from all over the

crowd, rising up like bubbles in the frothy waters of the Great Spring on Andor. And on their heels came calls for quiet, so everyone could hear.

But the ambassador didn't raise her voice to make it any easier. She went on in that same subdued tone.

"What is your name?" she asked the human.

"Trimble," he told her, as if mesmerized by her searching eyes, her gentle speech. "Lars Trimble."

She nodded. "I make a promise to you, Lars Trimble. I make it here and now, not as the Federation's ambassador to this world, but as Stephaleh n'Ehliarch, daughter of Andor. I promise you that I will do everything in my power to keep you and your family from harm. *Everything.* Do you believe me, Lars Trimble?"

The human regarded her. Numbly, he nodded.

Later he might remember the potential profits he had lost as a result of Kirlosia's afflictions. He might even curse himself for not having throttled her when he had the chance.

But for now Lars Trimble was ensorcelled by the spotlight he'd abruptly found himself in. And by the invitation-to-trust demeanor it had taken Stephaleh years and worlds to perfect. Of course, it hadn't hurt her credibility any that she'd meant every word of her promise to him.

"Good," said the ambassador. "With your help, I will find us a way out of these troubles." She placed her hand on his upper arm, squeezed it reassuringly. Then she turned and went back the way she had come.

Once again the crowd parted for her—this time a little more willingly. In her wake, she heard the shouts rise up again—pleas to know what she had said. Demands to know whom she had spoken to and why.

It had been a mistake to address the crowd's

leaders—she knew that now. Its leaders had been its head; by far, it had been wiser to appeal to its heart.

For a time now they would puzzle over what she had said to Lars Trimble. It would keep them off balance, keep their minds focused somewhere other than on their fears. At least temporarily, she had defused an explosive situation.

But it was hardly a permanent solution. She would have to get to the bottom of these incidents—before Lars Trimble and all the others like him took matters into their own hands.

Chapter Ten

Ilugh couldn't sleep, no matter how many times he shifted his position on the hard, molded mattress. It was no surprise—he had too much on his mind.

Specifically, the attack on the embassy—for he was certain it had been an attack and no accident. An act of sabotage that had endangered the lives of Ambassador Gregach and his entire staff.

Maybe the other guards could put it out of their minds. To them, this was just a job, an easy way to extend their military service without putting their hides on the line.

But they didn't know Gregach as Ilugh did. As far as they were concerned, the ambassador was just another soft, slimy bureaucrat, living from one spilat dinner to the next.

Nor were they completely wrong—even Ilugh had to concede that. The ambassador dearly loved his homeworld delicacies.

However, he hadn't always been like that. Once, the ambassador had been *General* Gregach, commander of the K'Vin forces at Titrikus IV and author of the victory over the invading Eluud. Once, the ambassador had been a hero of sorts, an up and coming star in the K'Vin military hierarchy.

Ilugh knew this because he had served under Gregach. Perhaps only as a common soldier, but he'd learned enough about the general to develop a healthy respect for him. Not only was Gregach a winner, but he logged his winnings without wasting K'Vin blood. Many of his peers had grown up in the school of Victory at Any Cost, but Gregach had been inclined to keep his losses to a minimum.

What Ilugh *didn't* know was what had happened to take the luster off Gregach's career—to earn him this unenviable position in the diplomatic service. Perhaps some enemy of his had gotten the upper hand in homeworld politics—who could know? Certainly not a lowly soldier.

But when Gregach was transferred here, Ilugh had asked for a transfer to Kirlos as well. He had applied for a berth as one of the general's—no, the *ambassador's*—personal guards. Out of loyalty, out of respect, and though he would never say it out loud, out of affection—the kind one can only have for a great leader.

As he tossed and turned, Ilugh could hear Big Stragahn snoring at the other end of the barracks. It had started out as a small sound, on the edge of Ilugh's consciousness, but now it was too loud to ignore.

And he knew it would only get worse. That was the way with Stragahn, particularly on nights when he remembered too well and had to get drunk to forget. Pretty soon everyone would be up, swearing softly at Stragahn, but too timid to wake him up for fear he'd put them through a wall.

If Ilugh had had any illusions about getting to sleep

tonight, they had been dispelled. The only one who would sleep was Big Stragahn.

"Damn," came the first curse, from the bunk below him. Onaht stuck his head out and peered up at Ilugh. "He's at it again. This is the fifth night this month!"

Ilugh grunted. He leaned over, rested his tusks on his forearm. "You don't remember—it used to be worse. When he first got here, Stragahn used to do this every other night. It's only in the last couple of years that he's mellowed."

That didn't seem to pacify Onaht. Not at all.

"I didn't sign up for this wretched place to lie awake at night," he groused. "If I'd wanted to do *that,* I could have asked for a berth on the Border."

The snoring was getting louder, right on cue. There were bodies stirring all over the barracks.

Onaht muttered another curse—a rather colorful one that Ilugh hadn't heard before. He had to chuckle at it.

"Go ahead and laugh," said Onaht. "Maybe you can go without sleep; I can't." And with that he threw his legs over the side of the bed. He stood, glared in Stragahn's direction, then started to walk.

"Wait a minute," said Ilugh. He leaped down from his own bed and padded after Onaht on his bare feet. "Where do you think you're going?"

Onaht didn't look back. "To wake the soulless bastard," he said.

Ilugh caught him by the arm. "Are you crazy?" he asked. "He'll tear your arms off and feed them to you whole."

Onaht snorted. "So what? Can it be worse than listening to this *sound* night after night?" And more roughly than he had a right to, he shrugged Ilugh off.

Ilugh bristled a little, feeling his tusks jut out. "Go

ahead," he said. "Be a young hothead—it's *your* death song."

He thought the other guard would turn back at the last. After all, *no one* woke Stragahn.

However, to his amazement, Onaht didn't stop. He walked right up to the big one and shoved him.

"Shut up, you big lummox," said Onaht, adding insult to injury. "We're trying to get some rest here."

Ilugh held his breath. So did Hulg and Tazradh, sitting up now in their bunks. In fact, the barracks building itself seemed to tense in anticipation.

But Stragahn didn't move. He seemed oblivious to Onaht's intervention.

Onaht had to be the luckiest soldier in the Hegemony.

Even more miraculous, Stragahn's snoring had stopped. There was quiet now in the barracks—an almost eerie quiet.

Something about it made the skin crawl on the back of Ilugh's neck. He walked past a self-satisfied Onaht and took a closer look at Stragahn.

Rolled him over—and saw the awful strangled expression on his face. The way his tongue lolled, the way his eyes appeared to pop out of their sockets.

"Gods," whispered Onaht.

"Call a physician," barked Ilugh. Someone went rushing out to comply. He put his ear to Stragahn's chest, winced a little at the lack of a heartbeat. With the heel of his hand, he pounded at the big one's breastbone—but to no avail. Stragahn was halfway to his ancestors.

"Ilugh!"

It was Hulg—he recognized the voice, whirled angrily. Then he saw the reason for the cry.

Hulg was leaning over Dronagh's bed. And Dronagh wasn't moving either. His eyes, like Stragahn's, seemed to be fighting their way out of his head.

It couldn't have been organ failure—not in two of them at once.

Then what?

Poison? But Stragahn and Dronagh hadn't eaten at the same place today.

Suddenly he knew.

"Gas," he said out loud.

But the word was hardly out of his mouth when a look of horror raked Onaht's face—worse by far than what he'd looked like when he realized Stragahn was dead. He started wheezing, gasping for air—and in the space of a moment he had collapsed on the barracks floor.

The others were petrified—too appalled, too fascinated, to move. Ilugh shocked them out of it with a snarl: "We've got to get out of here—*now!*"

And as his comrades scrambled for the door, he grabbed a still-gasping Onaht under his arms. Mustering all his strength, he dragged him toward the exit.

They had almost reached it when Ilugh began to feel light-headed. His throat was constricting; he felt as if someone were trying to strangle him.

Still, he kept on going, too frantic to stop—out past the door, into the fresh air.

But the struggle to breathe didn't get any easier—instead, it got worse. And as the others gathered around him, trying to decide how they could help, he felt himself succumb.

"What?" roared Gregach.

Gezor stared at him. The Sullurh seemed taken aback by the outburst.

But then, what had he expected? What would *anyone* have expected after announcing such a thing?

The ambassador forced himself down into his chair. "Details," he said, his jaw working so that his tusks swung forward and back. "I want details."

His assistant complied. "Four dead, eight survivors —and of the eight, two are comatose. The physicians have yet to complete their tests, but they seem to agree that there was a gas involved. Most likely, plethane."

Gregach rolled the information over his tongue. *"Plethane?"* he spat. "In concentrations sufficient to kill and maim my personal guards—right there in their barracks?" The ambassador knew that the gas occasionally escaped from underground—but only a wisp here and there. Never enough to create a danger to the populace. He found that his fingers were clenched into fists; he unclenched them. "Where did it come from?"

The Sullurh shrugged that elaborate shrug of his. He seemed to be trying to hide from Gregach's wrath.

"So far," Gezor said, "there is no evidence of a leak, which would seem to rule out a natural occurrence. The only other reasonable conclusion is that someone smuggled a self-destroying container filled with gas into the barracks. In other words, sabotage."

He appeared to be on the verge of saying something else. But he chose not to give voice to it.

Of course the ambassador could not let it lie. "What?" he said. "Is there something more?"

"Your pardon," said the Sullurh. "I was about to offer an opinion—and the ambassador had asked only for facts."

Gregach grunted. "All right, then. Give me an opinion."

But still Gezor hesitated. "It may not be one you wish to hear," he said at last.

"You mean," said the K'Vin, "the opinion that the Federation is behind these incidents?"

"Yes," said the Sullurh. *"That* one."

"It makes no sense—*still.* Why would Stephaleh attack me—and deny it?"

"Perhaps," Gezor suggested, "to see how far you can be pushed."

The ambassador didn't like the sound of that. "Explain yourself," he said.

"It may be," answered the Sullurh, "that this is some sort of test—of the K'Vin's propensity to defend themselves. After all, it has been more than three decades since the Federation had any real contact with the K'Vin Hegemony. Perhaps this is their way of determining whether you have any fight left in you."

Gregach leaned forward, unable to keep his voice from rising in frustration. "Toward what *end,* Gezor? To what *purpose?"*

His assistant didn't flinch this time. He spoke the words calmly, with a certain amount of purposefulness: "In preparation for conquest, Ambassador."

The K'Vin eyed the smaller being. He made it sound so simple, so reasonable. But of course it was neither of those things. It was a concept so huge and arrogant that Gregach would never have considered it on his own.

And yet . . . could he afford to ignore it? If there was even a wisp of a possibility that his assistant had mined out the truth?

"You are saying that Kirlos is a . . . a testing ground, Gezor? A laboratory?"

"Yes, Ambassador. And if we do not respond with appropriate quickness and strength, we will be inviting the same sort of events on a larger scale. Eventually, perhaps, the fall of the entire Hegemony."

Gregach cleared his throat. "And the disasters on

128

the Federation side? The complaints that we received concerning them?"

"Distractions," said the Sullurh. "Attempts to explore our capacity for clear thinking. Or else the Federation's efforts to justify their atrocities in the eyes of some interested third party—whom we cannot, of course, identify at this time."

The ambassador sighed. He was almost sorry that he had opened the floodgates on this copious flow of conjecture.

At bottom, he still did not give credence to any of it. He did not believe that his choices here and now would determine the fate of the entire K'Vin civilization.

However, *his* beliefs were not all that mattered. He also had to consider the beliefs of his superiors, anticipate *their* reactions to the news of this second incident on K'Vin soil.

And it was possible, just possible, that one or more of them might conclude, as Gezor had, that these incidents of sabotage were a prelude to invasion. In which case he had better appear to be taking steps to forestall such a possibility.

But what might those steps be? Unable to think of any himself, he asked his assistant.

Gezor wasn't slow in answering. Obviously he had thought this all out beforehand. "There is only one measure that will absolutely prevent any further incidents, Ambassador. And that is to assume control of the Federation embassy."

Gregach's stomach churned at the very idea of it. "Do you know what you're saying, Gezor?"

The Sullurh nodded, undaunted. "Yes. But I repeat —it is the only way to ensure an end to these disasters."

The ambassador snorted. "It is unacceptable. There must be other ways of securing ourselves against these attacks—at least until we can be certain who is perpetrating them and why."

This time it took Gezor a moment. "To begin with, a more rigid enforcement of the line dividing Kirlosia; any Federation-sider even caught *near* K'Vin territory must be incarcerated. Second, a *passive* display of military force—perhaps the positioning of embassy guards along the Strip, to show the Federation that we will not tolerate further acts of aggression . . ."

Gregach growled.

The Sullurh straightened. "On the *chance,* of course, that the Federation *is* responsible for the incidents. Third, a tightening of security in and around the embassy and other potential targets. And fourth—"

"Gods of blood and destruction, Gezor! There is a *fourth?*"

That wide-eyed stare. "You asked for recommendations, Ambassador."

Gregach took a deep breath, blew it out. "Yes, of course I did. Proceed."

"Fourth," resumed the Sullurh, "the institution of martial law. To confine the reaction of the populace when they learn of the gas attack on your guards."

Now that Gregach thought of it, there *had* been stirrings of unrest among the K'Vin. Nothing like what was rumored to be taking place on the Federation side—but then, the K'Vin were a more disciplined people. Any unrest at all was probably something to be concerned about.

It was uncanny how Gezor sometimes seemed to know the ambassador's people better than the ambassador did. Quite uncanny.

"Very well," he told the Sullurh. "See to it that these measures are carried out."

Gezor inclined his head. "Of course, Ambassador."

Business at Busiek's had dropped off somewhat since all of the trouble started. Fights had been breaking out between sentients who had previously been content to give one another a wide berth. Now the slightest look, the most minuscule offhand gesture, was cause for hostilities. As a result, many of the regulars had stopped coming in.

Sullurh business, however, had picked up. Busiek was not particularly thrilled about that, because Sullurh tended to order one drink and sit at a table forever. Waitresses ignored them, yet they kept on coming. Other customers belittled them, bad-mouthed them, and made their lives miserable, but they kept on coming.

And still, thought Busiek ruefully, when every other sentient race in Kirlosia had found someplace else to go, or maybe another building to blow up, the Sullurh kept on coming. And there were more of them now, because the races that had been picking on them weren't around to do so anymore.

Now the Sullurh were paying the bills. Funny how it all came around.

The Sullurh all tended to blend together to him. So Busiek thought nothing of the fact that Gezor sat at a corner table hidden in the shadows, because Gezor meant nothing to him. Nor did the individual with whom Gezor was conversing.

But if the K'Vin ambassador had seen that his aide, Gezor, was having an urgent, huddled conference with Zamorh, Stephaleh's aide, then both Gregach and Stephaleh would have been very interested to know just what those two worthies might be discussing. Gregach and Stephaleh were not there, however—a fact of which Gezor and Zamorh were quite aware.

The ice in their drinks had long since melted when Gezor and Zamorh finished their discussion after what, to Busiek, seemed like hours. As they rose from their seats, leaving money on the table for the waitress, a soft, pulsing sound came from Gezor's pocket.

The two Sullurh looked at each other significantly as Gezor pulled out a small unit.

"Well, that was to be expected," said Zamorh slowly. "We'll have to make some preparations, won't we?"

"I can arrange it," said Gezor. "Give me five minutes to send word ahead, and then we'll leave."

Zamorh nodded approvingly and sat back down.

Behind the bar, Busiek sighed. He'd thought they were leaving. Couldn't get rid of the damned Sullurh, even when you really shouldn't want to.

"How do we know they're in there?" rumbled Worf.

The away team and Thul, who had insisted on coming along, stood in the shadows of an alley directly across the street from Busiek's.

"It's elementary," replied Data.

Worf stabbed a finger at Data. "I am not certain," he said tightly, "why you are speaking in that odd manner, with that peculiar accent, and saying 'It's elementary,' 'Come, come, Watson,' and 'The game is afoot.' I do know that it is beginning to seriously annoy me."

"Ease up, Worf," said Geordi. "Or are you going to threaten to shoot him?"

"Do not tempt me," said Worf ominously.

"I shall endeavor to refrain from using Holmesian phrases," said Data. "I suspect, however, that Gezor remains the link to all of this. Possibly Zamorh as well. I believe that Gezor's appearance at the embassy may have been a signal to someone else to perform the act of sabotage, or perhaps he was carrying a detonation device that had to be within a certain range. I believe that he and Zamorh have been prodding the ambassadors to make moves that would lead to war."

"But why?" said Geordi.

"I am not certain," admitted Data. "Since they are both seconds-in-command, they may be maneuvering to dispense with their superiors in the hope of obtaining higher rank."

"I suppose it's possible," said Geordi, though he had some rather large doubts about Sullurh being elevated to lofty positions.

"Striving for power has always been a legitimate motive in the Klingon Empire," agreed Worf. "On the other hand, the Sullurh do not seem aggressive enough to—"

"Look!" Data said suddenly. They ducked back into the shadows.

Gezor was emerging from the bar.

"I knew it," said Data. "The meeting at Busiek's the other day was not happenstance. It must be a regular meeting place, where Gezor can confer with—ah!"

Right behind Gezor came Zamorh.

"How intriguing," said Worf. "The seconds for both ambassadors. It would seem," he admitted, despite his earlier judgment, "that Lieutenant Commander Data's supposition of collusion was correct."

"Elemen . . . uh, thank you."

Geordi was suddenly struck by a thought. "Thul," he said slowly, "they're Sullurh, like you. Have you by any chance heard of—"

"Heard of any of this?" said Thul, shocked. "I can assure you, Mr. La Forge, I was loyal to Dr. Coleridge.

133

Some of these young people"—he gestured toward the retreating forms of Gezor and Zamorh—"get crazy ideas, crazy schemes. I don't know what goes on in their heads. If I had heard anything, I assure you I would have notified the proper authorities. Of course, who would listen to a Sullurh?"

"Obviously, the ambassadors would listen," said Geordi. "Data, come on, they're getting away."

"Not this time," said Data calmly, and he held up a tricorder. "I've locked on to their life readings so that we will be able to track them while staying completely out of sight. I believe that Gezor knew we were following him last time, because he spotted us in the bar. On this occasion, they will be given no opportunity to see us."

This time Gezor did not go down Embassy Run but instead went directly into the back streets behind Busiek's, with Zamorh right behind him. And right behind the two of them were the Federation trio and Thul.

They made their way through the shadows, following Worf's lead, for he was easily the stealthiest of them. Having a track on the life readings of those they were pursuing certainly simplified matters.

"Clear the streets! Curfew! Everyone off the streets!"

The voice was coming through a public address system. The away team and Thul hid themselves in an alleyway as a squadron of K'Vin made their way toward them with their weapons slung, but clearly prepared for trouble. The seal of the K'Vin Diplomatic Corps was emblazoned on their shirts, and Worf realized immediately that they were from the embassy. It was easy, the Klingon mused, to be diplomatic when you had superior firepower.

He was holding his phaser at the ready, prepared to

start firing on the patrol if necessary, but Data noticed and gave a quick shake of his head.

Slowly the patrol passed by them; they waited until it was a safe distance away before they continued.

Geordi was extremely glad that the tricorder was guiding them. They were deep into the back streets when he remembered something Nassa had said—*says,* present tense, he reminded himself, thinking of the way she had spoken of her husband. If there was an afterlife then they were deservedly together— about how easy it was to get lost in the back streets. She had been quite correct. Nothing was marked, and the streets seemed to intersect and crisscross according to no perceptible pattern. Probably laid out that way on purpose, he reasoned, to keep outsiders away.

But Data's pursuit was steady and certain as he led them around one corner and then another.

"They've stopped moving," Data said suddenly. "Perhaps they've arrived at their destination. And they are not very far ahead of . . ."

He paused.

"What is it?" said Worf urgently.

"We are being followed," said Data. "I hear them."

Worf did not, but that was no surprise. His hearing was not as acute as that of the android. "How many?"

"Four. Perhaps five." He spun suddenly. "And from in front. More."

"Why didn't the tricorder pick them up?" said Worf in annoyance.

"I had to keep it narrowcast to only those two," replied Data. "Otherwise I would have picked up the life readings of everyone around us in the city."

"Quickly, this way," said Worf, and he pointed to an alleyway heavy with shadows. The others followed him in.

They huddled against the walls, watching carefully.

135

Moments later, Worf and Geordi heard what Data had heard earlier, and then the street beyond the alleyway was crowded with at least a dozen Sullurh, muttering to one another. Half had come from behind the trio, while the rest had come from in front—and the two groups seemed surprised to have run into each other without running into the *Enterprise* men.

Moments later they vanished back into the enfolding darkness of the back streets.

"What were they saying?" Worf asked.

"They were speaking very quickly," said Data, "but I believe I caught the word 'above' several times."

"Above?" said Geordi. "Above *what?"*

And with preternatural silence, the Sullurh suddenly dropped down from above.

Within an instant the alleyway was filled with struggling people.

Three of them were attempting to overpower Data, and yet the android's first priority was to glance at their feet. They were barefoot, and the soles of their feet were curiously padded. They had managed to sneak up overhead after removing their boots. Data found that intriguing as he scrambled to his own feet, lifted two of the Sullurh over his head, and hurled them into the street.

He spun quickly to face the third; the Sullurh was aiming some sort of device at Data. The android moved toward it with blinding speed—but not fast enough to stop the Sullurh from pressing a button.

Instantly, an explosion seemed to go off inside Data's head. He spun, imagining that sparks were leaping from his eye sockets, and when he tried to call for help it came out as a bizarre, high-pitched chirp.

The alleyway swung sideways and Data hit the ground, stiff as a board.

Geordi saw Data go down—and that was the last

thing he saw, for somebody landed a right cross into his face that sent his VISOR flying. Terror ripped through Geordi: in the blind alley, he was suddenly *truly* blind. "Damn!" he shouted, or started to. Then he was clubbed from behind and went down as well.

Worf had no time to mark the fate of his comrades, for the Sullurh were concentrating their resources on him. The phaser had been knocked from his grasp in the first assault, but fortunately the Sullurh seemed to be unarmed.

A couple leaped on his back and threaded their arms under the Klingon's; in front of him, several more were pounding on his chest and stomach. With a roar, Worf drove his elbows back, breaking the hold of those behind him and getting a grip on them at the same time. Then, bending forward quickly, he sent the two Sullurh hurtling over his head and into the others, who went down like tenpins.

Abruptly, he was grabbed from behind by his heavy link sash. Before he could react, he was swung around and sent smashing into a wall.

Whoever held him still had a grip on the sash, and like lightning Worf dropped down and slid it off. Kneeling on the ground, he drove his fist into the nearest target, which happened to be the crotch of one of the Sullurh. The Sullurh screamed and went down, writhing in agony, and Worf grabbed up his sash just as the others regrouped and charged him.

He started to whirl. Two Sullurh came in from the side, and the heavy sash crunched against them. One of them caught the brunt of it and went down with a fractured jaw; the other was merely floored.

Worf swung the sash again and heard a satisfying scream. If he could find his phaser, he would be all set. . . .

Someone else found it first.

The phaser flashed in the darkness, blasting Worf back against the wall. Consciousness fled and, sagging to the ground, he rolled over on his side.

Thul lowered the phaser and turned toward the others, shaking his head. "Another minute or so and he would have finished you all."

One of them grumbled, "We had him staggering."

"You had him *laughing,*" observed Thul.

There were footsteps at the head of the alleyway, and Gezor and Zamorh appeared there. Gezor nodded approvingly.

Thul nodded back.

"Thank you for alerting us to our pursuit," said Gezor, inspecting the three inert forms on the ground. He held up the small box that had beeped at him back at Busiek's. "I see that the pulse generator worked as expected on the android."

"It did," confirmed Thul. "Of course it might have gone more smoothly if we had had enough phasers to go around. But then, our inexperience with the weapons might have proved our undoing."

"What would you have us do with them?" asked Zamorh.

Thul grunted. "Isn't it obvious?" he asked. "They are saboteurs, prowling the K'Vin back streets to perpetrate more mischief. They—along with their humble servant, namely myself—must be brought to the authorities immediately. That is how law-abiding citizens always proceed."

Chapter Eleven

ESQUAR HUDAK preferred the ambience of Busiek's to what he saw around him—the flawless new plastiform tables, the cheap modern art, the freshly fabricated walls and ceilings and floors. He would take the eccentric time-worn quality of the big place on the Strip over the sterile regularity of this one any day. What was this pub called, anyway? He couldn't even remember its name.

However, it was the very anonymity of this place, its lack of popularity among the Federation-side merchants, that had qualified it as the perfect venue for this meeting. For while it wasn't exactly a *secret* convocation, it wasn't the type of thing they wanted to advertise either.

He would say this much on the pub's behalf: management had gone out of its way to make the merchants feel at home. All of them had drinks before them. Of course, that was just good business, wasn't it? The sooner the drinks were served, the sooner the merchants would be ready for seconds.

Out of the corner of his eye, Hudak noticed Stephaleh's Sullurh aide sitting in the farthest corner of the room. How long had he been here? Inwardly the Pandrilite laughed. It was so like a Sullurh to remain as unobtrusive as possible, even when he was supposed to be the embassy presence at the meeting.

The Pandrilite cleared his throat and immediately drew the attention of those assembled. He was not surprised by the efficacy of that simple action. When one towered over one's fellows, one commanded a certain amount of respect.

"You all know why we're here," he began, watching the reaction of each face in the gathering. Most of the merchants were humans, but a half-dozen other races were also represented. "The atmosphere that has developed in Kirlosia is hardly good for business, and boneheaded stunts like storming the embassy are only going to make matters worse." He stopped for a moment while a perfunctory wave of applause rose and fell. "Our only chance to salvage our livelihood— our future—is to stand behind Ambassador Stephaleh, as this group has done in the past."

"The past," said a wiry little Tetracite named Keeglo, "is a little different from the present, don't you think? Make no mistake, I don't put any faith in these crahglat droppings about the Federation wanting to start a war, but *someone* is doing *something,* and I haven't seen Stephaleh make the first move to stop it. At least, I haven't seen any results."

Hudak had taken the occasion of the Tetracite's speech to chug down some of his drink. It was an old Pandrilite ploy—diminish the opposition's argument by appearing to do something else while the argument was presented.

Actually he couldn't help noting that the drink wasn't half bad. It went down with a certain amount of fire. Were the proprietors getting it from some-where other than the usual sources?

"With all due respect," said the Pandrilite, "we cannot gauge the effectiveness of the ambassador's efforts at this point." He indicated the Sullurh with a thrust of his chin. "Am I right, Zamorh?"

The aide got up and suffered the stares of the merchants. "What Esquar Hudak says is true. The ambassador is exercising all her power to protect you and your business interests."

The Pandrilite wondered if he hadn't made a strategic error by bringing Zamorh into the conversation. He'd hoped for something a little more convincing; it was as if the Sullurh didn't have much faith in his own words—or anyway, that's the way it sounded to him.

"However," Zamorh went on, "it is difficult to know if her actions have borne fruit. The measure of success can only be the passage of time without further incidents."

A Vulcan named Stokk stood and addressed the Sullurh. Hudak cringed a little, though he didn't show it. Now he was *sure* he shouldn't have involved Zamorh.

"Why did Stephaleh not attend this meeting her-self?" asked Stokk. "Did she not consider it important enough?"

"I can answer that," said the Pandrilite. Again all eyes were on him and the Sullurh was all but forgot-ten, except perhaps by the Vulcan. "Don't forget, we are but a small part of the citizenry that lives under the aegis of the Federation. Stephaleh is the official representative of the Federation on Kirlos. She cannot seem to attach herself to any one group. That, in a sense, would be to say to all the other merchants that they do not count, that she and her chosen few will make all the decisions, and that their opinions are

141

worthless, even if—and you will pardon my straightforwardness—they *are.*"

"I see," said Stokk. "And this principle prevails even though *we* offer Stephaleh support while everyone else wishes to tear her limb from limb?"

Hudak decided to meet the Vulcan's argument head-on. He couldn't afford to linger on this point, not if order was to be restored and the K'Vin sector was to be reopened as a viable marketplace.

With his new *shrol'dinaggi* deal hanging in the balance, perhaps that meant more to him than to some of the others—but they *all* had a lot at stake here, Stokk included.

"You *know* it does," he told the Vulcan. "There is no other way. And now, if we can at least agree among ourselves that we must remain aligned with the ambassador, we can . . ."

At first he thought it was just another objection rising up to meet him, this time in the form of Yudal Malat, his fellow Pandrilite. After all, the merchant had stood up and opened his mouth as if to speak.

But the sounds that came out weren't words, not by any stretch of the imagination. They were strangled cries, garbled incoherencies from deep inside, as if something were eating away at Malat and doing so in the most painful way possible.

For a terrible second or two, the assembly just watched, too shocked to come to the Pandrilite's aid. In the meantime, Malat began to froth at the mouth, and the froth was tinged blue with his blood.

"Ancestors," rasped Hudak, launching himself through the other merchants to reach his racial brother. But before he could get there, Malat's head jerked back and he slumped against the human beside him.

"A physician!" roared Hudak. He pointed to the

man nearest the door. *"You,* go find the—" He never finished his instructions.

The pain that suddenly erupted in his gut was like nothing he had ever felt before. He tried to fight it, to somehow deny it its right to exist in him. But it was too great. It spread down to his intestines, reached up to clutch at his heart.

Burning . . . like a flame inside him, an acid, a blade twisting into each organ where the tender nerve endings were closest together . . .

"Eaghhh!" The cry was torn from him, wrenched from the smoldering pit of his stomach.

He was dying—he was certain of that. And with a Pandrilite's insight into such things, he was certain what had caused it. The drink had been poisoned.

All around him now, other merchants were rising up, screaming or choking silently on their own blood-stained bile. The room was a madhouse, a scene of carnage that would have sickened even the most eager warrior.

And there in the corner, Hudak saw through red veils of agony, was the Sullurh. Unaffected, calm, aloof. Almost tranquil as he looked on.

So it was that before the Pandrilite died, his mouth full of his own white-hot insides, he knew not only what had killed him . . .

But also *who.*

This time the burden weighed too heavily on her. She could not snap out orders, though Zamorh awaited them as eagerly as ever. Stephaleh could only sit with her head bowed over her desk and try to trace the thread of events that had brought them to this pass.

Hudak had not truly been a friend, only a political

ally. He had seen merit in supporting her, and in turn she had helped him prosper, just as she had attempted to help all the merchants prosper, within the bounds of her Federation-granted powers. It was just that Hudak had been so much better than the others at *accepting* that help.

So when she grieved, it was not solely for the individual, though she would certainly miss him. Just as much, she mourned what he represented—a sanity in the ranks of the merchants. A partnership that she had worked long and hard to cultivate.

And now her greatest supporters—perhaps the only supporters left to her in these troubled times—had been decimated. Only a few of the merchants still lived to tell of the incident, and they were too shaken to be of any use. Zamorh's account had been the only coherent one.

She felt as if she were standing naked in an Andorian windstorm, her skin slowly being flayed off her still-living bones. For there was pain for her in this . . . this failure. All her life she had prided herself on her diplomatic skills, but the present situation seemed to defy her abilities.

"Ambassador?"

She looked up, saw Zamorh still waiting in the center of the room.

"Have you come to a decision? I told Chief Powell I would give him his instructions as soon as possible."

Stephaleh took a deep breath, let it out. She straightened. "Yes," she said. "Of course. We must have martial law. It's the only way, as you so eloquently point out. But that is as far as I will go."

The Sullurh regarded her. "Evacuation will take time, Ambassador. We must contact Starfleet now; later we may not have that option."

She smiled inwardly at the urgency in her aide's

voice. Sometimes she thought Zamorh cared more about her responsibilities than she did.

"Be that as it may," she said, "I will issue no evacuation order. The Federation did not establish a presence on Kirlos casually, Zamorh. This planet is our only real link with the K'Vin and their Hegemony. If the K'Vin are responsible for all this, and we leave now, we show them that we are weak; there are leaders among them who will see our departure as an opportunity to wrest certain contested planets from us. If the K'Vin are *not* responsible—as I am still inclined to believe—then evacuation will destroy our only chance for a rapprochement with them, and the outcome will likely be the same. In either case, we face a greater disaster than any that has taken place so far on Kirlos."

"But, Ambassador, *murders* have been committed. No doubt, many more are in the offing."

It was unlike Zamorh to speak so forcefully. But then, his family was part of the endangered populace.

She stopped herself suddenly, shaken by her callousness. Would the Sullurh be so wrong if that was his motive? After all, what did *he* care that some other world would be spared a bloodbath if the lives of his loved ones were forfeited in the process?

A face swam to the surface of her thoughts, that of Lars Trimble, the bearded man in the crowd. She had made a promise to him, hadn't she?

It forced her to rethink her position. By keeping the Federation's objectives before her, by making them her priority, was she playing fast and loose with the welfare of those who lived here? Was it possible that after all these years of trench diplomacy, she could look at her job as a game of dyson—an abstraction, wherein each individual part had no real meaning except as a means to an end?

Then again . . . did it really matter *how* she arrived at her conclusion—feeling the heart-wrenching difficulty of her decision or distancing herself from it? In the end, the result was the same.

There was so much potential for bloodshed here, and so much there, how could a thinking being come to grips with those possibilities other than to measure them as accurately as possible—and to take the action that would bring about the fewest casualties? Cold as it was, she knew no other way.

Forgive me, Lars Trimble.

"No," she told Zamorh at last. "There will be no evacuation. We will not run from this. We will find those responsible and we will stop them. Is that clear?"

The Sullurh didn't hesitate for long. "It is your decision," he told her. "I can but advise, Ambassador." Then, with a slight bow, he backed away and went to relay her instructions to Powell.

Chapter Twelve

THE TWO OFFICERS stood side by side on the bridge of the *Enterprise*. Both were staring intently at the viewscreen.

"Well, Ensign Davies?"

"You were right, Captain," said the geologist. He stepped closer to the image of mottled green and swept his hand across the surface, tracing a pattern with his finger. "Those are definitely the outlines of an ancient quarry."

Wesley Crusher sighed. He had seen the same image as the captain, but he hadn't noticed those details. He could barely make sense of them even with Davies's promptings. "But how can you tell?"

"Personal experience." Picard had felt the tug of old memories even before he remembered the time and place. "As a child I often played in the remains of a Roman quarry. Parts of it were flooded, while other sections had been filled in with dirt; all of it was covered with trees and grasses. Yet I can remember my astonishment the first time I flew over the area in a hovercraft. Even after thousands of years the scars in the land were still visible. The signs on Tehuán are fainter, but familiar nonetheless."

"These quarries are much older than those on earth," announced Lieutenant Dean, walking down the ramp to the command center. His face was flushed with embarrassment. "After cross-checking with the planet's geological data, I've uncovered a reference to the excavations buried in a footnote in the original planet survey. The first scout team confirmed that Tehuán has never possessed an indigenous intelligent life-form, but they were unable to determine the identity of the space-traveling race that opened the quarries. And since the site was abandoned some five thousand years ago, they evidently didn't consider it worth mentioning in the planet brief."

The science officer tensed, as if bracing himself for a rebuke at his oversight. Picard eased the frown off his face. He could hardly upbraid the man for not being an android; even Data might have missed the significance of that footnote. But probably not.

"What was being excavated?" asked Picard.

Davies leaned over Wesley's shoulder to examine the readings on the Conn console. "Sensor scans indicate recrystallized dolomite with trace amounts of iron oxide and diopside. This particular compound is sometimes referred to as arizite."

"Arizite?"

"It's a decorative marble, not very common in—"

"I'm familiar with it," said Picard. "In fact, I have a statue carved from arizite sitting on my desk." His thoughts jumped back to Kirlos and Professor Coleridge's archaeological project. "Could the ancient Ariantu Empire have included this sector? Could Tehuán have been the source of arizite for the Ariantu sculptors?"

Dean was quick to answer. "There's no direct evidence to indicate a connection. However, the preliminary dating of the site indicates the rock was being removed during the era in which the Ariantu were still in residence on Kirlos."

"All of which may be of interest to Professor Coleridge," said Picard slowly, "but I don't see the relevance to—"

"Captain!" Wesley's fingers skipped over the Ops console. "I've re-analyzed the tricorder readings from Commander Riker, the ones he took from the area where the colonists were killed by a disrupter blast."

The ensign paused for dramatic effect, then announced, "A large percentage of the rocks in the landslide are composed of arizite."

Wesley appeared somewhat crestfallen when the captain accepted this news calmly, and more than a little resentful when the other officers insisted on double-checking his analysis.

"Patience, Mr. Crusher." Picard moved to the command chair and sat, relaxed but alert, while Davies and Dean conferred over the data.

"Confirmed," said Davies finally. "The phaser attack on the mountain peak uncovered a vein of the marble. But then, any stray phaser blast in the valley would probably do the same. The entire mountain range is composed of metamorphic rock." The geologist aimed a sympathetic but somewhat condescending look at the young ensign. "It could simply be a coincidence."

Wesley hunched down into his chair.

"But what if it's *not* a coincidence?" asked Picard. Despite his outer reserve, he had experienced the same thrill of discovery that had excited Wesley. "What if *this* is why the raiders beamed down to Tehuán?"

"I don't see how," said Davies. "The vein was small and the rock simply isn't that valuable. A ton of it would barely pay back the cost of fuel for a single ship to make the trip, much less a *fleet* of ships."

Picard recognized the force of the geologist's argument, yet the only distinctive feature of Tehuán was the presence of this ancient quarry. And it was tied, if only faintly, to the death of three colonists who had come face to face with the attackers. If they hadn't landed to gather arizite, what *had* they come for?

Burke's voice broke the silence. "I'm receiving an alert transmission from Kirlos." Then, as he scanned the incoming message, his brow furrowed in alarm. "Captain! Ambassador Stephaleh has declared martial law on Kirlos."

"On speakers," ordered Picard.

He listened intently as the heavily accented voice of Zamorh, the ambassador's Sullurh assistant, dispassionately recounted the recent series of catastrophes on Kirlos. And the death of Professor Coleridge.

When the message had concluded, one clear thought remained in the captain's mind.

"Arizite," he muttered softly, as if to himself. "I don't understand why, but it is the one common thread in everything that has happened here and on Kirlos."

Picard pushed himself out of the captain's chair.

"Staff meeting in five minutes. Ensign Crusher, recall all senior officers from Tehuán."

He hesitated for a moment, then headed for the ready room. There was just enough time to collect one very important item from his desk.

The Ariantu warrior crouched in the center of the conference-room table, gripping its knife and biding its time. Picard could almost see it twitch as the room

150

filled with people. Its slitted eyes seemed to follow their movements and mark them as prey once they had chosen seats. He was still half absorbed in studying its form when he announced his proposal.

"Leave? Now?" Dr. Crusher stared at the captain, then began to shake her head. "No, absolutely not! I'll need at least one more week to clear sickbay of critical cases."

"We can take them with us," said Picard evenly.

"But it would mean separating critical-care patients from the family members who have returned to the planet. And outpatient treatments are still going on. Not to mention we're constantly treating the new injuries that have occurred since the colonists started rebuilding."

She paused for breath and Riker immediately jumped in.

"Captain, I'm also concerned about the away team on Kirlos, but we can't leave the Tehuán settlement unprotected. Another attack would wipe out everyone."

"Sensor scans indicate the fleet has left the sector." Picard looked to Burke for confirmation and the security officer nodded in agreement, but Riker was obviously still unconvinced.

"We don't know that they're gone. They could have cloaking devices."

"I doubt it," said Burke scornfully. "If they're still using disrupter pistols, they won't have cloaking devices. I'm surprised they even have transporters. In my opinion, Tehuán was probably attacked by space drifters looking for some easy profit. The Gatherers, perhaps. Since they didn't find anything worth stealing, they'll head for the nearest trade center next and resume their usual petty thefts."

Riker grunted. "That's only conjecture! We can't

risk the lives of several hundred colonists on such slim evidence."

Burke dismissed this suggestion with a shrug, but he did not offer a rebuttal. Turning back to Picard, Riker said, "Captain, I gave my word that the *Enterprise* would stay to protect this colony."

"It wasn't your word to give, Commander." Picard quickly raised a hand, as if to blunt the sting of his reply. "However, it is not my intention to abandon anyone. The colonists on the surface will simply have to evacuate. They can remain on board the *Enterprise* until we return from Kirlos."

"That may save the people on Tehuán, but what about the populations of Devlin Four and Maynard Two? The fleet is probably keeping a low profile because of the *Enterprise*'s presence. As soon as we leave, they could attack one of the other outposts."

Picard's eyes were drawn to the Ariantu statue. He wondered what price it would bring on the black market. Had someone expected to find similar artifacts on Tehuán?

"I believe that Kirlos will be the next target." Yet he couldn't offer any rationale for that belief. He looked back in time to catch the skeptical look that passed between Riker and his chief medical officer. "But I admit that leaving this sector is a calculated risk."

"Whose risk?" demanded Dr. Crusher. "Not *ours*. We'll be safe on this starship. You're gambling with the welfare of thousands of people in this sector."

"Oh, but the stakes are much higher than that, Doctor. An attack on Kirlos would mean not only substantial loss of lives but a disruption in diplomatic relations between the Federation and the K'Vin Hegemony. The repercussions could affect the safety of millions of people."

Crusher settled back into her chair, arms crossed

over her chest in a gesture of defiance. His reply might have silenced her, but she remained as unconvinced as his first officer. Picard deliberately looked to the officers who had only listened to the debate.

"Any other objections?"

Ensign Crusher and Lieutenant Dean dropped their gazes from his, but did not speak. Only Deanna Troi locked eyes with him. She looked puzzled.

"You made up your mind before the conference even started, didn't you?" she said. "Nothing that has been said has made any difference."

"On the contrary, Counselor," said Picard. "The comments of my senior officers are always of interest to me."

He rose from the table.

"Mr. Riker, begin the evacuation of the Tehuán settlers. The *Enterprise* will break orbit in four hours."

Chapter Thirteen

THE FIRST THING Geordi became aware of was that he couldn't scratch his nose.

The second thing he realized was that he couldn't *see* it. Or anything else.

He sat up, staring into nothingness. "Data! Worf!"

"They are right next to you," came a rough voice.

Geordi recognized it immediately. He also recognized that they were in serious trouble.

When Gezor had brought in the three Federation men and the Sullurh who had been aiding them, he had seemed characteristically apologetic. "I know you have been trying your best, Ambassador. The cooperation with the dig, with the Federation in general. It pains me to have to bring this to your attention."

Gregach was staring at the three unconscious forms on the floor. The Sullurh, Thul, stood beside them. Gezor had admitted that he had been weak, and unable (or unwilling) to bring such furious force against one of his own in order to render him unconscious. Gregach could almost admire that, if it hadn't been so damned inconvenient.

"*Does* it pain you?" Gregach asked. "Are you sure you're not deriving some pleasure from it, Gezor? Some moderate feeling of I-told-you-so?"

Gezor looked stricken. "No, Ambassador" was all he managed to get out.

Gregach nodded, satisfied with the Sullurh's sincerity. His gaze wandered to the dyson board set up in the corner of his office, with which he had had so many pleasant and entertaining matches with Stephaleh. How had they come to this pass? he wondered.

He could wonder no more. He had already taken some degree of action by declaring martial law. That had to be the first step, but not the *only* step.

The Federation officers were starting to come around. The Earthman was coming to first, although the Klingon seemed not far behind. In his hand, Gregach was holding the curious curved eyepiece that the Earthman customarily wore. He wondered how it worked.

Then the human opened his eyes and Gregach saw those helpless, blank orbs floating in their sockets. Geordi clearly had no idea where he was or what was happening. There was fear on his face, and he started to shout for his friends.

"They are right next to you," said Gregach, trying not to sound sympathetic. A show of kindheartedness could not be tolerated. For that reason he elected to hold on to the eyepiece, at least for a brief time.

Now Geordi was trying to move his hands again and realizing why he couldn't. "We're manacled," he said.

"Yes," said Gregach.

Worf had not moved, but his low voice sounded through the office. "Is the great K'Vin ambassador so afraid that he must chain us like dogs?"

Gregach looked at Worf with open curiosity. "Is the Federation so craven that its representatives must resort to sabotage and trickery?"

"No," said Worf promptly. "But can *you* respond in the negative to *my* question?"

Gregach actually smiled at that. "Very well." He nodded toward Gezor, who half bowed in response.

Within moments Gezor returned with the keys to the manacles—and six guards, heavily armed, who kept their weapons leveled at the Federation men.

Data was still not moving, and slow alarm spread through Geordi as he tried to prod the android. "Come on, Data," and he felt around for the android's on-off button. He flicked it, but nothing happened. "Come on," he repeated. Nothing.

"I am curious," said Gregach. "Which one of you is in charge?"

Geordi tried not to dwell on the fact that the voice was coming from nowhere. It *wasn't* nowhere, he told himself. Gregach was . . . what, about five feet in front of him? He half lifted Data, who was still stiff, and said, *"He* is."

Gregach laughed at that, and turned to Worf. *"He* is? Really?"

"His performance is adequate when he is functional," said Worf sullenly.

"Well," said Gregach, "we can pretty much say that for *all* of us, can't we? So"—he circled around his desk—*"he* is the one who gives you the orders to commit sabotage."

"No," said Worf.

"Someone else does, then."

Worf frowned at that as he shook his hands out to

156

restore circulation. "Word games are beneath a warrior," he rumbled.

Gregach nodded slowly. "You are quite right."

"We didn't have anything to do with it," said Geordi, addressing a space about two feet to Gregach's left. "If you want to know who did, I'll tell you. It's that Gezor guy."

For the first time, Gezor spoke up. *"Truly?"*

Geordi cursed to himself. Of *course* Gezor would be standing there. They were obviously in Gregach's office, and where else would Gezor be? But because the Sullurh had said nothing, it hadn't occurred to Geordi that he was present. He felt like an absolute fool.

But he pushed on. "Yes, truly," he said tightly, hoping against logic that Data had been right. "Data figured it all out. Gezor and Zamorh are working together to push you and Stephaleh out and seize power for themselves."

"Seize power?" said Gregach incredulously. "Of *what?* An artificial floating ball of rock in the middle of nowhere? Filled with archaeologists and the scum of the galaxy? What do you think this is, some sort of secret power base? A stepping stone to the stars? Good God! *Seize power!* If he wants it, he can have it! Gezor, do you want it? I can pack and be gone inside of two hours."

"No, thank you, Ambassador," said Gezor politely. "I ran the embassy shortly after your predecessor's hurried and somewhat embarrassed departure after he amassed such great gambling debts. As I recall, I was quite content to turn the reins over to you."

"Are you sure you don't want them back? Think of it as an early birthday present."

"Quite sure, Ambassador."

Gregach sighed. "Can't blame a fellow for trying."

He turned back toward Geordi. "So . . . your commander there figured it out, did he? And did he have an even more plausible motivation for Gezor's alleged duplicity than the one you just put forward?"

Geordi thought, *I knew it was a stupid idea,* but said out loud, "I'm sure he was working on it."

"Yes, well, I'm certain he can continue to do so where you'll be confined. Gezor, take them down to the holding cell on the lowest level. Cell D."

"Cell D?" Gezor blinked. "Sir, we rarely use that. It hasn't been cleaned out in years."

"Yes, I know," said Gregach. "I do not take well to betrayal, and I enjoy duplicity even less. I see no reason to be charitable while I decide what to do with them."

"There is a great deal you do not see," said Worf, "because you are more blind than Lieutenant Commander La Forge. If you had any decency, you would return his VISOR to him. If you had any sense, you would listen to him. Or to me."

Gregach eyed him up and down. "You speak your mind at times when you can ill afford to do so."

"I speak my mind and let the times attend to themselves."

Gregach nodded slowly and tried not to smile. Then he said to Geordi, "Mr. La Forge, stretch out your hands please."

Geordi did so. And a moment later the VISOR was in his hands. Quickly he put it on . . . and saw nothing.

A shock of dismay ran through him. "It . . . it's not working. When it was knocked off me, or maybe when I was hit, the connectors—"

"I am many things, Mr. La Forge," said Gregach. "Warrior, ambassador, gamesman—but a technician I am not. I will provide you what tools we have, if you wish, and in your cell you may endeavor to repair the damage done to your equipment. And, for that matter, to your valiant commander. Perhaps you can replace the logic circuits that brought him to such an odd and erroneous conclusion concerning my trusted longtime aide."

The guards started to guide them toward the door, Geordi struggling with the weight of Data. Worf started to reach over to help.

"Not the Klingon," Gregach said.

Worf turned and stared at him, not showing surprise but certainly feeling it. Thul stepped in to help Geordi with Data, and they were hustled out the door.

"You," Gregach said to Worf, "will receive somewhat more suitable quarters than your compatriots. I would not dishonor a fellow warrior with the inhospitable accommodations of this building's ancient dungeons."

"I go with my comrades," Worf said.

"Very good," said Gregach. "I knew that would be your instinctive reaction. But think a moment, Lieutenant. Down there you will do them no good. Up here, spending time with me, who knows? You might be able to talk me into some degree of leniency with them. And with yourself, for that matter."

Worf said nothing, his eyes flashing.

Slowly Gregach nodded, and his gaze wandered toward the corner of his office. "Tell me, Lieutenant, do you play dyson?"

Stephaleh could not recall the last time she'd slept nor, for that matter, the last time she'd even relaxed. Of course, a number of times in the past, she had been involved in tense negotiations that could have dissolved into war. Each time she had managed to avoid conflict and bring about peace.

159

She took great pride in all that, despite the hours and the exhaustion that had gone into it. But *this* . . . this was a unique situation, one she had never dreamed could happen on Kirlos. There was death, destruction—and a rapidly crumbling friendship that had once held Kirlosia together as well as any official treaty.

She had trouble recognizing Gregach now, as he made the transition from diplomat to soldier. His martial side was one she had never really seen before, and she found it distasteful. Particularly because she feared that when this was all over, they would never be able to restore things to the way they had been.

Most troubling, at present, was the absence of the officers from the *Enterprise.* They had gone off on their own the night before, looking for answers. She was glad to have them, since in their own way they were better trained for this sort of problem than she and Powell were.

Worf was right: Powell had never fired a phaser in the line of duty and appeared somewhat skittish about doing so. He preferred it when things were nice and orderly; he was not unlike the ambassador herself in that respect.

Zamorh, who rarely left her side now, spoke up. "Ambassador, the people are frightened. Our broadcasts seem incapable of calming them down. Perhaps a direct appeal from you would . . ."

She shook her head. Stephaleh knew that few people on the Federation side of Kirlos cared about the embassy or the ambassador. These were inconveniences they had tended to ignore—until recently. When she sent out orders, the people obeyed, but they grumbled. She had even walked among them to try to resolve matters, and had come away feeling that she'd wasted her time. Public opinion, she knew, was fickle; the smallest of things could sometimes turn a crowd into an ugly mob.

"No, Zamorh. I do need to do something, but exactly what it is seems elusive."

The ambassador rarely admitted weakness to the Sullurh, so he was somewhat taken aback by the admission. He thought and then responded, "Perhaps you need to take the initiative rather than follow in Gregach's footsteps. Act rather than react."

This made some sense. She drummed her fingers restlessly on the desk, noting how much less stiff they were than usual. The motion actually felt good. In fact, many of her aches and pains had subsided as the crisis had drawn more and more of her attention.

She felt like one of her ancestors, ignoring her wounds in the course of some great battle. She tended to downplay the warrior instincts in herself; all Andorians did. But maybe they were not so different from the K'Vin after all. But what if she were to change her strategy just a bit? Confront Gregach as one warrior to another?

Inspired, she tapped her console and asked for a direct line to the K'Vin ambassador. Her people had apparently anticipated her move; there was an active channel ready and waiting.

"Ambassador Gregach, I hope I am not disturbing you."

Gregach looked as if he had been napping, and she wanted to poke at him, keep him a bit off balance. And of course Gezor was right there, on the periphery of the communications field. "As it happens, I was in conference," the K'Vin blustered.

"I won't keep you, then. I'm calling to ask if your

people have seen the Starfleet officers." She'd needed *some* reason to call him, to reopen their dialogue. This one was as good as any.

He grunted. "You mean the ones who just might have caused this mess?"

"You know better than that, Gregach," she said calmly. "They arrived at our request and with your approval. Your documents are most thorough, and you know they have no interest in Kirlos beyond scientific curiosity."

"So you say. Anyway, they are indeed here. I have detained them pending satisfactory questioning."

This came as a shock to Stephaleh. She summoned some bravado and went after Gregach with a sternness that shook the K'Vin. "You held our representatives and did not bother informing this embassy? How *dare* you violate the treaty so blatantly! We've always had an understanding, Gregach, and now I begin to wonder if either of us truly understood the other. Why are they being held? What have they done?"

"Done? Well, according to our people here, they were found in our territory, looking around. 'Acting suspiciously' is the phrase used in the report. And I thought it would be best if I talked with them personally."

"Fine. Talk with them—and then *release* them. You know they have done nothing. And you also know that as members of the Federation, they are entitled to counsel."

The K'Vin made a derisive sound deep in his throat. "You have no judge advocate general's office to rely on in this sector," he said. "You use a simple attorney who, I believe, is resting quietly in a medical facility at this moment. Under the circumstances, Ambassador, I merely asked the Starfleet officers to waive their right to counsel."

162

"And they agreed?" she asked incredulously.

"In a way. Do you doubt me, *old friend?* Well, it doesn't matter now, Stephaleh. What *does* matter is that someone has been causing havoc on this world, and I will see to it that we find an *answer.*"

"Even if that answer might already be staring you in the face, though you choose to ignore it? The K'Vin have never been known for their deductive reasoning. They prefer to go ahead and take whatever they like."

Gregach shrugged. "Just as we should have taken Kirlos a long time ago. We have tolerated the Federation presence long enough. Maybe this will open some eyes back on the homeworld—and conclude the charade of negotiation."

Stephaleh liked neither the tone of the conversation nor the naked feelings she and Gregach were displaying. She knew better than to emphasize differences, but she couldn't seem to stop herself. She was allowing her personal resentment to cloud her judgment.

Get a grip on yourself, Stephaleh. Is this all you've learned in so many years of playing the diplomat?

"This world actually belongs to the Ariantu," she reminded Gregach, "not to anyone who lives here presently. Now, when may I expect the release of the Starfleet officers?"

"When I am satisfied I have heard all they know."

She curbed her anger at that. "Very well. My protest will be filed with your government within the hour. I do not want them harmed, Gregach. I want this to come to a *satisfying* end. A *fast* and satisfying end."

Now it was Gregach's turn to pause and think. He was actually a careful thinker, and Stephaleh regretted her earlier comment. Perhaps he would ignore it as something said in the heat of the moment. Perhaps not. Perhaps their friendship was torn asunder.

"Then let me return to my guests for a fast and *satisfying* conversation. Gregach out."

Gregach turned from his chair and looked at Gezor, who was silently waiting near the door of the office. "Well, Gezor, what do you think of that? My good friend Stephaleh accuses me of treaty violations!"

"Technically she is correct, Ambassador. However, I think it is best to stress that the Starfleet officers were found in K'Vin territory, making them the first transgressors."

"Damned right, Gezor. And she dares to resort to protocol at this stage. We're on the brink of a war that could engulf Kirlos and she wants more words!"

"But what will you do now, Ambassador? What is the best course of action?"

Gregach stopped to think. His first inclination was to summon his old friends and have an old-fashioned war council. But he had learned that several of them remained purposefully ignorant of the goings-on and he did not want to waste time with repetitious briefings. He hungered for action—but *what?*

Zamorh waited until he thought the ambassador had regained her self-control and then chose to speak. "It is most disturbing to have Lieutenant Worf and the others in custody. Could they know something?"

"They know something, yes, but it may not be what Gregach wants to hear. Instead, it may anger him. And in this time of increased hostilities, that may be dangerous."

"You know, of course, that the K'Vin have been known to use methods of torture—"

"Never!" Stephaleh snapped. "Gregach would never torture members of Starfleet. Why, the diplomatic repercussions would . . ."

"Would what, Ambassador? As I see it, the relations are as bad as they can get, short of armed conflict."

"You may be right, Zamorh. However, I will do whatever it takes to prevent arms from entering this. It's bad enough Powell and his men have to walk the streets."

"Something needs to be done, if I am correct."

"You are, Zamorh, but I wish to the deities I knew what it was. I can't produce the culprits behind this mess and I certainly can't explain why Starfleet officers were in K'Vin territory, in violation of our treaty."

"But we *can* help expedite their release," Zamorh said, with his head bowed a little. He was obviously being hesitant, and Stephaleh knew she would have to draw him out.

"We can file protests and motions," she said, "but there is no one here on the planet who can effect their release through diplomatic channels. In fact, those channels may have just closed indefinitely."

"As you know, Ambassador, my people were here long before the K'Vin or the Federation."

"Of course I know that, Zamorh. Do you have a point?"

"We studied the old ruins before they were occupied by officials and traders. We know of tunnels and passageways that connect many buildings. The tunnels were part of an early system of transportation, or so we thought."

"Yes?" Stephaleh was growing a little impatient. She wanted to do something, and Zamorh was deliberately taking his time.

"One such tunnel leads from Busiek's, the pub near the border, to the K'Vin embassy. It may not have been damaged during the explosion."

"Are you suggesting we send someone in to liberate

165

the officers? That would be just the provocation Gregach needs to break our people apart—or maybe even kill one of them. Relations, which have always been cordial here, would be shredded. Likewise, relations between the K'Vin and the Federation would be damaged beyond repair."

"I'm sorry, Ambassador. I am only trying to help by suggesting a course of action."

Stephaleh looked at her aide and wondered. Was this her only option? And if so, whom could she possibly send? Powell? Ekrut, who was certainly small and agile enough? She shook her head and put both hands flat on her desk. "No, Zamorh. We will not make a rescue attempt. It lacks the subtlety of diplomacy. Instead, I will have to choose carefully the words that will win their release, or at least placate Ambassador Gregach."

Gezor waited a few more moments and spoke again. "Sir, is not a response of some kind in order? If I understand the K'Vin way, that is."

"Yes, it is, Gezor, but it must be the *right* response," Gregach said. "The K'Vin way is deliberate, and we must not overstep our place."

"Would some use of the hostages be appropriate?"

"They are not hostages, Gezor. That is a poor choice of words. They are more like guests, as I told Stephaleh. Did you place Worf in a better room?"

"Of course, Ambassador."

"Excellent. Maybe a fellow tactician can be of help." With that, he turned and strode from the office.

Alone in his room, Zamorh had time to think. According to the chronometers, synchronized nightly now, he was certain the time was coming. He had worked carefully to orchestrate his part of the plan, and he was pleased to see that Gezor had been useful, too. However, though things had reached a boiling point, neither side seemed able to take the next step. He understood the importance of that step and wondered if either side could be budged, setting the stage for the final act. Maybe, he considered, the time had come for a clear military action on the part of the Federation, one that might shake up the K'Vin a little, cause them to take Stephaleh's position more seriously. He got to his feet, looked in the mirror, and was pleased to see he was well groomed. With a purpose to his step, he walked down the hall to Stephaleh's office.

The Andorian was seated at the desk, as he expected. She was busying herself with paperwork and did not notice his entrance. She rarely did, given the Sullurh way of being quiet around others.

"Ambassador, if I may be so bold, a thought has occurred to me."

Stephaleh looked up from her desk and felt a crick in her neck. It hadn't been there this morning, but now it felt as if it would never leave. "Yes, of course, Zamorh. Speak your mind."

"I may have been mistaken about a rescue attempt, and for that I apologize."

"It's all right. None of us are thinking clearly in this matter."

"Be that as it may," Zamorh continued, "since you are seeking some action to take, it may be best to consider reassessing our fortifications and supplies in case we ourselves are attacked. A heightened state of readiness may be called for here."

Now that was a productive contribution, she thought. In fact, it surprised her that this was the first time she ha considered checking the defenses. Even Powell had said nothing about it. Compared to Worf, Powell left something to be desired. She made a note to herself to review his performance once this was over. "Yes, Zamorh. Please ask Chief Powell to tend to it. And thank you for your suggestion."

Worf was seated on the hard bed, wondering about the special treatment afforded him. He would have been perfectly content to remain in the small cell with Geordi and Data. The spartan conditions had suited his tastes, and the company would have been welcome, since there was much to figure out. Even if the android got on his nerves from time to time, Worf had to admit that as a superior officer, Data had acquitted himself fairly well.

These thoughts were interrupted by the sound of a key in a lock. The door swung open and in walked Ambassador Gregach. Worf immediately stood and Gregach patted the air, indicating that the Klingon should sit down. On a small table beside the bed was a half-finished game of dyson. Gregach had beaten the Klingon in their first match, reminding him of his bet with that Keenan woman on the *Enterprise* and the infuriating defeat that had landed him on Kirlos in the first place.

At least Worf's game was improving a little. So far, this second match was too close to call.

"I have come," said the K'Vin, "to talk about things."

"Things?"

"Yes, Worf. We are facing times of action and perhaps desperate measures. I find my own colleagues wanting; they are old men now and have no fire left in them. The Sullurh serve me well, but as far as I know they have never been in any armed conflict. You, on the other hand, must have seen considerable action."

"I have," replied Worf, wondering where this was going.

"The Klingons have always fascinated me, and I am sorry that we never met in a full-scale battle. I would have liked that. Never mind, though. I'm here to talk to you about the situation. Obviously everyone is pointing fingers, but no one is certain of anything."

"Actually, Ambassador, a few things are clear. One, the attacks on both sides seem to have been timed exactly and appear to indicate a planned attack. Two, since both sides have been attacked and people died in both Federation and K'Vin territory, this assault was not aimed at any one government. Three, the goal appears to be something on Kirlos itself; there must be some aspect of this world that has escaped everyone's notice."

Gregach stopped Worf by coming over and looking at the officer. "Something on Kirlos? Such as what?"

"We do not know. But the fighting is for some*thing*, not some*one*."

"Do you have any other conclusions?" Gregach genuinely admired Worf's clear thinking.

"Yes. Finally, we have reason to believe the conspiracy involves your aide, Gezor—but that is an assumption you seem to ignore."

Gregach walked about the small room, noting that he had never been here before. It was used by visiting dignitaries and in his years on Kirlos, he had never been visited. That had been all right with him; he had never missed the visits—until now. Could this Klingon be right? Could Gezor be part of a conspiracy? Worf spoke plainly and clearly. His first three points made sense, but this fourth . . . Why would Gezor betray his employer?

"Why would Gezor be behind this?" he said aloud.

"He may not be behind it, sir. He may be a part of some larger conspiracy."

"You're certain of this, aren't you, Lieutenant?" He

169

turned to look directly at Worf, to see for himself the obvious sincerity behind the words. Worf merely nodded and looked straight ahead severely. "What, then, would you suggest I do?"

"You could apprehend Gezor and ask him all the questions you seem intent on asking me and my fellow officers."

"And then?"

"Get answers. Deal with the problem and be done with it. We should either stop the destruction or find a reason to fight—and then fight."

"You would *like* to fight, wouldn't you?"

"I enjoy battle, yes—but it must be a battle worth fighting, not one over bruised feelings; wasted efforts have been the downfall of many an emperor. The Klingons' best battles occurred when worlds were at stake."

"You've gone through a lot of emperors, I would imagine."

Worf grunted. This aspect of his people, the calculated killing for mere political gain, seemed pointless to him. He was a purist. He wanted a battle to mean something.

"You have given me much to think on; I thank you. Please get some rest. I imagine the coming days will tax us both."

Gregach turned and knocked once on the door. A guard opened it and allowed the ambassador to leave. Worf sat patiently on the bed, knowing that his time to act would come.

Chapter Fourteen

ILUGH WOULD HAVE PREFERRED to be near the K'Vin ambassador, where he belonged. But Gregach had deemed it more important for him to patrol the Strip.

And now, finally, events had proven Gregach right. No sooner had Ilugh gotten word of the riot than he had commandeered a ground car and taken off in that direction. It wasn't far enough away to think about transmatting and besides, that was no longer a viable option, what with vandals having wrecked some of the booths in the area.

As his driver tore through the winding city streets, Ilugh felt light-headed, dizzy. As if the plethane were still in his system. Of course, that was impossible—all traces of the gas had been purged from his blood-stream. No doubt this was one of the psychosomatic incidents his doctors had warned him about. What had they called them? *Recurrences?* But they'd said the incidents would be mild and of short duration.

That showed how much they knew, he told himself,

fighting off a wrenching wave of vertigo. Ilugh watched the street corners whiz by on either side of him. Maybe the doctors had never had an incident in a fully accelerated ground car.

Not that he was going to complain about it. It had been difficult enough getting himself restored to active duty; he wasn't going to ruin that now.

Moments later, they hit the fringes of the riot. In keeping with his training, the driver didn't slow up in the least. He bore down on the rioters until they finally noticed the car and gave way. Only when the crowd had grown too dense for anyone to move quickly did he decelerate and give the citizens more time to scatter.

Ilugh was in the thick of the crowd before he realized the extent of the riot. It was big—much bigger than he would have guessed. So much for the vaunted K'Vin discipline; in times like these, it seemed, it was shed like an old skin.

He and his driver spotted the beleaguered border guards at the same time. Even from a distance, Ilugh could tell that a couple of them had gone down. And if training had held, at least twice that number of civilians had been stunned in retribution.

The guard in charge looked glad to see him. Ilugh knew him by sight, but not by name.

"What's going on?" he snapped as his ground car screeched to a halt. He leaped out in the space that the car's arrival had cleared.

The border guard indicated the mob with a tilt of his head. Ilugh could barely hear him over all the shouting.

"It was that bit of business on the Federation side. The crowd expects some sort of retaliation." The guard frowned, pushing his tusks out in the process. "So they're thinking that they'll strike first. If

Stephaleh wants to spur them into overrunning her sector, they'll be only too happy to oblige."

Ilugh grunted, eyeing the rioters as they coalesced again into a solid mass. He raised his blaster, making it obvious that he wouldn't hesitate to use it. It seemed to have no effect, however; the mob continued to advance slowly.

"There should be others here by now," said the border guard. "Shouldn't there?"

"Don't count on too many others," advised Ilugh, though he would have welcomed some additional reinforcements himself. "This isn't the only trouble spot, though it seems to be the—"

He never finished his sentence. With a roar, incited by something or someone in their midst, the rioters surged forward all at once.

Ilugh fired. Again. And again.

Rioters fell and were trampled by other rioters. Nor could the blaster beams keep them at bay. There were too many of them, and they were too caught up in their fear and hatred to stop.

Slowly, and then less slowly, the guards found themselves yielding ground. Before they knew it, they were in the middle of the Strip, and then beyond it, on what was officially the Federation side.

Ilugh tried to keep his head, to shout orders to the guards who were close enough to hear him. But it was no use. Their retreat became a rout.

He managed to squeeze off one last volley before the blaster was ripped from his hand. There was an impact to the side of his head; he felt himself falling. . . .

The next thing he knew, he was propped up against the ground car, the taste of metal in his mouth, wondering how long he'd been unconscious. A couple of guards were kneeling beside him; one of them was his driver. Their blasters were in the ready position—for all the good it did. The mob, unstoppable now, was flooding past them on both sides, as a river flows around a great boulder in its path.

Ilugh got his legs underneath him, raised himself so he could see a little better, as the rioters poured across the Strip and into the Federation sector. He grunted, spat blood.

And found himself pitying the poor Federation-siders who got in the mob's way.

"You're a fool, Trimble! Almost as big a fool as that Andorian in the embassy tower!"

Lars Trimble faced the small clot of merchants who stood just outside the half-open door of his residence. Their expressions were twisted, angry, all their merchants' subtlety gone, replaced by a burning need to escape.

"We've got to force her hand—*make* her issue the evacuation order."

Trimble spoke as calmly as he could. "According to what I've heard, the order has already been issued. Evacuation vessels are on the way."

Mand'liiki shook his narrow Rhadamanthan fist. *"Lies,"* he hissed. "All lies. Stephaleh has been behind this from the beginning. She's not about to let it end so easily. Not by her own choice, anyway." He turned to the others. "I'll believe she's given the order when I've seen it with my own eyes!"

That got a rise out of the assembled merchants. They pummeled the empty air and bellowed in agreement.

"Lars," came a voice from behind him. Trimble glanced over his shoulder and saw his wife's face, racked with fear. As gently as he could, he urged her back into the residence.

"She charmed you, Trimble! She enslaved you with that act of hers—or you'd be out here with *us* now!"

He confronted the merchants again. "No," he said. "She has no hold on me."

"Then join us!" cried the Rhadamanthan. "Prove to her that you can still think for yourself!"

The human shook his head. "This is wrong—useless, and worse than useless. The Federation doesn't start wars; you know that as well as I do. And Stephaleh doesn't start wars either. At first I might have doubted that, but I've had some time to think about it. To *reason*." He licked his lips. Words didn't come easily to him; he had to search for them. "It has to be the K'Vin. They're trying to turn us against one another, put us at each other's throats. And it's working. We're doing their dirty work for them, so they can march in here when it's over and claim what's ours. So they can have Kirlos and her trade routes all to themselves, without spilling a drop of K'Vin blood."

"The K'Vin have bled, too!" shrilled one of the merchants. Inside, one of Trimble's children cried out at the sound, and something went taut within him.

"That's right," added another. "They've spilled more than a drop, Trimble. They've lost more people than we have!"

"And you believe their reports," said the human, "before you'll believe those of your own embassy?" He shook his head. "How do you know that K'Vin have been killed? Did you *see* them? And even if they have been, are you saying that their government wouldn't have sacrificed them? Just as—according to *you*—the Federation is sacrificing us?"

That surprised them—almost as much as it surprised *him*. For he had never taken his reasoning quite so far—and certainly had never thought about how to

175

express it to a group of angry merchants. And yet his arguments had the ring of truth.

For a moment they were quiet. Then Mand'liiki spoke up again.

"Pretty words," he spat. "Just like Stephaleh's. But we know the truth. We saw the Starfleet officers arrive, and soon after that the troubles started. Are you going to tell us it was a coincidence, as *she* did?"

Trimble sighed. "I don't know," he said. "Maybe there *was* a reason for their coming here—something we're not privy to. But it wasn't to bring on these disasters. It wasn't to start a war with the K'Vin."

"Of course not," agreed the Rhadamanthan. "And Kirlos doesn't revolve around a sun."

There were shouts of encouragement, laughter, and solidarity. And suddenly the merchants were stirred up again.

They didn't want to believe the truth, Trimble realized. They wanted to believe whatever was easier for them—and it would be easier to storm the embassy than to confront the K'Vin.

"Last chance," said the Rhadamanthan, pointing at Trimble with a long, slender finger. "Are you with us or not?"

The human didn't hesitate. "Not," he said.

Mand'liiki expressed his disdain with a broad, sweeping gesture. "Come on," he said, whirling to face the others. "We don't need him. There are others who will jump at the chance to join us!"

And with that, they started off down the narrow, twisting street. Trimble watched them go.

"Lars, are they gone?"

He looked back at his wife, his sons. "Yes," he said. "They're gone, but—"

He was interrupted by the strangest of sounds. A

ponderous rumbling that seemed gradually to surround them, though it also seemed to remain very far away.

Then it began to grow louder and closer, and Trimble could hear other sounds bristling on its surface—cries and shouts, frantic screams charged with a terrible energy.

Could Mand'liiki have gathered a mob so quickly? Or had one been gathering even as they spoke? No, for as the noise expanded, grew louder, it became plainer and plainer that it was not made by Federation-siders.

Without thinking, Trimble ran out the door and into the street. But he didn't have to go far before he got the answer he sought.

The cross street, straighter and wider than this one, was flooded with K'Vin. They charged from right to left—bellowing, rending, destroying. As he watched, they smashed the windows of a tavern, beat down its door, and tore away the supports of its overhanging roof.

Meanwhile, Mand'liiki and his followers—what was left of them—were beating a desperate retreat in the humans' direction. And there were K'Vin in close pursuit, many more of them than the Rhadamanthan and his companions could possibly have handled.

Trimble just stood there, paralyzed by dread and fascination. It was a bizarre scene, one that couldn't be real. He had lived on this street nearly all his life, and never had he seen a single K'Vin set foot on it. Not one.

"Lars!"

His wife's cry roused him. Forcing his knees to unlock, his feet to carry him, he started back to his residence.

A thought: maybe he could help Mand'liiki and the

others. Then another: there was no time. Even as he watched, two more merchants were taken down from behind.

He climbed the steps, felt his wife's grasp on his forearm. She half pulled, half dragged him inside and slammed the door after him.

The children were crying, but Trimble couldn't help it—he had to press his face against the window, to watch in horror as the Rhadamanthan raced past, the only one still on his feet. There was horror scrawled on his face, fear for his very life.

It was sickening and riveting all at once. And of course Lars knew that the K'Vin had seen him, that they might at any time turn and leap up his steps and throw their massive bodies against his door.

But for the time being, he and his family were safe. The intruders seemed content to wreak havoc on the shops alone.

On their way to . . . where? *The embassy?*

Yes. That was the direction in which they were headed. Evidently they believed, as the Federation-siders did, that Stephaleh and the Starfleet officers were somehow behind the spate of disasters.

He thought of the ambassador and what they might do to her. It sent shivers up his spine.

"My gods," breathed his wife as the K'Vin barreled past. "My dear gods."

Chapter Fifteen

BEVERLY CRUSHER SANK DOWN into the soft cushions of the sofa, one leg curled beneath her, and waited for Troi to order refreshments. They were in the doctor's cabin, but she was too tired to play hostess. She was almost too tired for company, but lately there had been so little time to spend with friends that she craved companionship as much as sleep.

Deanna lifted two long-stemmed goblets off the food dispenser shelf. They were filled with a golden liquid that threatened to spill over the brims as she walked across the room. Handing one of the glasses to Beverly, the counselor continued their earlier conversation.

"Actually, most of the colonists seem relieved to be away from Tehuán. The evacuation has enabled them to remain with the injured, and shipboard accommodations are quite luxurious compared to living conditions in the settlement. Since it's only for a short time, they don't feel as if they are abandoning their commitments."

Beverly sipped at her drink, savoring the cool, sweet juice. Troi was still standing, so it was easy to avoid eye contact.

After an awkward silence, Deanna added, "Unfortunately, the same can't be said for the crew."

"Is it that obvious?" asked Beverly, knowing that it was all *too* obvious to the empath.

"I wasn't speaking specifically about you, Beverly. A number of officers seem to harbor . . . reservations about our change of plans."

So Will and Deanna had discussed this as well. Beverly wondered if Deanna was acting as the ship's psychologist in bringing up the subject or if she was off duty now. "And you don't have any reservations about our return to Kirlos?"

This time Deanna looked away. "I'm not entirely comfortable with the captain's actions. Fortunately, command decisions aren't my responsibility."

Before Beverly could reply, the counselor had turned toward the door of the cabin. A chime sounded. And immediately following the chime, Wesley Crusher stepped through the portal.

The cabin controls were set to admit her son automatically, but since Wesley no longer lived with her, a certain awkwardness had arisen about the protocol for these visits. His token warning was part of an unspoken compromise between a sense of family and the growing recognition that both of their lives were becoming more private.

"Am I interrupting?" Wesley asked. Although he liked Troi, a frown had creased his face when he saw someone else here with his mother. He quickly masked the reaction but his mother knew him too well to miss the signs of tension in his lanky frame. And he would be unable to hide his true feeling from the empath.

180

Setting her drink down on a table, Deanna said, "I was taking a short break from work, but I should be getting back to my office."

The counselor made a tactful exit from the cabin, leaving Beverly alone to deal with her son. He was obviously troubled, but to Beverly's dismay she felt a stab of irritation that he should choose to seek her out now. Then she remembered how long it had been since they had talked, really talked, and concern overrode her weariness.

"What's up?" She could usually muster more subtlety, but fortunately her direct approach seemed to be just what Wesley needed.

"It's about Captain Picard."

Her fingers tightened around the stem of the goblet.

"He's wrong," cried Wesley. "Everyone knows it: you, Commander Riker, Counselor Troi. Why is he taking the *Enterprise* to Kirlos anyway?"

Why indeed? "Because he's the captain. And even if we can't understand his reasons, we have to trust that he knows best."

Beverly watched her son struggle to make this leap of faith, one that she herself had been unable to make this time.

"That's what I've always believed," he said. "I mean, Captain Picard always knows so much more than anyone else that I figured he couldn't make a wrong decision."

"Until now?"

Wesley nodded.

"No one is perfect," she said, echoing the arguments that had run through her own mind over the past days. "Not even Captain Picard. But he's one of the finest captains in the fleet. And because his judgment is right more often than it's wrong, it's our duty to follow his orders at all times."

"Even if it means that the people on Devlin Four are killed?"

"Yes." No matter what her doubts, that had to be the answer. If it wasn't, Beverly knew she would have to rethink her entire career in Starfleet. And she was definitely too tired for that right now.

Wesley dropped down to sit beside her on the sofa. She resisted the urge to hug him. He would see it as a maternal gesture and not realize she was in need of reassurance herself.

"I'm glad I'm off duty," he said at last. "I don't want to be on the bridge right now."

Picard had listened to the message twice. It was short and to the point. There was no need to stay in the ready room any longer. Nevertheless, he had not moved from behind his desk and he felt no desire to do so. He tried to dismiss this inertia as fatigue but finally admitted it was self-indulgent brooding. This self-knowledge only darkened his mood. He had made his decision and acted on it, so agonizing after the fact was futile; he should return to the bridge.

And still he did not move.

A moment's respite alone in this room had left him unguarded for the first time since starting this train of events. With his defenses dropped, memories of the scene in the conference room teased at his mind. He heard the voices of his senior officers, listened once more to their arguments, and countered them all again.

Instinct had whispered that the key to recent events was on Kirlos and had urged a return to that planet. Against the advice of his crew, he had trusted to that instinct. But what if he was wrong? What if the self-confidence that was essential to command had been distorted into arrogance? He wouldn't be the

182

first starship captain to slide over that fine line without feeling the shift within himself.

Having finally admitted those doubts, Picard thrust them aside. They were not sufficiently strong to make him change his present course, so any further examination would be not only self-indulgent but dangerous. For now he believed, he *must* believe, that the final outcome would prove him correct.

But the waiting was hard.

The door chimed. "Come," said the captain.

The doors to the ready room whisked open. Looking up, Picard saw his first officer cross the threshold. The doors snapped shut; Riker froze in mid-stride.

"Captain?"

Only then did Picard realize he had been sitting in the dark. He tapped the room controls, then blinked at the sudden flood of light. Riker stepped forward and snapped to attention.

"We're approaching the Sydon solar system, Captain."

"Thank you, Number One."

That announcement hardly justified a detour to the ready room, but they both knew it was only a convenient excuse for Riker's presence. Under ordinary circumstances, the first officer would not have bothered to cover his curiosity about the contents of the Starfleet transmission. His tact was a symptom of the strain that had arisen between him and the captain since the conference. Picard offered the information first, before Riker had to ask. Or worse, before he left the room without asking.

"The message contained Starfleet's official reaction to the *Enterprise*'s unauthorized return to Kirlos." And the admiral's chilly delivery had made the unofficial position just as clear. "Given the recent outbreaks of violence, and Ambassador Stephaleh's decision to

183

impose martial law in the Federation sector of the planet, my decision falls within the murky area of captain's discretion."

"Then they approve," said Riker in a voice stripped of inflection.

"They approve if I'm right," replied Picard. "But if I'm wrong, my actions will be difficult to justify."

In all likelihood, it would mean the loss of his command. He would be transferred to a desk job at a starbase, where captain's discretion was limited to deciding which stack of printouts to read next. And he would stay a captain for the rest of his career.

The sudden flash of a yellow alert saved him from further contemplation of that fate.

"Captain to the bridge. First officer to the bridge."

They both raced from the room, but Riker had a head start and reached the bridge first. He called for an explanation as Picard settled in the captain's chair. If the missing fleet of raiders was in this region, then he had made the right decision.

But his sense of relief was shattered by the security report.

"Long-range sensors have picked up a K'Vin warship, class-D combat unit. Course heading indicates they are also bound for Kirlos." Burke broke off, his eyes tracking the panel readout. "Correction. They've changed course for an intercept with the *Enterprise.*"

"Raise shields," ordered Picard immediately. Some races would interpret the raising of shields as a provocation; they would assume aggression where none was intended. However, according to Ambassador Stephaleh, the K'Vin saw a lack of defense as a positive invitation to attack.

"The ship is now within communications range." A shapeless bright dot appeared in the center of the viewscreen.

"Establish contact." Picard sucked in a lungful of air, preparing for the high-volume bluster that the K'Vin expected in a standard greeting.

"Hailing frequencies open, sir. But they are not responding."

He let loose his breath. As one, he and Riker turned to each other and exchanged a silent question. Was this typical K'Vin posturing or an attack approach?

"Ten minutes to intercept. . . . Sensors indicate weapons system activity."

"So they're going to attack," said Riker. Picard heard a mixture of anger and surprise in the younger man's voice.

"Yes, it certainly looks that way." His mind raced through the few options open to him. If he ordered a change of course, the K'Vin would give chase. And a class-D warship could match, possibly even exceed, the *Enterprise*'s warp speed, with sufficient power left over to unleash a few photon torpedoes. There was no time to curse Ambassador Stephaleh for the absence of his chief engineer and his best weapons officer.

However, even if escape was possible, such a retreat would leave the warship free to resume its journey to Kirlos. Which meant the K'Vin would arrive at that planet with thwarted blood lust and a heightened suspicion of the Federation.

So there was really only one course of action. Picard would have to call their bluff. If it was a bluff.

"Red alert. Battle stations."

Flashing red lights and a brief flurry of activity marked the change in status. When all movement was stilled, a tension remained. The crew members' attention was riveted on their panels, but Picard and Riker studied the main viewer. The outlines of the warship sharpened; the image filled more and more of the screen.

185

"Ten minutes to intercept."

"I owe you an apology," said Riker softly. Only the captain could hear him. "The trouble on Kirlos is escalating. If you hadn't ordered a return, the Federation sector would have been left defenseless."

"I don't see it that way, Number One." He couldn't keep the bitterness out of his voice. "Without opposition, the K'Vin might have been content simply to flaunt their superior military power. However, this confrontation will probably destroy any opportunity for a diplomatic reconciliation. As a direct result of my decision to leave Tehuán, I've endangered my ship and the colonists on it, and possibly triggered an interstellar war."

He had been wrong after all.

Chapter Sixteen

GEORDI PUT DOWN the narrow tool and slowly, almost fearfully, replaced his VISOR.

The first thing he thought was *Oh, God, it's still broken.* But then he realized he was seeing something —the wall of the cell. It was just that there wasn't much to look at.

Tentatively he swung his gaze in the direction of Thul—and let out a yelp of joy. There was a comforting agglomeration of colors, although not the usual spectrum of heat suffusions that came from, for example, a human. That was natural—different species had different readings. Nevertheless, Thul was most certainly there, and Geordi felt relief sweep through him.

"I knew it!" he said. "All I had to do was get the proper alignment on the connector and—"

Suddenly he turned, for he had been at work on the damaged VISOR for so long that he had almost forgotten. "Data!" he said, and sure enough, there was the still insensate android.

Geordi pulled open the front of Data's uniform and went to work. Thul watched in open amazement. He had never seen anything even remotely like Data in all his years, and was quite certain that he never would again.

Geordi moved swiftly and surely, his confidence restored along with his sight. He tried to push the bleakness of those hours away from him. He had only the here, the now, and the future to worry about and . . .

And what the hell was Data lying on?

The engineer stopped working, and Thul said in confusion, "Is something wrong? What's happening? Can he not be repaired?"

"What? Oh . . . sure," said Geordi. "I'm almost finished, but . . . look at that," and he pointed at the floor.

"At what?" asked Thul.

"Oh. Right, I'm sorry," Geordi said. His hands started to move again through Data's circuitry. "You can't see it. There's a variance in the heat emission in the floor, in an area about, oh, I'd say about twenty feet square."

"What does that mean?" Thul said, genuinely confused.

"It means there's something that's a different temperature underneath the floor, which basically means there's some sort of entrance to a passageway. And as soon as I have Data up and running—there!"

And on that word, as if on cue, Data's eyes snapped open.

His eyes promptly adjusted to the darkness, and Data said slowly, "Are we in danger?"

"Of course," said Geordi affably. "But we have a way out."

"That is to be preferred."

188

Within moments Geordi had closed Data up and he was indicating to the android officer the approximate perimeter of the area he had sighted. It was directly in the middle of the floor. "What do you think is under there?" Geordi asked. "And why hasn't it been noticed earlier?"

"What might be there, I do not know," said Data. "Remember, Geordi, that this embassy was built on the site of Ariantu ruins. Since this area was chosen as the embassy site, naturally no digs were permitted here."

"Well, we start digging now," said Geordi. "How long do you think it will take to get through?"

Data was kneeling over the floor, considering it. Then he abruptly drew back his fist and smashed it straight down. The rock crumbled beneath the impact and his fist and arm went straight through, sinking all the way up to his shoulder.

"Not long," he said.

Within half an hour they had cleared away the stone that had covered over the passage entrance. It was hot work. Geordi was starting to feel the dehydration that Dr. Crusher had warned them about.

He stared down into the hole, and his VISOR told him that there was a floor about six feet straight down. He certainly hoped that his VISOR was in proper working order and wasn't failing to inform him that the floor was actually sixty feet away.

"Perhaps I should go first?" offered Thul.

"This one's mine," replied Geordi.

The android took him by the hands and lowered him into the passageway. Once Geordi's extended foot touched the ground, he told Data to release him.

The air was thick and musty, barely breathable. The floor was covered with dust that seemed inches thick.

189

But all of that was of secondary importance to Geordi.

What caught his attention was a gleaming metal door.

Immediately Geordi's mental alarm went off. Last time he'd encountered a gleaming metal door in a strange place, he'd almost been turned into a puddle of goo. Nevertheless, he approached it—very slowly, very carefully, ready to leap back at the slightest hint of trouble.

The doors slid open without a sound, and what was inside was unmistakable.

"Data!" he called back.

"What have you found, Geordi?"

Geordi shook his head. "You gotta see this."

Within moments Data had dropped down, and so had Thul. The only light was that provided by the torches in their dank cell overhead, but it was more than enough.

Data cocked his head in fascination. "A turbolift."

"So it would seem. Do we take it? You're in charge, Data."

"Yes, I am," said Data. "Although very little is required in the way of decision-making. I do not see any alternative."

"Okay, then. Let's do it."

They stepped into the turbolift. It was quite different from the ones on the *Enterprise*. Much larger, and covered with ornate symbols and unreadable glyphs —unreadable to Geordi, at least; Data was already busy studying them.

The doors slid shut, and the turbolift started to move at a remarkable speed—sideways.

Geordi, having a brief flashback to the time the *Enterprise* turbolift had gone berserk during the computer virus, gripped the handrails. Data and Thul did likewise.

The turbolift sped along on its course and then came to a stop.

"That was easy," said Geordi.

Suddenly it dropped.

Geordi and Thul gasped in shock; Data merely cocked his head curiously as the turbolift seemed to fall like a stone. But instinctively Geordi knew that the car was being cushioned through whatever was powering it, that it was not plummeting out of control, and that they were not going to wind up like pancakes.

At least he *hoped* not.

The car fell for what seemed a mind-bogglingly long time, the air hissing past them; then it slowed to a stop. Geordi braced himself, certain that it was going to leap off diagonally or in some other equally hideous direction.

Instead, the doors slid open, and the turbolift discharged its passengers.

The three of them walked slowly through the wonderment of what would eventually—should there be an eventually—come to be known as the omega level.

Ahead were rows and rows of gleaming consoles with huge curved screens and gleaming black touch-activated panels. And all of it was covered with more of the elaborate glyphs that had decorated the inside of the turbolift. The ceiling seemed to stretch upward forever, like the roof of a cathedral.

Geordi realized that he'd forgotten to breathe. "What is this place?"

Something tapped him on the shoulder. He turned and jumped back several feet.

Data was standing there with a gun strapped to him—a gun that was almost as big as he was.

"I believe," he said, "this is the weapons level."

Thul, meantime, was staggering around as if in ecstasy. He ran his fingers over the lettering, and he was muttering in reverential, prayerful tones. Looking around, Geordi said, "Thul . . . does any of this mean anything to you?"

"It's the nerve center," he was gasping. "It's what I . . . I and Dr. Coleridge were looking for. The center of Ariantu technology."

As Thul spoke he seemed to have more power, more urgency, in his voice. "The Ariantu were a proud warrior race," he said. "Weaponry, power—that was what they worshiped, what they cherished above all else."

Geordi, hardly listening, ran his fingers across one panel. A screen just above it lit up, and he realized that diagrams were flashing past him, a new one every few seconds. *Incredible.* Diagrams of what? Engines, he thought. But they weren't based on warp drive. "Data, take a look at this."

Data shifted his gun around to his back and stood next to Geordi. The speed at which the diagrams appeared did not intimidate Data, who could have assimilated the information at ten times that rate. "Intriguing," he said. "Shunt drive."

From behind him, Thul said, "What?"

"Shunt drive instead of propulsion. These designs are based on the concept of transporting yourself from one point to another point to another repeatedly."

"Of course!" shouted Geordi. *"That's* how they did it! Don't you get it, Data? That's how they accessed the delta level! The space-port level! They didn't need doors because they just transported right through. From outside to inside in an eye blink."

"Pity," said Data. "I thought your wormhole theory was rather interesting."

"Maybe they have that, too. Who knows? But right now we've got to get topside and out of here."

"Yes, but the elevator will only take us back to the dungeon of the K'Vin embassy," said Data reasonably. "I don't see how our situation is improved."

"I do." And Geordi smiled.

Data looked down at his gun. "Oh. Of course. We're armed."

"Heavily. I'm gonna find one of those for me. You figure out if it has a stun setting. I'd really rather not disintegrate a platoon of guards if we can help it."

The turbolift returned them to the hole beneath their cell, and the three of them clambered up into it. Geordi could not help but notice that a change had come over Thul. He moved with new certainty of purpose, with new strength. Could he really have shared Nassa Coleridge's dreams so intensely? How long had he known her, anyway? Something was strange, but Geordi did not have the time or the inclination to find out what it was.

The moment the others were behind him, Geordi said, "Ready? Okay. Let's get the hell out of here."

He swung the gun around, aimed at the door and fired.

A burst of light leaped from the gun and smashed through the door, splintering it into a thousand pieces.

Quickly he powered it down a bit, because at that intensity it would demolish sentient beings, and Geordi did not want to be a murderer. He braced himself, Data behind him, and waited for the running feet, the response from the guards who were stationed just outside the door.

Nothing.

A trick? Were they hiding just outside the door?

"Data," he whispered. "Do you hear any breathing?"

Data paused. "Aside from the people within this cell?"

"Yes."

"No, I do not."

Geordi frowned at that, and at that moment his communicator beeped. He tapped it. "La Forge here."

"Where have you been?" Worf's deep voice demanded. "I've been trying to contact you."

Now *that* was interesting. Whatever was down there, it was interfering with communications. "Preparing our jailbreak," said Geordi. "But nobody's here to challenge us."

"Of course not," said Worf. "They're all running about and squawking like headless chickens."

"I do not think that is possible," Data put forward. "If chickens are headless, squawking would not be—"

"Not *now,* Data," sighed Geordi. "Worf, what's happening?"

"All of the planetary alarms went off at once," said Worf. "And sensors have run amok. Something huge is heading our way, a fleet of unknown origin. Speculation is running rampant. Everything from a Romulan attack to the Borg."

Data was the picture of calm. "Lieutenant Worf," he said into his own communicator, "you are with Ambassador Gregach now?"

"I have access, yes."

"Stay with him. If everyone is as distracted as you say, our departure from captivity should be simplified. We will return to the Federation embassy and will remain in touch with you."

There was a pause. "A good plan," came Worf's reluctant admission.

"I know," said Data evenly. "Data out."

"Data out" was right. Within minutes, the android and Geordi had blasted a hole in the outer wall of the K'Vin embassy. They had encountered no resistance whatsoever, for the K'Vin soldiers had been deployed somewhere else. In the immediate vicinity, there were only K'Vin citizens, gripped by an air of desperation, as if they believed the end of the world was rapidly approaching and the only thing left to do was mark time.

It was, thought Data, a singularly *human* way to think.

"We must get to Ambassador Stephaleh and obtain more information on this mysterious fleet," said Data. Geordi nodded briskly. "Thul," said Data, "I want you to . . ."

He stopped, looked around. Everywhere people were running around, pretty much as Worf had described them. Nowhere did they see Thul.

Geordi was looking around, too. "I know he came out with us."

"Perhaps he has returned to his family," suggested Data.

"Sure. That's probably it. Who can blame the guy? If the end of the world was coming, I'd want to be with my family."

"Really? I would want to be stopping it."

"Good point." He clapped Data on the shoulder and said, "Let's go."

Thul rushed through the winding back streets, breathless, his legs aching with fatigue. He had never been so excited in all his life.

No, that was not quite true. He had been equally excited the first time he laid eyes on the Ariantu.

He would never forget. There had been four of them—tall and proud and bearing themselves like the

195

hunters they were. Dressed in robes that tended to obscure their appearance, but Thul had seen through their disguises. And no wonder—had he not been waiting for them all his life, like his fathers before him, nurturing the slim hope that their patience and faith would someday be rewarded?

And suddenly, wonderfully and inexplicably, there they were. In *his* house, beneath *his* roof, coming to see *him*.

It had been like a dream, a waking fantasy. So numbed had he been by their presence, by their reality, that he could not find words to greet them. It was only after they had spoken a greeting themselves —in a tongue that was at once strange and comfortingly familiar—that he had remembered his manners and asked them to sit.

His furniture had been a bit too small for them, a source of embarrassment to him. But then, they were *true* Ariantu, and Thul—like the other Sullurh, the ones who had remained here after their kinsmen withdrew from Kirlos—had declined somewhat in stature over the millennia. They did not need the measuring stick of their ancestors' physiques to know that; it was plain even from one generation to the next, a result of the acute inbreeding that had likewise diminished the length of their tails, rendering them mere stumps. And even the stumps were removed during the *enio'lo* ceremony, so that the Sullurh would not be identified with the Ariantu who had once ruled here.

The *enio'lo* was a condition of their stewardship, decided long ago by the leaders among the Sullurh—a word that meant "Those Who Stayed" in their ancient language. For long after the other Ariantu left, aliens began to visit and settle on Kirlos—only a few at first, then greater numbers. And many of them, the K'Vin in particular, had been at odds with the Ariantu. So the only way to survive was to lie low, to assimilate, to encourage the genetic drift that had already made them appear different from their forebears, and to perform the tail-severing ceremony.

But as much as they had changed outwardly, the Sullurh were still Ariantu at heart. Fiercely proud, watching over their race's greatest possession—its farthest flung world when its empire was great and glorious. Protecting it against the ravages of mercantile invaders as best they could and in the only way available to them—by insinuating themselves into the power structures of the alien cultures that had come to take over the planet.

Assimilation had meant hardship—and sacrifice. And when Lektor and his companions had had trouble sitting in Thul's chairs, it had reminded him of just how great the Sullurh's sacrifice had been.

However, his visitors had been gracious. They had overlooked the size of his furniture. Indeed, they had overlooked all of the differences between Thul and themselves. Lektor himself had declared that it was of no account who had stayed and who had gone. The time had come for the Ariantu to regain their former splendor—and the Sullurh would have their rightful share in it.

In fact, Lektor had informed him, the Ariantu had already come a long way toward rebuilding their culture. But their people longed for Kirlos, the soul and the emblem of what they had once been. The memory of it had gotten into their blood, had become a crucial and necessary factor in their empire's resurrection.

Thul had found himself nodding. Yes. Of course.

197

That was what the Sullurh expected, what they had worked for decade after decade and century after century.

However, Lektor had told him, the recovery of Kirlos would not be an easy task. It could not be accomplished by military might alone, for together, the Federation and the K'Vin were too strong. No, it would be necessary to employ subterfuge—to divide and conquer.

And that was the reason the four Ariantu had come. To sow the seeds of dissent and distrust. To pry the Federation loose from its holdings here, so that only the K'Vin would be left to face their ancient enemy— an enemy once again as strong as the Hegemony or stronger.

But to do this they would need the help of the Sullurh. The Ariantu had no way of influencing the Federation and K'Vin ambassadors; but Those Who Stayed, over the long years, had earned the ambassadors' confidence. Finally, all their hard work could find a purpose.

Thus, it was decided. The Ariantu—Lektor and the others—would devise the plots of sabotage and assassination. Thul, as leader of the Sullurh subcommunity, would work with Gezor and Zamorh to bring about chaos and conflict between the embassies.

Toward what end? To pave the way for the arrival of the Ariantu fleet, which would soon return to reclaim the gem in its crown of worlds. Nor, once it set out, would there be any contact or coordination with the fleet—not with both embassies routinely monitoring planetary communications. It would be blindly dependent on the Sullurh's success.

But their plans had gone awry. The ambassadors had stubbornly resisted all efforts to pit them against each other; Stephaleh had been too slow in calling for an evacuation of her sector.

And so, when the Ariantu fleet arrived, it encountered a Kirlos that it could not easily bend to its will. The Sullurh had failed in their efforts—efforts they had begun a long time ago, before they ever had an inkling of what would come of them.

All for nothing. It was a bitter pill to swallow.

Then Thul had stumbled on the way out of their difficulties—the knowledge that would place Kirlos in Ariantu hands once more, despite the failure of their original plan.

And the irony was that the *Enterprise* officers had led him to it. He had allowed himself to be subdued along with them and imprisoned, so as not to give away his alliance with Lektor's group.

At the time the Sullurh had already known that their plan was doomed—that the fleet would arrive before their efforts came to fruition. But it still seemed to Thul that by keeping their alliance a secret, the Sullurh could still be of use.

How right they had been, Thul remarked now to himself. How *very* right.

For if he had not been imprisoned, he would not have accompanied Data and Geordi in their escape. And he would never have found the legendary omega level.

Lektor's residence was just ahead, on the other side of the street. He crossed over, headed for it—scarcely able to contain himself. This news would make up for everything. It would redeem the Sullurh and restore their right to share in the new empire.

The female was in front of him before he knew it. He had almost collided with her before he saw her and, seeing her, noticed that she was pregnant.

What's more, he realized, he knew her. He had performed the *enio'lo* on her daughter only a year or so ago.

"Master Thul," she said, reaching for his hand out of respect. It was plain that she was frightened, what with all that was happening.

"No time now," he said, speaking in short, staccato bursts. "Too busy to stop—sorry."

And with that, he sidestepped her and continued up the street. Perhaps, he told himself, if all goes well, that baby of hers need not undergo the *enio'lo* as her sister did. With any luck, it will keep its tail.

Strangely, that seemed a sad thought. The rite had been a badge of shame among the Sullurh, a denial of their heritage, at least to the outside world. But in a way, the Sullurh experience, including even the *enio'lo,* had become a heritage in itself.

The thought was lost to him as he descended the steps to Lektor's flat. He knocked on the door—four times, so that they would know who it was.

At first there was no answer. Finally a strip of light showed beneath the door. It opened.

Not Lektor, but Eronn. The Ariantu looked down at him. After a moment, he indicated with a gesture that Thul should enter.

A little cold, the Sullurh mused. But that will all change when I tell them what I found.

They made their way down a short corridor, turned left into a small room. Lektor was sitting inside, along with Naalat. Pirrus was apparently out somewhere.

"Thul," said Lektor, rising. Only here, in the privacy of his residence, could he let his visage go uncowled. His eyes, dark red—almost maroon— presided over a short snout filled with a predator's pointed teeth.

How different from the average Sullurh, in whom

each of those characteristics was only a faint echo. And yet they were brothers, descended from the same ancestors, spurred by the same instincts. Weren't they?

"We escaped," said Thul, underscoring the obvious. "Or rather, the *Enterprise* officers did, and I came along."

Lektor nodded, his eyes narrowing. "I see. They have returned to the embassy, then? With their knowledge, now certain, that Gezor is our tool?"

He made it sound as if Thul should have prevented it somehow. Or was that the Sullurh's imagination?

"Two of them have gone back to the embassy," he answered. "The third, the Klingon, is still in Gregach's grasp."

Lektor exchanged glances with the other Ariantu. No words, just glances; Thul wished he could communicate that way, as his ancestors must have.

"But there is other news," he blurted. "Good—no, *great* news."

That got their attention. Thul took a deep breath before beginning.

"To make good our escape," he explained, "we had to delve deep into the gamma level—so deep, in fact, that we found a level below it."

"Below it," repeated Lektor.

"Yes," said Thul.

The Ariantu did not respond as he had expected. They looked at him, at one another—but there was no excitement evident in their expressions. No more than in Data's face, or Geordi's, when they had noticed the conduit.

Then it came to him. Perhaps the spacegoers had not nurtured the same legends as the Sullurh. Perhaps, removed by time and distance, they had forgotten some of them.

"Have you never heard of the omega level?" he asked. "Of the secret that lies within it?"

"We have heard," said Lektor—a bit dryly, it seemed to Thul. "Just as we have heard of the stars that steal unruly younglings, and the never-ending feast enjoyed by warriors in the afterlife. Legends, all of them, with no basis in fact."

Thul shook his head. "No. You have been away too long—you cannot know. The omega level is not just a legend—it *exists*. And it holds a way for us to achieve victory—even now!"

But the Ariantu were unmoved; they put no credence in what he said. Worse, they were looking at him as if he were deranged.

"I saw the place with my own eyes," insisted the Sullurh. "I saw weapons—powerful blasters. What more proof do you need than that?"

Lektor shrugged. "So there's a lower level, and it contains some weapons. That doesn't mean it contains *the* weapon—the one the legends prate on about."

Thul was stunned. How could they refuse to even investigate? He put the thought into words.

"It is simple," Lektor answered. "With the ship here, matters will proceed quickly now. We must make ourselves continually accessible to those above, which will leave us no time at all to pursue a Sullurh's fantasies."

A Sullurh's fantasies. The phrase emphasized the distinction between the spacegoers and their Kirlosbound cousins. Not *mere* fantasies, or *empty* fantasies, but those of a Sullurh—as if Thul's beliefs were somehow worth less than those of Lektor and his kind.

And this time, he assured himself, it was not his

202

imagination. The slight, if unintended, was nonetheless real.

By the same token, however, Thul found himself reassessing his faith in the omega level. He couldn't help it. The Ariantu were so knowledgeable, so experienced . . . by the gods, they traveled the stars! And he, like all Sullurh, had been tied to Kirlosia all his life.

Could it be that they were right? That the omega level had never existed—except in the lore of Those Who Stayed? That what he had found was only some backup life-support facility, or something even more mundane?

But the weapons . . .

No. As Lektor had been quick to point out, that was not proof either. Any ancient Ariantu facility would have had weapons handy; after all, they were a warlike people.

It was hard to accept it all, especially after his excitement at discovering the place. But in the cold light of reason, Thul had to admit that Lektor's view might be the correct one.

Still . . .

It was then that Pirrus returned. He hardly acknowledged Thul's presence, so eager was he to report to the other Ariantu.

"There is chaos everywhere," said Pirrus, his exertion barely evident in his voice. The Ariantu, Thul had learned, hardly ever got winded. "The populations on both sides are pressing their embassies to surrender—after all, they haven't a prayer of standing against our ship. But the ambassadors have sequestered themselves."

"And what of the ship itself? Has there been any word from our brethren?"

203

Pirrus shrugged, his bushy mane creeping up around his ears. "None. Apparently they are still adjusting to the situation."

Lektor snarled deep in his throat. It was a sound that Thul had never heard him make before, and for that reason—though not that reason alone—it was startling.

"Then we wait," he said. "They will send us word when they need us." He looked at Thul. "You, too, must wait until those in the ship decide what to do." His eyes hardened. "But you cannot wait here. Go back to your house; we will send for you."

Thul almost asked *why* he could not wait there. However, he told himself, Lektor had enough on his mind without having to explain to *him* what his motivation might be in every little thing. So he let it pass.

"Very well," said the Sullurh. "I will be there when you need me."

Lektor nodded, once. Then he turned away and muttered something to Naalat, and Naalat answered, and they were engrossed in the making of some plan that concerned only them.

Thul left, emerging into the Kirlosian night with a feeling of unreality in his stomach. He felt . . . unnerved. And not just by the fact that his hopes regarding the omega level had been dashed. The greater shock was the ease with which Lektor had dismissed them.

More and more, he was forced to see that the differences between the Ariantu and the Sullurh were often greater than their similarities.

And it disturbed him that this should be so.

Chapter Seventeen

A SHIP APPEARED in space where moments before there had been nothing but vacuum.

The corona of a nearby white dwarf flared. Fiery tendrils lifted up from the star's surface and twisted wildly, thrown into disarray by the disruption in the fabric of space.

Darting closer to the star, the scout released a signal and waited.

A tightly packed cluster of ships burst into space, then dispersed in a radiating star pattern. The largest vessel lay at the center of the fleet; it was surrounded and protected by eight fighters that formed a shield around the heart. But one of these ships assumed its outlying position too quickly and without thought; it crossed through a feathery plume of the white dwarf and was consumed by fire.

Arikka curled a lip to show her displeasure at the report of the loss, but the scoutmaster only flicked his ears. At least his eyes were respectfully cast aside. Baruk might not be cowed, but he was not so brave as to meet her gaze, even on a viewscreen.

"These navigational charts are ancient," he said. "Stars have drifted from their designated positions."

"What good is a nose if it can't sniff danger?" Her tail arched in contempt, fur bristling outward, but unfortunately Baruk could not see it.

"Rorrul was too eager. She didn't wait for my warning signal before moving her ship."

"Then you didn't signal fast enough," replied Arikka. "It's your job to warn the paac of trouble in time for us to change our path."

Baruk lifted his chin to bare his neck. In accepting her reprimand, he brought discussion to an end, so she moved on to a practical redress of the situation. "Since your senses are so dull, you'll serve better as the tail."

Arikka felt some satisfaction in seeing her grandson shudder with humiliation at the reassignment, but the demotion would not bring back the burned ship or its dead crew. Rorrul's kin had been eager hunters, well suited for the flank position that served as an extension to the main paac. After some thought, Arikka promoted Howul from the belly to the scout position and shifted the remaining ships to cover his vacancy. No one would replace Rorrul, just as no one would replace the ship that had been destroyed days earlier.

Her own heartmaster, Teroon, transmitted the orders without argument, but when the communications with the other shipmasters had ended, he turned to her and said, "That was harsh punishment, Mother. We're new at this; errors are to be expected."

The control cabin was small and cramped for space, but the astrogator and the pilot were too absorbed in their work to eavesdrop. She revealed her misgivings. "Baruk didn't make a mistake. He made a fast kill."

"I thought we left our feuds behind on Ariant."

"So did I," said Arikka, ruing the loss of the ships almost as much as the kin they carried. "Yet my family, not my enemy, shrinks before my eyes."

All the worldly possessions of her paac had been sold or bartered for the fleet of twelve fighting ships. Her family could not afford even the most decrepit cargo freighter, but these ancient remnants of the Ariantu empire-builders were too small to be of commercial use and were sold as scrap. Under her direction, that scrap had been restored to its original purpose.

"Ah, well," she sighed. "At least this treachery shows spirit."

Her hand moved to the talisman that dangled on a chain around her neck. The chip of unpolished stone was rough-edged and raw, like her paac. She had not birthed any effete artists who could carve and polish arizite into a form fit for the marbled halls of the High Paacs of Ariant. Nevertheless, those noble families were still on the home planet grubbing in their fields while she soared beyond the stars. Arikka and her kin were the true spiritual descendants of the ancient Ariantu empire-builders; she would fashion her descendants into a new noble paac. And they would prove their prowess by sinking their teeth deep into K'Vin flesh.

K'Vin. The very utterance of that name was like a choking bark of combat. The K'Vin had dared to take up residence on what by rights was Ariantu territory —but Arikka would avenge that festering insult.

No High Paac noble would dare condescend to her ever again. Instead, they would crawl in her presence, with tails dragging in the dirt.

"Signal the paac. We jump to Kirlos next."

Teroon grunted with surprise. "So soon, Mother?"

"Yes, before my children destroy themselves with their petty bickering."

Arikka would have preferred to put them through additional maneuvers, additional drills. Aside from providing her with a High Paac pendant of arizite, the attack on the quarry planet had been meant as a taste of real battle for those who had only listened to tales of ancient glory. Who could have guessed that the settlement lacked any weapons with which to defend itself? The single fleet casualty had occurred because two fighters crossed paths just as a weapons salvo was released. Another convenient accident. Despite the ease with which it had been carried out, the victory had left her feisty offspring feeling cocky. Much *too* cocky. They needed a tougher target to teach them some humility—and give them a few wounds to lick.

But when Teroon had pored over the star charts, searching the branching network of shunt coordinates for an exit near a planet with modest defense capabilities, there had been no suitable targets that could be reached in less than a week. And since each day's delay gave her children time to remember old planet-born rivalries, to turn on each other again, she was forced to move on to their ultimate destination sooner than she had planned.

Still, she told herself, *Lektor has had plenty of time to carry out our plan. Kirlos should be ours for the taking.*

The second Ariantu scout was more careful, or perhaps less vindictive, than its predecessor. Following scoutmaster Howul's lead, the paac ships of the Ariantu jumped into space at a safe distance from the

208

star known as Sydon. Maintaining the tight formation of their passage through the jump tunnel, Arikka directed her fleet toward the outermost planet from the sun.

On Kirlos, the long-range sensors that scanned the sector surrounding Sydon missed the sudden appearance of ten ships within the confines of the solar system. A stealthy approach to the planet's eternal-night side registered on a few short-range sensors, but these local detectors were supervised by Sullurh employees. And Sullurh hands reached out to silence the alarms before higher-ranking members of the K'Vin and Federation could hear the sound. Unchallenged, the Ariantu armada slipped below the orbiting defense systems of both sides.

Crossing out of the darkness into light, the fleet hovered to a stop over the land that covered Kirlosia. There was no one living on the harsh surface; thus no one looked up and saw the invaders. Except for the Sullurh, none of the inhabitants of the town even knew they had been conquered.

They would know soon enough, thought Arikka as she stroked the arizite pendant at her throat. She was the first of a new line of Ariantu rulers of Kirlos. How many paac mothers would wear her talisman before it had been rubbed smooth? How many generations of her blood kin would walk the tunnels of the subterranean world built by long-dead Ariantu?

Heartmaster Teroon signaled her with a silent wave of his tail. He had established direct contact with their operative on the planet, the one who had prepared the way for the arrival of her paac.

Arikka leaned close to the video monitor, recognizing Lektor. She bared her teeth and said, "We are ready to hunt!"

But her kinsman did not look glad to see her. She could tell by the curl of his lip, the slight quivering of his ears.

"But you've come too soon, Mother. Our preparations are incomplete."

She was surprised. "Then complete them *now*. How long can it take even your Sullurh fools to set the K'Vin rabble at the throats of Federation curs?"

Arikka saw Lektor's eyes widen at the rebuke. At least his blood instincts had not been lost during his stay among the degenerate Sullurh.

"We are *all* fools," he told her.

The fur on her tail and on her mane bristled, but she had sufficient self-control to keep her eyes hooded. Lektor's remark bordered on a blood insult; it was not like him to be so careless.

"A Federation warship is on its way back to Kirlos," the spy went on. "And the K'Vin embassy has requested a warship from the Hegemony. When the two ships cross paths, they will likely fight each other—but not if they hear of an attack on this planet. The threat of a third force could overshadow their hostilities; they might join forces against us."

"Let them! My children are eager for battle." Arikka was not about to show fear to *anyone*. Her kin were young and inexperienced, but the blood of Ariantu hunters ran through their veins. They would rend their enemies by instinct alone when the time came.

"Your fighters are no match for two starships," Lektor went on. "But there's no need for a confrontation. If you withdraw the fleet and hide behind the moon Demodron—"

"Enough! This world is mine now. I will not retreat."

Lektor had apparently gone as far as he dared.

210

Baring his throat, he acknowledged her right to decide. "As you say, Mother. What are your instructions?"

It had only been hours since Thul had left the Ariantu, but it seemed like days. He paced the rooms of his residence, a place no bigger or more comfortable than any of his people's residences, despite his standing in the community—for among the Sullurh, there were no class distinctions. The only difference between Thul's home and anyone else's was the ringing fact of his solitude.

Sullurh rejoiced in family life; it was considered a joy to pass on the mantle of stewardship to each new and eager generation. More than a joy—a sacred trust.

Thul's other duties, however, had always stood in the way of marriage and progeny. He had been busy with the affairs of the community, *enio'lo* ceremonies being the least of his burden. The Sullurh had their own laws for settling disputes among themselves, and as their chosen leader, Thul was expected to interpret those laws, to plumb them for a justice that would satisfy all parties concerned.

At the same time, he had responsibilities outside the community. His labors on behalf of Nassa Coleridge, which had enabled him to obtain data regarding the Federation outside Kirlos—data he could never have obtained any other way.

Of course, it had been anything but unpleasant working for the human. At times he had even enjoyed it, and her company as well, to the point that his grief at her passing had been genuine and unadulterated with guile.

Yet he had never lost sight of his reasons for doing what he did. Never had he forgotten that he truly

211

worked for *his people,* that his efforts were an invest-
ment in the day the Ariantu would return.

Then why did he now feel alienated from that
purpose, as if it had been taken away from him? Or,
worse, had never really been his to begin with?

It made him feel lonely where he had never felt
lonely before. It drove home his lack of family with
unmerciful force.

And strangeness of strangenesses, the face that kept
trying to fill the void was that of Coleridge. Or was it
so strange at that?

Other Sullurh had their kin to look to for companionship. Whom did Thul have to look to day after day,
other than the human archaeologist?

What's more, she had been good to him. So many of
the aliens treated the Sullurh like inferiors or ignored
them, as if they somehow didn't exist—which was,
after all, the condition they had worked to achieve.
But Coleridge was different in that regard. She had
respected Thul, even liked him, or appeared to.

And *he* had liked *her.* Why not admit it? If he had
been forewarned about the museum sabotage, if he'd
had any idea where and when the next incident was to
take place, he would have made certain that Coleridge
wasn't endangered by it. He would have found a way
to save her.

Unfortunately, Lektor had not wanted anyone but
his group of four to have that foreknowledge. Nor had
Coleridge's presence at the museum made any difference to him; to the Ariantu, she was just another
trespasser on Kirlos. Another alien to tread underfoot
in their recovery of their ancient outpost planet.

Thul found himself resenting the Ariantu. If he had
had any immediate family at all on this world, it had
been Coleridge. And it was Lektor's bunch that had

212

destroyed her. It sounded bizarre when he thought of it that way, but it was true, wasn't it?

No, he told himself. *It is insane. Coleridge was an alien, and the Ariantu are your people.* Kinship was not a matter of casual choice; it was buried in the blood, deep and undeniable.

Granted, he felt no real bond with the Ariantu—a disappointment indeed. But it did not mitigate the fact of their common ancestry. Nor did it excuse his resentment toward Lektor and the others.

The Ariantu had done their job, no more, no less. They had held up their end of the bargain; it was up to Thul to do the same.

Suddenly he could no longer tolerate the confines of his residence. He could no longer wait patiently while Lektor bore the entire burden of what happened on Kirlos.

If there was planning to be done, he would help. If work was required, he would do that, too.

Then, if something went wrong, he would have no one to blame but himself.

This time, he didn't have to knock on the door. Just as he was about to, it opened, startling him.

Lektor, apparently, was just as surprised. He'd drawn his hand back to strike before he realized it was only Thul.

Lowering his arm, he ascended the steps to the street level. Pirrus was right behind him, then Eronn and Naalat. None of them gave the Sullurh a second glance.

"Where are you going?" asked Thul, trying not to sound as if he was begging for the information. "Has something happened?"

Naalat looked at him then, breaking stride for just a

moment, and snarled. "Something *indeed.* We are leaving. We have been called back."

The words were slow to sink in. And before Thul could absorb them in their entirety, the Ariantu had come to stand in the middle of the street. One of them, Pirrus, looked up at the dark, domed sky.

"I don't understand," said Thul, following them. *"Why* are you leaving?"

When Lektor regarded him, it was with narrowed eyes, baleful and bloodred in the darkness beneath his hood.

"Because it has become dangerous here. There will likely be violence—destruction. And since there is nothing else we can do, there is no reason to risk us." The corners of his mouth pulled back to reveal sharp white fangs. "Do you understand now, Sullurh?"

Thul understood—but wished he didn't. "What about *us?* What of Those Who Stayed? Surely we will be beamed up as well."

Naalat laughed; it was an ugly sound. "Only Ariantu may board an Ariantu vessel." His eyes were crimson, ablaze with an unholy light. "And you are not Ariantu. Can it be said any more plainly than that?"

Lektor glanced at him as if to silence his arrogance. But Naalat would not be silenced. "Why shouldn't he know?" he asked. "What difference can it make now?"

Thul addressed Lektor, his voice faltering in his throat. "What does he mean?" he asked.

The Ariantu made a ripping sound in his chest, but something about him seemed to yield. To soften.

"What he means," explained Lektor, "is that we used you. The Sullurh were never partners in this. You were tools."

214

"Tools?" repeated Thul. Now there was a heat growing in him—in his belly, in his face. "But we are Those Who Stayed! We are the ones who sacrificed!" He sputtered. "No one is more Ariantu than we are!"

Lektor snorted. "Really? Look at yourself." He pulled back his cowl. "Then look at *us*. And tell me that *you* are Ariantu."

Thul shook his head. "You never had any intention, then, of making us participants in your conquest? Of welcoming us into your empire as brothers, as equals?"

Lektor eyed him. Was there shame in his eyes as he answered? "None," he said. "And if you were truly Ariantu, you would have known that from the beginning."

Then the figure of Lektor began to sparkle from within, to generate a swarm of frantic ruby-colored particles. And the same thing was happening to the others.

They were departing, leaving the Sullurh to face the threat of the Ariantu ship, alongside the aliens—the trespassers. For in the eyes of the Ariantu, the Sullurh were an alien race as well.

And aliens, Thul knew, were seen only as an inconvenience, just as Coleridge had been an inconvenience back there in the museum.

He could no longer contain the heat that was building inside him. He lashed out in Lektor's direction, grabbing for his robes, hoping—he didn't know what. To make him stay? To make him take the Sullurh with him?

But it was too late. The Ariantu had become immaterial—a ghost, sparkling like the embers of a spent hearth fire. And in the next moment, Lektor was gone altogether. They *all* were gone.

215

Thul dropped to his knees right there in the street. He felt rage, fear, a sense of having been violated—all at once, all commingled.

He thought of the other Sullurh. What would he tell them? That their brethren from the stars had betrayed them? That Thul's trust in the Ariantu had brought down this shame upon them?

Could he face that prospect? He didn't think so. His standing in the community was all he had. Without that, he was nothing.

He had to strike back at the ones who had humiliated them. He had to regain for the Sullurh a measure of their self-respect.

But how?

Abruptly the answer came to him, as if delivered by the ancient gods of his people. And as he got up off his knees, he knew exactly what he had to do.

Chapter Eighteen

STEPHALEH REGARDED THE ANDROID. She had grown to like the inquisitive and talkative machine. Sometimes, in the hectic rush of events, she even forgot that he was a construction.

But she had been unprepared for his request. After all, if a seasoned diplomat like her, with all her proven instincts and tactics, couldn't persuade the Ariantu to lay down their arms, what chance did an artificial being have?

Then again, she told herself, *he can hardly fail more miserably than I have.*

"All right," she said finally. "You have my permission, Commander Data."

The android nodded once. "Thank you, Ambassador." Seating himself at her desk, he reengaged the communications channel with two deft taps on her keypad.

La Forge stood off to one side watching silently but intently. He almost looked as if he was holding himself back, Stephaleh noted. As if he'd have liked to offer some advice, but was restraining himself. She thought about that. Why would he hold back? Out of respect for Data's rank? Or because of something more personal—a decision to let the artificial man stand on his own, perhaps?

"Ariantu," said the android. "This is Commander Data. Please respond."

Suddenly the screen filled with an image of the bridge of the Ariantu heartship—an image dominated by a single figure, though others stood or worked in the background.

"This is Arikka, paac mother," said the main figure. She looked very much like the statuette that Coleridge had beamed up to Captain Picard—the one that Stephaleh had admired so much, but officially ignored. Arikka was long and graceful, with a wolflike snout and fierce eyes. Her attire was severe and ostentatious at the same time—the garb of a warrior, recognizable in any culture.

"It is about time that you presented me with a military authority," said the Ariantu, "not some spineless civilian with no power to back up her words."

Stephaleh flinched a little at the insult, but took it in her stride. Right now she had other things on her mind.

They obviously respected Data because of his title and his uniform, she noted. How interesting.

"Paac Mother," said the android, his brow wrinkling ever so slightly, "I am not a mili—"

It was Geordi who stopped him, both hands raised. Silently, he mouthed the words: *Play along, Data. You are military—for now.*

Data immediately chose another entry into the dialogue.

"Paac Mother, it is our hope that we can resolve this conflict without bloodshed."

Arikka's eyes narrowed. "You speak strangely," she said, "for a warrior."

"Nonetheless, that *is* our desire."

She looked at him. "Fine, Commander. You wish to avoid bloodshed? Then leave this world. *Now.*"

Data seemed unimpressed by the threat. "First of all," he said calmly, "that is not possible. There are not enough transport vessels in the vicinity to evacuate all of Kirlosia. Second, we are not *inclined* to leave. At least not until your claim to this world has been verified." A pause. "And the best way for you to do this is in face-to-face talks, which I am sure could be held right here in the embassy."

Stephaleh was impressed. She could hardly have put it better herself.

On the monitor, the Ariantu seemed to be mulling over Data's words. Was she actually considering beaming down? Had the android succeeded?

"You are not military," concluded Arikka.

Stephaleh's heart sank—along with Geordi's, if his expression was any indication.

"You make the same inane noises as that other one," added the paac mother. "The one you call 'ambassador.'" She turned her head and spat. "There is nothing more to talk about. You will leave the planet now—or you will die. It is all the same to us."

"You permit no room for compromise," observed Data. "Certainly if there is a chance to avoid needless suffering—"

The screen went dark.

"Well," Geordi said, "at least they're an open-minded bunch."

Data turned to the ambassador. "I did not accomplish very much," he said apologetically.

219

"That's all right," the Andorian assured him. "You came closer than I did. You have nothing to be ashamed of."

But all the same, he *had* failed. Data's attempt at negotiation had had a promising beginning, but it had ended the same as hers: in defeat.

Stephaleh glanced out her window. The panic in the streets was getting worse, and there was nothing she could do about it.

A beeping in the room. La Forge tapped his communicator. "Geordi here."

"Any success with the Ariantu?" It was Worf's voice; the ambassador could not help but recognize it.

"Not much. They're a very . . . single-minded people. But I guess we'll keep trying until a better option comes along." He frowned. "Or until they make good on their threat—whichever comes first."

At the K'Vin embassy, Worf was looking out a window, too. Given his proximity to street level, the chaos outside seemed even closer, more threatening. He growled low in his throat.

"What about the populace?" he asked Geordi.

"What *about* them? They're scared to death. They're smashing everything they can get their hands on—even each other, I'm afraid."

"They must be kept in check," said the Klingon.

"Sure. Got any suggestions?"

Worf considered the problem for a moment. "We could always shoot them—stun them unconscious—and stop the rampage."

There was silence on the other end. "Worf," said Geordi finally, "I don't think Starfleet Command would approve of us phaser-stunning the whole Federation side of Kirlosia. Have you got any other ideas?"

The Klingon grudgingly reconsidered. "Yes. Have Powell and his men execute Disaster Plan Beta. Tell him it is in the manual."

"Gotcha. Thanks, Worf. We'll keep you posted."

And then Worf was alone again, with only his frustrations for company.

The gap that they had created in the outer wall of the K'Vin embassy was still there. With the arrival of the Ariantu ships, its repair had no doubt become a low priority for Gregach.

What was more, there were no guards around. Or at least, none that Thul could see. Had they all been dispatched to the Strip?

The Sullurh slipped through the opening, negotiating a path through the debris. Still, no one challenged him. Before long, he found the cell in which he and the *Enterprise* officers had been incarcerated.

Here, too, things had been left as they were. The well that the android had fashioned in the center of the floor still gaped wide, though with all the dust in the air, it was difficult to see to the bottom.

Ironic, wasn't it? The K'Vin were sitting directly on top of the very thing that might drive off the Ariantu fleet. And yet, preoccupied by the return of their ancient enemies, they had not yet investigated the prisoners' escape—or they would have discovered the gleaming doors of the turbolift and plumbed its mystery.

If they had gone that route, they would have posted a guard here. Perhaps many guards.

And Thul would have been prevented from doing what he was doing now—lowering himself into the space beneath the cell and dropping to the floor. It was no easy task, considering his lack of familiarity with

221

physical exertion; in fact, he almost turned an ankle in the process. As it was, dust puffed up in great clouds around him, filling his lungs and making him cough.

He took a moment to steady himself, catch his breath, come to terms with the reality of the turbolift and the significance it held for him. Then he approached, watched the doors slide aside, and entered.

Knowing what to expect, he had thought, would make the journey less terrifying for him. He was wrong. When the lift completed its horizontal passage and began to plummet, his knees turned to jelly and he sat down on the floor. After a second or two, he slid into a corner and wedged himself there, glad that the Starfleet officers were not here to disapprove of his squeamishness.

Thul tried to ignore the rasping of air outside the car, the dizzying speed of his descent. He distracted himself by reading the glyphs on the walls, which were similar to the written language of the Sullurh.

Would Lektor and his comrades have been able to read these glyphs with such ease, as divorced as they were from their own history? He wondered.

Suddenly he was seized by an irresistible sense of impending doom, and he was certain that the lift was going to crash. That the braking mechanism had failed, and that he would be mangled with the rest of the lift when it collided with the bottom of the shaft.

Instead, the cubicle came to a gentle halt. The doors opened, revealing the weapons level to him a second time.

Thul gazed at the banks of sleek, shiny consoles, the impossibly large curved screens, the sheer size and power and grandeur of it all.

How could he ever have doubted that this was the omega level? How could he have let Lektor or anyone else shake his faith in the promise of this vision?

If they had only agreed to come here, to see it for themselves . . . but no. It was too late for that. Much too late.

He walked out into the middle of the floor, intimidated by the potential of the place—the potential that he somehow had to unlock. The glyphs all around him offered a variety of data and directions, but none of it was immediately useful. The words were familiar enough; it was their usage that was a little puzzling.

He had some familiarity with computers—much more than the average Sullurh, anyway, thanks to his association with Coleridge. With any luck, these machines would follow the same logic as those used by the Federation.

But where to begin? He found himself drawn to the largest of the consoles and followed his instincts.

Then he got close enough to see the boldface glyphs on the machine. His blood started pounding in his ears as their meaning slowly sank in.

This was the *ultimate* weapon—the one the legends had named "the Howling God." The stories had been truer than he'd dared to believe!

With a sense of reverence, he stood before it, savored the sight of it. As if it were a shrine.

For it *was*, in a way. A shrine to the might and the destructive capacity of his ancestors.

There was a seat before the control panel—perhaps a bit too high for him. Nonetheless, he clambered up and scanned the monitor. All it showed was an empty grid.

He read a glyph that was marked "begin." Placing his hand on the round, silvery surface below it, he found that it was warm to the touch—almost as if the machine were a living thing.

He waited—but not for long. The image on the screen didn't change, but other screens lit up around it, one by one. Each had the same sort of grid as the large screen, but superimposed on each grid was an array of blips: one big white blip in the center and a variable number of smaller colored blips surrounding it. No two screens showed the same configuration.

What was all this? And then he knew.

The Ariantu had been a spacefaring race. More than likely, these were sectors in space—no, solar systems! The large central blips would be suns; the smaller blips would be planets.

It opened up a whole new line of possibilities. Thul shivered with the immensity of it.

He had come here with but one thing in mind—to gain revenge on Lektor's people. To even the score for the humiliation they had inflicted on Thul and his kind.

Surely, he'd believed, the omega level would give him the means to blast the Ariantu out of orbit. To serve notice that Kirlos wasn't theirs, could never be theirs. That it belonged to the Sullurh—the only *true* Ariantu—and to no one else.

But now a grander scheme was taking shape in his mind. For if these *were* solar systems he saw before him, they had to include one particular system—the nearest, in fact, to the one occupied by Kirlos.

The home system of the K'Vin Hegemony.

Thul located the glyph that instructed him to "select." He pressed the round surface below it. Like the other one, this panel was warm to the touch.

Almost instantly the large grid displayed features similar to those of the one to the left and above it. Thul knew nothing of astrogation, but it was plain that this was not the K'Vin system. The glyphs on the bottom of the screen identified it as the home of a race called the Eluud.

He touched the "select" panel again, and the large

monitor borrowed a different image. This one was wrong also, however: it was the system that had given birth to the Pandrilites, a member people of the Federation.

A third time he laid his palm on the panel, and a third time the image shifted. Thul inspected the data below, poised to make yet another selection.

It turned out to be unnecessary. *He had found the K'Vin!* Found them where they lived, in the heart of their distant Hegemony!

The Sullurh's heart was beating so hard that he thought it would damage his rib cage. He felt his mouth going dry as he stared at the monitor.

The K'Vin home system. And *he* had the power to destroy it!

Questions sprang to mind—some fully formed, some less so. For instance, if this weapon was capable of destroying the hated K'Vin, why had it not been used before? And was it really possible to blast something so far away?

It didn't take Thul long to give up on finding the answers. He had no knowledge of such things—or pitifully little.

And what difference did it make how the machine worked? All that *really* mattered was *if* it worked.

Licking his lips, the Sullurh scanned the console for a panel corresponding to the next step in the process. He found one marked "empower" and pushed it.

The effect was dramatic. Suddenly every machine in the place seemed to come to life, as if they were all enslaved to *this* one and had only been waiting for its instructions in order to serve it.

Each monitor was illuminated, a series of high-contrast images flitting across it in rapid-fire succession. There was a low whirr, the sound of dormant mechanisms reviving themselves.

So far, so good. Thul searched for the next likely command in the sequence—and found it: "activate." He hesitated, but only long enough to remember the way the Ariantu had used him—used his *people*. There would be time enough to deal with them *after* they saw how wrong they had been about the Sullurh.

He pressed the panel.

But what followed was not what he had expected. The entire omega level began to vibrate—not just the sleek black machines, but the entire place.

It's all right, he told himself. *The machines are old. The vibrations will diminish.*

They didn't. In fact, over the next few seconds the tremors grew worse.

Thul's chair was shuddering—*shuddering!* He had to get down off it for fear he would be thrown off.

But it was no better standing on the floor. He could feel the vibrations in his bones, to the point where they almost hurt. And more—he could hear a grumbling below the soles of his feet. The very bedrock of the planet seemed to be shifting about, as if the whole world was coming apart.

And Thul knew—with a certainty that exceeded the bare facts, that came from the pit of his stomach rather than from his brain—that he had done something horribly, *horribly* wrong.

Chapter Nineteen

GREGACH TUMBLED FORWARD, and only Worf's strong arms prevented him from hitting the floor.

The two of them staggered to a window and looked out over Kirlosia. There was a steady vibration, as if the entire planet was surging with some sort of barely controlled energy. Buildings were trembling, and from their vantage point, Gregach and Worf saw people falling over one another, trying to run to safety when there was no safety.

"What's happening?" whispered Gregach.

"What in the deity's name is going on?" demanded Stephaleh, in that intense and yet soft tone she had.

Her view of Kirlosia was no better than Gregach's. Her sensitive antennae were already throbbing with the intensity of the steadily building vibrations. Behind her, Geordi and Data were looking on in confusion.

"A power buildup of some sort," said Data.

"Power from where?" demanded Geordi.

Data began to pace quickly, his mind racing. "Power . . . power building up. A weapon from outside, possibly. The Ariantu, trying to destroy Kirlos. But why? It makes no sense. Why would they come all this way just to destroy the planet?"

"Maybe they would," said Geordi. "Who knows?"

"I do not believe it," Data said. "For the sake of argument, let us eliminate it. That would mean the buildup is coming from within the planet rather than without."

"But that makes even less sense," said Geordi. "Where would the power be building from, and—"

His voice trailed off, and he realized what was happening a second after Data did.

"That level we discovered earlier," said Data. "If any place has the weaponry to accomplish it, it would be there."

"A weapon to destroy the planet? But why? Some sort of suicidal maneuver?"

"I do not know," said Data, his calm voice never speeding up, despite the urgency. "I doubt mere suicide is involved, however. The Ariantu, from all we have learned, are a very aggressive and warlike race. If they were to destroy Kirlos, they would not do so without a reason. And whatever that reason is, it must lie in that level. We must hurry."

"Back down there?"

"Back down there." Data tapped his communicator. "Data to Worf."

"Worf here," came the brisk reply.

The situation was slipping away, and Data felt that he had to take control, had to be the leader, the commander. Data said, "Worf, we are returning to the K'Vin embassy."

"That may not be wise."

228

"But it is necessary. Prepare to meet us in the lowest level, by cell D. Data out."

He cut off the communication before Worf could question it.

"What are you going to do?" said Stephaleh urgently.

Data looked her straight in the eye. "Save this world," he said.

It happened so quickly that none of the ships had a chance to react or even to fully understand what was occurring.

On the dark side of Kirlos, the perfectly round, flat area known as the Valley began to glow with a strange, lambent energy. The edges flickered to life, rippling and surging with power. The power emanations became more and more intense, and the ships of the Federation, the K'Vin, and Ariantu looked on with growing nervousness.

Suddenly the entire planet trembled, as if vomiting up something massive, and a huge cone of energy leaped from the edges of the Valley, coming to a point in space miles above Kirlos's surface.

The cone was a dazzling swirl of colors, emitting energy readings that blew all the scales of every ship in the sector. The commanders of the *Enterprise* and the K'Vin vessel decided they were much, *much* too close to the point of the cone and started to move off.

And at that moment, space began to warp around the tip of the cone, as if it were drilling a hole right into the fabric of reality.

The warp was invisible to the eye, but all the instruments immediately picked it up, and lined schematics leaped into existence on all the boards. A massive graphic whirlpool image was widening faster and faster, narrowing into a huge sinkhole. Small at first, only several hundred miles wide, but becoming larger with every passing second.

The defense shields of the K'Vin warship glowed a dull red. Within the shimmering fog were the blurred outlines of a bullet-shaped vessel studded with rounded metallic cylinders. One of those cylinders loosed a glowing ball of fire.

"Hard aport!"

Picard's shout rose above the high whine of the ship's engines. He braced for the pressing g-force that should have followed his order. And felt nothing.

"Helm, respond!"

The deck lifted even as he spoke, pushing him down into the captain's chair. The *Enterprise* had veered up and to one side, but slowly, much more slowly, than he expected. Picard knew with a numbing certainty that the accelerating torpedo blast would hit its target. A simple evasive maneuver, one that should have carried the *Enterprise* out of harm's way, had failed. In the few seconds before impact he jumped ahead to his next action, devising a response to the devastating blow that could not be avoided.

The photon pulse filled the viewscreen.

"Conn, all power to . . ."

He never finished the command.

Because the energy bolt never made contact.

Against all expectation, against all sense, it missed the *Enterprise.* The torpedo curved away, still gathering speed, and faded into . . .

Nothing.

"Where did it go?" demanded Riker. Then, half rising from his chair, he pointed toward the viewscreen.

The K'Vin warship was spiraling and twisting in

space. And receding. Its image was growing smaller as the distance between the two ships widened.

"What the hell?" Picard stared at the image. He tried to understand why his ship was still intact, his opponent immobilized. He should have been relieved, but the anomaly was more frightening than reassuring.

"We're being pulled off course," cried Ensign Nagel from the Ops station. Her fingers rapped a frantic pattern across her panel. "Turbulence ahead."

"Maintain heading!" ordered Picard.

Bridge lights flickered. A voice from the aft deck called out, "Engines are drawing on auxiliary power."

"Why?" demanded Picard. "What's going on?"

"Captain!" Lieutenant Dean looked up from his sensor scan; his face was drained of color. "Sir . . . there's a wormhole out there."

"Merde." Dean's answer made the captain yearn for the simple threat of a photon torpedo. A wormhole was far more treacherous.

"Drop shields!" he ordered briskly. "Priority one emergency energy restrictions. Redirect all nonessential power to engineering."

Bridge lights dimmed. Console systems dropped their chatter to a whisper.

"Holding position," Nagel said as she labored over her controls. "Barely."

Picard rose from his chair and stepped to the science officer's side. "Lieutenant?"

Dean shook his head, answering the unspoken question in a low voice that only the captain could hear. "We're far too close. There isn't enough energy in this ship, in ten starships, to break free of the wormhole's pull. The vortex diameter is thousands of miles wide and growing very quickly, unleashing incredible power. Very soon . . ." His voice faltered

231

for an instant; then he continued, "Very soon it will be capable of pulling Kirlos out of its orbit around Sydon."

Picard tried to make sense of the catastrophe, but his mind balked at the immensity of the forces at work. He barely registered the approach of his first officer.

"The K'Vin are stubborn fools," said Riker. "They're still maintaining their defenses instead of redirecting energy to their engines."

A soft black cloud had enveloped half the warship's length. Then the glow of the shielding snapped off. The ship shot forward, but not far enough to escape the hungry void, which still nibbled away at the edges of the ship's image.

"Too little too late." Yet Picard knew that only a matter of minutes separated his ship and crew from that same fate. Considering the circumstances, he had no obligation, but . . . "Helm! Attach a tractor beam to the K'Vin ship."

"There really isn't much point, is there, sir?" asked Riker under his breath. "We're only postponing the inevitable . . . for all of us."

"If we are to die," answered Picard just as softly, "we shall do it as civilized beings."

He and Riker watched in silence as the tractor beam locked on to the K'Vin ship and dragged it out of the cloud of darkness. The warship hovered just on the lip of the vortex but did not slip back inside.

Instead, the *Enterprise* was pulled closer.

"Where's the damned turbolift you told me about?" shouted Worf, not particularly thrilled that the vibration of the ground beneath him was increasing.

Worf, Geordi, and Data were beneath the floor of the prison cell. Far above them, from the streets high overhead, the sounds of widespread panic could be heard. But there was no course except that which they were pursuing.

Data was standing in puzzlement in front of the lift doors, which refused to open. "I do not know," he said.

"Stand aside," said Worf, pulling out his phaser, ready to blast the doors apart. But Data was blocking the way and was now shoving his fingers into the narrow crack between the doors. Applying his strength, he shoved the doors apart . . .

And almost stepped into nothingness.

A deep shaft yawned before him. There was no turbolift car to be seen.

"We have a problem," said Geordi.

"Getting down to the weapons area quickly seems to be our only hope for preventing disaster on this planet," said Data. "And I can see only one way down."

He looked at Geordi and the engineer realized what he was thinking. "Oh, no, Data, please," he said. "Not that."

"I saw several abandoned just outside the building."

"Not that. Please."

"Several what?" asked Worf.

Five minutes later Geordi was once again clutching a speeder sled for dear life.

Data was flying with machinelike precision, and Worf was right behind them on a second sled. The sides of the shaft rushed by them at dizzying speed.

They got to the drop-off curve and angled straight down. The g-force pushed Geordi back in his seat. If he could have forced himself to release his grip for a moment, he would have yanked off his VISOR.

He bit his lip and thought, *This one's for you, Nassa.*

The high-speed descent continued, and then Geordi's VISOR screamed a warning at him. "The bottom!" he shouted as loud as he could, praying that the rushing air wouldn't rip his words away. "It's just ahead of us!"

He needn't have worried. Data's hearing was sharp, and the words carried back to Worf. In perfect synchronization, both of them slowed the forward thrust of the speed sleds and leveled them off. They alighted gently on a gleaming metallic surface that Geordi immediately realized must be the top of the turbolift.

There was an emergency hatch directly beneath Data's feet. Gripping it firmly, the android yanked it upward. It came free with a screech of metal, and one by one, they dropped through the hatch and into the turbolift car.

The doors were open; they ran into the weapons room. Then they stopped, not believing what they were seeing.

All the screens were lit up. On one was a visual of the Valley with the undulating energy cone. On another was a graphic of a rapidly forming wormhole. On a third was a visual of the *Enterprise* and a ship that seemed to be of K'Vin design, the two of them struggling desperately in the grip of the wormhole. On yet another screen was a diagram of a star system that Geordi did not immediately recognize. Everywhere lights were flashing as instructions were processed and moved forward with determined speed. The vibrations were less violent in this room, but the officers still felt them increasing as fast as the massive spatial sinkhole that was threatening to swallow the *Enterprise*.

And in the center of it all was Thul, bent over a

console, shaking his head, apparently dazed. When he turned toward the *Enterprise* officers, his eyes seemed to have shrunk in their sockets.

"I wanted to destroy them," he muttered, his voice flat and eerie in the huge chamber. "I wanted to obliterate them, but instead I've destroyed myself, my people, everything! Everything, gone!"

"Daaata," said Geordi, extremely nervous. "What's happening here?"

Data's mind was racing frantically, taking it all in, looking once more at the glyphs, which had smatterings of other alien tongues mixed in. Looking at the visuals, the graphics, and information pouring from a dozen other screens tracking energy levels, celestial navigation, and gravity fields—

"Of course!" shouted Data. "It's elementary."

Worf came toward him, growling, and Geordi tried to hold him back. Data didn't even notice.

"This," he said with a sweep of his hand, "this whole planet—it has doomsday capability. Look," and he pointed at the starchart. Computer-generated lines were lancing across it. "This is the K'Vin star system. This planet is the K'Vin homeworld. And it is being targeted."

"Targeted for *what?*" said Geordi, and then he realized. "Oh, my God."

"Exactly," said Data. "This machinery is generating that wormhole."

"We'll be sucked in," said Geordi.

"Yes," said Data. "The other end of the wormhole is going to be generated *there.*" He pointed. "Right within range of the K'Vin homeworld. Rather startling technology, actually. When the wormhole is large enough, this entire planet will be sucked in and hurled through the funnel like a stone from a slingshot. Just

235

as this happens, a hole will be created at the other end and Kirlos will hurtle out and crash into the K'Vin homeworld. The effect will be almost instantaneous."

"We can't stand around admiring it!" said Geordi. "We have to stop it!"

"Of course," said Data. "And we'll have to do it quickly." Even as he continued to speak, his hands began to fly over the controls. "The *Enterprise* is clearly using its tractor beams to prevent the K'Vin ship from being sucked in, but they will not be able to save themselves much longer. If they are sucked in before the wormhole is ready, they will be crushed in the gravity well. And even if they manage to maintain their distance, they are still between Kirlos and the wormhole. So they will be shoved inward when we are drawn in, and crushed between us and the K'Vin homeworld. Neither possibility is promising." He nodded toward another bank of instruments. "Geordi, go to those controls and do exactly as I say."

Chapter Twenty

PARTICLES OF DUST that had drifted lazily through space for countless aeons now collided in their mad rush to fill the deep rent in the fabric of space. They were joined by asteroids and odd bits of debris, a thickening cloud of matter pulled from the Sydon solar system. And here and there along the perimeter of the vortex, the ships of many worlds—Xanthricite, Randrisian, Andor—were buffeted by the incoming stream. Mired in the sucking pool, they struggled to escape.

Some failed.

The Ariantu ships had also fallen victim to their ancestors' machinery. Tail first, the entire paac was being dragged closer and closer to the widening maw of the wormhole. Baruk's ship was the first of the fighters to be whisked away.

Arikka stared at the swirling vortex that filled the viewscreen of the heartship. Ariantu technology had built the mechanisms that created the wormhole; Ariantu equipment could sense its presence.

"The Howling God lives!"

"Of course, Mother," said Teroon. "We've heard the legend of its creation all our lives."

"Yes, but I thought it was a lie the High Paacs used to scare gullible farmers into submission."

It had certainly scared her paac. The cabin crew was paralyzed, staring transfixed at the swirling patterns of energy. Only Teroon was calm, his fur unruffled. He began to recite in a soft voice: "The Old Ones could mold the universe to their will. They used the threat of that power to defend their empire. The price would be the destruction of Kirlos, but the planet was made for that very purpose."

Words from the half-forgotten narrative resurfaced in Arikka's mind. She continued the tale. "But the Ariantu artisans grew too fond of their crafted world, and when the K'Vin rose against them, they could not bring themselves to destroy the planet after all."

The crew of the heartship tensed as a second ship of the fleet was pulled to the lip of the maelstrom. It struggled to escape, jerking and twisting as if in pain, then vanished within the turbulent cloud.

"We are doomed," whispered Arikka. She had the courage to fight the K'Vin, but there was no way to fight this curse of her ancestors.

"It is only a tunnel, Mother," said Teroon. "A tunnel through space. And until Kirlos is sucked through, we can travel safely to the other side."

She almost dismissed his words as madness until she remembered that he had distant kin connections to one of the lesser High Paacs. For the first time in her long life she glimpsed the nature of true nobility: Teroon had not only heard the old legends; he had understood them.

"Where does it lead, this tunnel?"

Her shipmaster bared his teeth. "To the K'Vin homeworld."

"Ahh!"

She wondered if he was telling the truth. Or if, in fact, any living Ariantu knew the truth of the Howling God after five thousand years. Perhaps the answer was unimportant. Rather tha wait for death, Arikka would leap forward to meet it with a drawn dagger.

"Heartmaster, prepare to jump."

Geordi worked as quickly as he could, following Data's instructions. The android was giving it everything he had as he decoded computer commands, tried to disarm systems and drop down energy levels.

Thul had had two pieces of remarkable and somewhat questionable luck. The first was that he had been able to activate the doomsday weapon in the first place. Geordi was chalking that off to the concept that the entire doomsday system was on a hair trigger anyway.

The second bit of Thul's luck, Geordi remarked to himself, was that he was not already dead. Worf had even grumbled that if they were all going to die, Thul should go first—though that had no doubt been another example of Klingon humor.

Data stopped.

"What's wrong?" Geordi shouted, for the sounds of impending destruction were becoming louder and louder.

"The computer is rejecting my shutdown code," said Data. "I will have to find alternatives. Also, we cannot just recalibrate the guidance system, we have to eliminate it entirely. Otherwise we will simply be hurled somewhere else."

"Data, how long is it going to take?" demanded Geordi.

Data started to work faster. On the screen the *Enterprise* was losing what might be her final battle. Both the starship and the K'Vin ship were being dragged closer and closer to the wormhole.

"How long?" Geordi said.

"I am not sure," said Data.

Geordi felt as if the floor had been yanked out from under him. "Not *sure!* How long has the *Enterprise* got?"

Data glanced at the rate of progression of the wormhole. "Two minutes, thirty-four seconds."

Geordi mouthed it, but couldn't say it.

Data's hands moved quickly as he desperately searched for a solution. He scanned the glyphs, ran a million combinations in a second.

"Will you make it?" pressed Worf.

"I do not know," said Data again. "It will be three minutes, perhaps four until I can stop it."

"That's too long!" cried Geordi.

Data never slowed. "Perhaps it will take less time. I cannot be certain."

"You have to be certain, or everyone on the ship is going to die—and maybe us too!"

"I am working on it."

"Data!"

Time ticked past.

Geordi was at Data's side, doing as he was instructed, obeying the android's clipped directions, but things weren't slowing down. Energy levels were building.

"It is still not accepting the matching codes," said Data, his voice inhumanly calm. "I know it is an eighteen-glyph sequential based in—"

"Data!"

On the screen the *Enterprise* seemed to be distorting, the nacelles stretching, the saucer section distending. It was slipping backwards as gravity sucked it into the wormhole. Geordi could hear the screams of his friends in his head. *"Data! Are we going to make it, yes or no?"*

Data looked up, saw the starship's peril, felt the planet rumbling, saw the energy buildup. He might make it, he realized. The whole system would shut down immediately if he could just find the right code. He might make it.

He might not.

The *Enterprise* started to spin toward the wormhole, the K'Vin ship right behind it. Only seconds remained.

And from behind Data a low voice rumbled, "Permission to do something, sir."

He might make it still, Data thought. But he might not.

What could Worf do? Well, certainly the answer was obvious. And if Data was wrong, if Worf was wrong, they would all die. If Data waited and solved the riddle himself, they might still make it.

Or they might not.

Time.

No time. Out of time.

Now, Data's mind demanded, decide *now*.

All of that took less than a second to process. Seemingly without an instant's hesitation, he turned to Worf.

"Make it so," he said.

Worf raised his phaser and fired.

The beam struck the instrument banks on the far left. Worf kept firing and swept his phaser along, the beam slicing through the equipment. Geordi and Data hit the floor, and Worf kept going. From everywhere sparks flew as circuitry bubbled and hissed, metal melted, and explosions erupted from deep within the machinery.

Worf completed the arc on one side, dropped to one knee, spun, and started on the other side. The screens blew out, as did the gleaming black control panels. The glyphs disappeared in the eruptions, never to be translated. The computer banks cracked apart, and from all around them came one detonation after another, like a string of firecrackers, only far more ear-shattering.

Thul was screaming, but his screams were drowned out by explosions and phaser fire. Then Worf dropped to the floor, too, as panels leaped across the room, propelled by concussive force. Flames licked out of the cracks, and acrid stinging smoke filled the air. All around them was chaos and calamity; the end of the world was at hand, there to be touched and feared.

The eruption of the computers continued for what seemed forever but in actuality was only seconds, seconds filled with fear and hope and prayer and a certainty that these were their last moments and damn, what a stupid way to die—as part of a dooms-day weapon from a long-ago conflict.

And then, one by one, the explosions died down, and soon there was nothing but the heavy-hanging smoke.

The ground had stopped rumbling.

Slowly, amid much coughing, Geordi sat up, as did Data. Thul was still trembling, but they ignored him. Their faces were streaked with grime and ashes.

"Worf?" whispered Geordi. "You there?"

There was a loud cough and then "Yes."

They all sat there in silence as the smoke slowly dissipated. Worf was seated nearby, his face also covered with ashes.

He was glaring balefully at Data.

"Good work, Lieutenant," said Data hopefully.

Worf made no reply. Instead, he got to his feet and started to dust himself off.

"Data," said Geordi, "now that you've had your first real command . . . did you learn anything from it?"

Data considered the question. "I believe I have learned that command is far more difficult than I thought it to be. And you, Geordi?"

Geordi shrugged. "I learned that I need to try to keep cooler in high-pressure situations . . . and maybe find a way to keep my VISOR on tighter."

"I have learned something," said Worf.

The two of them looked at him in surprise.

"I have learned," said the Klingon, "that if I had been allowed to shoot things when I wanted to shoot them in the first place, we would have had significantly fewer problems." And with that, he turned on his heel and headed for the turbolift.

Chapter Twenty-one

THE HEARTSHIP'S PLUNGE into the mouth of the Howling God had electrified the remaining Ariantu. Pulses racing, tails curling, they cried out in unison as they watched the ship disappear from view. Their paac mother's action was worthy of a heroic saga, one that would be recounted for generations to come.

Yet there would have to be survivors if the tale was to be told. Perhaps that concern explained the hesitation of her children in following Arikka's lead. Despite an upswelling of pride at her courage, the shipmasters still strained their engines to stay out of the vortex.

Then the wormhole collapsed.

Light and energy spewed outward, squeezed from the depths of the hole. Objects caught in the swirling currents of gravity waves were pulverized by opposing forces. Just as abruptly as it had formed, the cosmic disruption subsided. In the calm that followed, a different motion began.

Of the twelve ships that had left Ariant months before, only seven remained. Despite their dwindling numbers, those seven were still hunters. The paac members did not waste any time in mewling their relief at the Howling God's departure; they immediately cast about for worthy prey.

The fighters did not need to travel far. The ancient weapon of their ancestors had saved them the trouble by snaring a Federation starship. Anxious to erase any impression of cowardice that might linger in the minds of their close-lying enemy, the fleet closed in on the starship called *Enterprise*.

Life support had been the last system to lose power to the demands of engineering. Warmth lingered, trapped by the insulating layers of the hull, but the air grew thick very quickly. The lack of oxygen had already begun to dull his mind when Picard heard the whine of the engines fade into silence. He felt himself pushed back into his chair by the forward acceleration.

At last. It's come. And he braced himself for the crushing well of gravity that waited for the *Enterprise* in the depths of the wormhole.

The glide continued.

Picard's labored breathing grew easier; his head cleared. All around him, lights were flashing with greater speed and intensity. The soft chatter of computers grew louder.

"Status report," he demanded with a hoarse cough. Amid the welter of voices the captain picked out one reply in particular.

"It's gone!" said Dean incredulously. "The wormhole has closed completely."

"We're drifting at subwarp," Riker called out from

the aft deck. "Engines are dead; power reserves are almost depleted, but recharging. Sensors will be back on line in three minutes." He took a deep breath, filling his lungs with fresh air. "Damn, but that was close."

"Agreed, Number One." Picard looked to the viewscreen, which had regained its former luminance. The K'Vin warship was still in view. It, too, was drifting in space, but lights were beginning to flicker across its hull. So they had both survived after all.

A shadow whisked across the screen.

"Raise shields!" he yelled instinctively, but it was too late. The deck rocked under the impact of a phaser blast.

Seconds later, red alert sirens sounded and the newly restored lights blinked wildly as power was diverted to the defense systems. A second phaser blast was blunted by the shields, but the *Enterprise* trembled at the blow. The fighter ships that were crisscrossing the viewscreen were no match for a starship— under normal circumstances. They had chosen their moment well and caught the ship when it was most vulnerable.

"Do we have phasers yet?" demanded Picard.

"Power levels are too low," replied Riker. "We can't fight back without losing shields. And each time they hit us, the defense systems drain our new reserves."

Another blow rocked the ship.

"Aft shield weakening, Captain," said Burke, frowning at the readings on his console. "Emergency power diversion can't compensate without affecting life support systems."

Out of the corner of his eye, Picard saw new movement on the viewscreen. The K'Vin ship had moved much closer. The red glow of its shields was dimmed, but the photon torpedo it launched from its hull was all too bright.

"Dammit, we saved their lives!" cried Riker angrily. "We should have let them—"

The detonation of the torpedo bathed the bridge with a searing white light. And reduced the number of fighters by one. The others scattered, abandoning their attack on the *Enterprise.*

"You seem to have misjudged the K'Vin," said Picard with a smile. Though, for a moment, he, too, had assumed the warship was aiming at his ship.

"Captain," said Burke. "We're receiving a message from Captain Shagrat of the K'Vin *Throatripper.*"

"Courage, Captain Picard! Together we will bring death to the Ariantu!"

"The Ariantu?" asked Picard, bewildered by the reference to that ancient culture. Then the pieces of the puzzle finally fell into place. "But of course!"

"I recognize the ships of those bloodsucking vermin! They haven't changed their design in five thousand years. The disturbance on Kirlos is sure to be some of their mischief-making."

Shagrat's crew fired another torpedo blast and vaporized an Ariantu fighter that had ventured too close to their warship. The viewscreen tracked the movements of the remainder of the fleet; they were approaching the *Enterprise* again. Picard wondered if they were so foolish, or suicidal, as to keep fighting.

"Captain, we're being hailed by the Ariantu."

"So," said Picard. "Now that they're overpowered, they've decided surrender is the better part of valor."

"I am Lektor, paac leader of the Ariantu!"

To Picard's human ears the voice sounded arrogant, but he tried to dispel that impression and listen impartially.

247

"Kirlos belongs to the Ariantu," Lektor continued, "and we invoke our rights as an indigenous people to resist colonization. We demand Federation protectorate status and your immediate assistance in defending ourselves from the K'Vin Hegemony's imperialism."

"What! You've just attacked my ship and yet—"

"That is of no importance," said Lektor. And this time Picard had no doubt of the arrogance behind the words. "You must honor our request for aid; that is Federation policy."

The *Throatripper* unleashed a third photon torpedo, which rocked the *Enterprise* with its close passage, grazing the shields and ultimately missing its fighter target. Seconds later, the K'Vin reopened communications.

"My apologies, Captain Picard. My weapons officer is overeager to make another kill. He has been reprimanded."

"Thank you, Captain Shagrat," said Picard, careful to keep any sign of anger out of his voice. "Your *continued* restraint is greatly appreciated."

"Captain, we're being hailed by another of the—"

"This is Matat, paac mother of the Ariantu! I have heard the claims of the impostor known as Lektor. He is a male and has no standing in our family. Ignore him. All negotiations for a protectorate status will be directed to my heartship—"

Communications were briefly disrupted by the exchange of phaser fire between two of the Ariantu ships. Then Matat's voice resumed, though with greater static interference.

"And I demand that the traitor Lektor be taken into Federation custody!"

"Incoming call, Captain."

"Let me guess," sighed Picard. "Lektor requests a rebuttal."

"This is Keriat, true paac leader of the Ariantu! I demand—"

Picard ordered an end to the communications with a throat-cutting motion. Silence settled over the bridge as he took his place at the captain's chair. He tugged the hem of his tunic into place.

"Hail the Federation embassy on Kirlos. I believe this matter is better left to Ambassador Stephaleh."

The world had not ended. Stephaleh looked out her window and watched people scurrying in the streets —not in panic, as before, but in ecstasy that their lives had somehow been spared.

It seemed that the Starfleet officers had saved an entire world—though Stephaleh had no idea how. Of course, they were still far from safe. The Ariantu were still hovering overhead, ready to unleash who knew what else on them.

Nor would the invaders agree to speak with her, any more than they had before the crisis. Communications with them were absolutely dead.

However, she could use this time wisely—to restore some order to her half of Kirlosia. Focusing on that purpose, she turned to address Zamorh—and noted his absence again with a sharp pang.

When was it that he had disappeared? She still couldn't put her finger on it. But it had to have been before the *Enterprise* trio informed her that Zamorh had been conspiring with Gregach's aide and that he'd been involved in the attack that led to their imprisonment.

Of course the accusation had faded in the flurry of events that followed—the appearance of the Ariantu, the onset of the world-threatening tremors. Nor was this the first time she had turned, out of habit, to give

Zamorh some order—only to realize he was nowhere to be found.

With a shrug, she touched a plate on her desk.

"Chief Powell, this is the ambassador. What is our situation out there?"

Seconds passed before Powell's deep voice came on, with a great deal of noise in the background. "For the moment, everyone seems relieved—*very* relieved. And the bars have just reopened, so that'll keep them busy for a while. But it's only a matter of time before they remember those ships up there, and the panic starts all over again."

Stephaleh sighed softly. "Have you seen Zamorh?"

"No, Ambassador, I haven't. Come to think of it, I haven't seen any of the Sullurh in quite some time. Not in the embassy, not in the streets . . ."

How strange, she thought. No Sullurh to be seen anywhere. Then she recalled how the Starfleet officers had been taken—by a group of Sullurh. At the time, she'd dismissed it as the action of a radical faction. But if *all* the Sullurh seemed now to have vanished . . .

The magnitude of it was like a physical blow to her.

"Chief, I want the streets cleared so I can make an announcement in, say, thirty minutes. But in the meantime, I want you to watch out for the Sullurh. If you find any, bring them here to me." She had to pause; the words just didn't sound right, even now. "I have reason to believe that they may be behind some of what's happening to us. Don't ask me how—just watch out for them, all right?"

The silence on the other end told her that Powell was having a hard time believing it, too. "Well," he said at last, "if you say so, Ambassador."

"Thirty minutes, Chief."

"Thirty minutes," agreed the human.

Stephaleh sat back in her chair. What to do next? If her suspicions were correct . . .

Suddenly, surprising herself, she opened a channel to the K'Vin embassy. With unexpected speed, she was relayed through to Gregach, who seemed to be busy putting disks back on a shelf. He hadn't noticed yet that his screen was active.

"Ambassador Gregach," she said.

He turned at the sound of her voice, swallowed whatever shock he felt at the intrusion. "You are well," he observed. "That is good."

"Yes," she said. "I am well. And you?"

He shrugged. "My office was rearranged by the tremors, as you can see. But nothing worse." He restored the last of an armful of disks to their proper places on the shelf. "I gather Worf and the others had some hand in circumventing our destruction."

"So it would seem." She resisted the temptation to remind him that if he'd had his way, the trio would still have been incarcerated and Kirlosia might have become rubble by now. "But I have called you for a reason."

He scowled, nodded. "I know. The Sullurh."

The remark set her back a bit. "You've come to the same conclusion, then?"

"Yes. Gezor has been gone since the tremors started. In fact, all my Sullurh are gone. And Ilugh tells me there are no Sullurh on the streets, either. When I couple those two facts with Worf's accusation . . ." He shook his head. "Obviously there is a connection between the Sullurh and . . . what? The tremors or the arrival of the Ariantu? Or both?"

"Good questions," remarked the Andorian. She was pleased to be exchanging civil and productive

251

words again with her old friend. There was still a stiffness to the conversation, but it was progress— more than she had expected, at any rate.

"I have instructed Ilugh to bring in any Sullurh he finds," said Gregach. "Perhaps you should do the same."

"I already have," noted Stephaleh.

For a moment they were forced to acknowledge their respect for each other. *Great minds think alike,* she observed—but only to herself.

"Feel free to call again if you have any information you think might be valuable," said the K'Vin. "I will do likewise."

"Agreed," said Stephaleh. Then she terminated the contact.

It was a pity about her relationship with Gregach. More than a pity. But she couldn't allow herself to dwell on it. Ordering her thoughts, she began to mentally compose the message that she hoped would maintain calm among the citizenry and reestablish her authority at the same time.

She made sure that the *Enterprise* officers would get the credit they deserved for having saved Kirlos. Far too many suspicions had been cast on them—all unfairly.

She had finished no more than a couple of sentences, however, when her communicator beeped and a light flashed red. Recognizing what that meant, she combed back a stray lock of hair that had fallen out of place and prepared herself.

Picard's countenance appeared on her monitor. "Greetings, Ambassador."

"Greetings yourself," she told him. "I have been trying to contact you for some time."

"How are my people—the ones you borrowed?"

252

"I had hoped to hear from them by now," she said, "but you will be glad to know that it was they who closed the wormhole—and kept Kirlos from being destroyed." And she went on to tell him the details. "You should be proud of them, Captain."

Picard nodded. "Yes. I'll tell them when I see them—which I trust will be soon."

"In the meantime," said Stephaleh, "what's the situation up there?"

"Educational, Ambassador. To say the least. Do you have any idea with whom we are dealing?"

"Yes," she answered. "The Ariantu."

That took the wind out of his sails a little, but he recovered nicely. "Of course," he said. "You would know that. You have no doubt been in communication with them."

"But not lately," she told him. "They won't respond to my hails."

Picard grunted. "They seem only too happy to communicate with *me,* on the other hand. It appears that three of the Ariantu vessels, including that of their leader, were swallowed up by the wormhole effect. And each of the surviving ships is now claiming leadership of the paac. Furthermore," he related, a little wearily, it seemed to the ambassador, "each also insists that Kirlos still belongs to the Ariantu, and that we must evacuate our own people immediately."

"They have been insisting on our evacuation since they arrived," said Stephaleh. "But the rest is very interesting. It seems that the prospects for our survival have improved dramatically. Along with our bargaining position."

Picard shrugged. "Well, there are fewer Ariantu to deal with, if that's what you mean. But I would not discount them as a threat. What's more, the presence

253

of the K'Vin warship is complicating matters. As you know, the K'Vin and the ancient Ariantu had a blood feud that lasted for some time—and neither side is willing to let it go, even now."

"A fine mess," she commented, seeing what was coming.

"And one that cries out for your expertise, Ambassador."

Aha! I thought so.

"The Ariantu have not been eager to listen to me up until now," she told him. "Why would they change their minds?"

"If I indicate that you are the appropriate authority," said the captain, "I am sure they can be convinced."

Stephaleh nodded. "Very well. I accept the responsibility."

"Thank you," said Picard. "I will inform all parties involved. Picard out."

The Andorian took a deep breath, let it out. She placed her hands flat on the desk before her, took a moment to notice the increased number of lines and wrinkles that had formed in the past few months. Or was it days?

The Ariantu. Yes, indeed, the Ariantu.

She wanted very much to do this well. After all, it was the end of her career, and people were always remembered for what they did at the end, not at the beginning.

Stephaleh would have felt better if she'd had some idea how the Sullurh were connected to all that had happened. For more and more, it appeared that there *was* a connection. After all, the tremors had begun soon after the appearance of the Ariantu, and the Sullurh had vanished soon after that. How could there not be a connection?

254

Suddenly the need to find a Sullurh to provide an explanation loomed larger than ever.

Thul entered the house where his sister lived, followed by the three Starfleet officers. It was dark inside, but they could see well enough to notice that the furniture was in disarray.

"Little bit of a mess here," commented Geordi. Data and Worf were silent, but their expressions reflected the same sentiment.

Thul admitted to himself that his actions had caused much damage and strife. Grief filled him; he knew he had to cleanse his soul before he entered the afterlife. As he had told the *Enterprise* officers, he would do his best to set everything right again in Kirlosia—with the help of the other Sullurh.

On the way up to the city level, Thul had explained to Geordi how this house had been chosen for a meeting place in times of trouble. It was likely that Gezor and Zamorh, among others, would be here.

Worf watched every move Thul made; he was more than ready to use his phaser to keep the Sullurh in line. His patience had grown thin throughout the wormhole incident, and only the satisfaction of being proved right earlier had kept his mood from darkening. He disliked the Sullurh. He wanted to be done with the mission and return to the *Enterprise.*

"My friends, it is Thul. Are you here?" His voice sounded weak, and Data boosted his sensors to detect movement or sound. In moments he noted people coming from some back room. A crowd of ten Sullurh moved forward. There was a young girl, some women, one of whom was pregnant, and several men, including Gezor and Zamorh.

"Why have you brought them here, Master Thul?" demanded Gezor. Everyone seemed to cower a bit behind the brash Sullurh. His natural instincts were to be efficient but bellicose, and people were more than happy to let him lead.

"Because the time for hiding has ended. Our Ariantu brethren have abandoned us; we must make a stand for what we are and what we want. They have declared us unfit, and we must now make our own way. These representatives of the Federation saved our world, and we—no, *I*—owe it to them to make amends for what we have done."

Thul looked around. His people looked back with mixed emotions.

"Did you really go under the ground, Master Thul?" the little girl asked.

"Yes, Glora. And I unleashed a horrible weapon. The one that this world was designed to be."

"Then the legend was true," Thul's sister said slowly. The truth of those words spread among the group and they began chattering quietly among themselves.

"Silence!" cried out Worf. Suddenly, the group became quiet.

Data stepped forward and said, "We must understand who the Sullurh really are and what your connection is with the Ariantu. Only then can we begin to investigate the options available."

Zamorh glanced at Gezor, whose look was stern and hard, betraying no emotion. Apparently Gregach's aide wanted no part of the off-worlders, nor did he feel like helping Thul redeem himself.

But Zamorh felt otherwise. "You can hold your own counsel," he told Gezor. "I believe we have done enough damage to ourselves and our world. If the Federation officers can help, we should allow them to do so. I say speak, Master Thul."

Thul nodded his gratitude. Then he turned back to

the trio from the *Enterprise.* "The best place to begin," he said, "is no doubt at the beginning. With the departure of the Ariantu."

And he went on to tell how the ancient Ariantu Empire had collapsed of its own weight, having gone too far too quickly. Of how only a few—the forebears of the Sullurh—had stayed behind to serve as caretakers, until the empire could grow strong again and reclaim them.

"Originally," Thul said, "the stewardship was to have lasted only a short time. But years became decades, and decades became centuries, and centuries became millennia. During that time, we changed— partly by accident and partly by design, because we knew that it was only a matter of time before the K'Vin would reach out for Kirlos. And when they did, we did not wish to be recognizable as the descendants of their age-old enemies."

Finally, Thul told them, the K'Vin *did* come. "And other races came, too. They accepted us as Sullurh, never dreaming that our heritage was so glorious. Long before Kirlosia became divided, we were seen as a trustworthy and hardworking if humble people, quite suitable for employment in the embassies. Nor was it difficult for us to obtain high-ranking posts, ultimately as aides to the ambassadors themselves.

"But all our efforts were in preparation for the Return. Somewhere, we trusted, the Ariantu were still alive as a race, making ready to take back this planet that had once been theirs." Thul shook his head. "Suddenly our prayers were answered. Four came among us and renewed our sense of purpose. They were Ariantu—*true* Ariantu, like gods! They gave us a chance to reclaim our heritage, and we seized it as those who are starving might seize at a crust of bread."

Thul looked at his people, watching for nods or reactions. The little girl, Glora, listened intently. There was a smile on her face. His sister merely nodded, having heard all this before from Thul during private moments, before the troubles began.

"When Lektor told us it was time to retake Kirlos from the alien squatters, we agreed. Gezor and Zamorh and I helped him escalate the enmity between the Federation and the K'Vin Hegemony." He looked at the *Enterprise* officers again. "Then, with you three, I found the legendary omega level. I knew it immediately for what it was—the core of our beliefs, the reason Kirlos was so important to the ancient Ariantu. What I didn't know was just how horrible finding it would be—how it would push our entire world down a road to its own destruction."

Thul had to stop and collect himself. There were just too many emotions, too much remorse. It all threatened to overwhelm him.

- Then he went on—about the appearance of the Ariantu ships and how the Sullurh were eventually rejected by Lektor and the others, how they were deemed *inferior,* much to Thul's shame, and finally, how he had unwittingly set the doomsday machine in motion.

"However," Data interjected, "the doomsday device has been incapacitated. It is possible to establish a new beginning for yourselves. And the first step is to take this information to ambassadors Stephaleh and Gregach. To explain this to *them.*"

"No!" cried Gezor, trembling with anger—and with fear as well? "I will not face Federation charges of conspiracy and be jailed! I will not be taken from my family and lose everything dear to me!"

Thul walked slowly to the shaking Sullurh and took

him in his arms. "Gezor," he said, "look at me. I have acted as a conscience for our people, acted in what I perceived to be the true Ariantu way. What I have learned is that time has passed; things have changed. We have committed crimes—perhaps terrible crimes. But we must face the consequences with honor, with the nobility that the spacegoing Ariantu have lost. We must go back to the embassies and settle this once and for all."

Thul's words were gentle and reassuring, and they had the desired effect. They brought out the courage, the sense of responsibility in his fellow Sullurh.

"And now," he said, "we must go. Gezor and Zamorh and I." Like a true leader, Thul walked out of the room, expecting the others to follow.

Data held Worf and Geordi back until Gezor and Zamorh finally moved. Then the trio filed out behind them.

Thul led the group out of the house and down the street to the nearest transmat booth. On the way, Geordi asked Data what he now thought of Thul.

"He is obviously a spiritual leader to these people," said the android. "I did not suspect this. Did you?"

"No. In fact, this keeps getting weirder and weirder," Geordi replied. The group had arrived at the transmat station and Thul was programming in coordinates.

"Weirder? Please define the use here."

"Well, everything seems to be one thing and then, *pow*—it's something else. It's been happening from the minute we beamed down here."

"Ah. For me, this is not unusual. I am constantly revising my expectations as I observe humans on the *Enterprise.*"

"So nothing has surprised you on Kirlos?"

"Not true," Data replied. "As I said, Thul has surprised me, as did the wormhole device. And one more thing."

"What's that?" Geordi asked, as they stepped up onto the platform.

"That Lieutenant Worf had a better instinct for dealing with matters here than I originally credited him with. I will remember this the next time I command an away-team mission."

As the transmat machine began its process, Worf was heard to mutter, "Next time, I will send Keenan."

Chapter Twenty-two

"THAT IS CORRECT, CAPTAIN," said Data. "But the proceedings are about to begin. I can tell you more about it later."

"Very well, Data." The captain's voice was clear and calm as it came over the communicator, despite the potentially explosive situation he found himself observing. "But keep me posted, will you?"

"Aye, sir."

Just then the ambassadors reentered the room.

As she and Gregach came in, all eyes rose to meet them. There were six at the table—the three officers from the *Enterprise* along with Thul, Zamorh, and Gezor.

Stephaleh avoided Zamorh's gaze. On a personal level, she would never forgive the Sullurh for the deaths he'd helped cause or for the way in which he'd played her for a fool.

On an official level, however, she'd had to put all that aside. Neither Zamorh nor his people were subject to Federation jurisdiction, so their actions were technically closer to guerrilla warfare than to prosecutable crimes. And now that they'd made public their claim to self-determination, she could hardly let her own feelings get in the way of a just and workable settlement.

Gregach had agreed on this principle, though he seemed to have more difficulty adhering to it. Right now he was glaring at Gezor as if he would have liked to string the Sullurh up by his thumbs.

They took their seats at one end of the table, facing Thul. "We have come to a decision," she said. "Actually, more than one. And some recommendations as well."

"First," said Gregach, "the Sullurh claim to Kirlos appears to be authentic. At least we have discovered no shred of evidence to the contrary."

"Therefore," said Stephaleh, "under Federation law, the Sullurh must be granted the right of self-determination. It is their planet; they may do as they wish with it. And if they decide that everyone else is to leave, the Federation will comply."

Gregach grunted. "The K'Vin Hegemony has no law governing a situation such as this one. We recognize no right of self-rule; otherwise, we would be kept from conquest, which is our life's blood." He spread his heavy gray hands. "However, we do not feel *compelled* to conquer or to maintain dominion over any given place. Until the present time, Kirlos has had value to us. It has been a profitable operation, what with all the trade going on. But now that they know what Kirlos is, and the dangers posed by the Ariantu, K'Vin-side merchants are abandoning our markets in droves—so we no longer have a reason to stay here."

"Of course," said Stephaleh, "the Ariantu are now

262

in orbit around Kirlos and they have a competing claim. And there is a certain legitimacy to it. However, two facts dilute their claim: first, and by far the more important, their forebears left this world while yours remained, and possession, as someone once said—someone human, I believe—is nine-tenths of the law; the second fact is that the Ariantu are incapable of governing Kirlos. Divided as they are, they would likely destroy this world and themselves along with it, whereas the indigenous population could carry on in a more peaceful manner."

"In short," said Gregach, "Kirlos is yours—if you want it. However, we suggest that you allow the Hegemony and the Federation to aid you in smoothing the transition to Sullurh rule.

"To be sure, we have selfish reasons for wanting to do this. We of the K'Vin Hegemony do not care to have a weapon at our throats, and Kirlos will continue to be a weapon until all its doomsday machinery has been dismantled to our satisfaction. In the case of the Federation . . . well, perhaps they wish to keep a close eye on the K'Vin for a little longer."

"But the greatest benefit in an orderly transition," interjected Stephaleh, "will be to the Sullurh. Because when the Ariantu learn of our decision, they will not be pleased. And the Sullurh may need some help in defending this planet—at least, for a number of years."

"So the plan is *this*," Gregach continued. "For five years, Kirlos will remain under the joint protection of the Hegemony and the Federation. After that, the Sullurh may tell us all to go back where we came from."

"One more thing," said the Andorian. "On the Federation side, and possibly on the K'Vin side as well, there are those who've spent most of their lives on Kirlos. They've made homes here; their children have grown up here. You may wish to consider allowing them to remain, but you don't *have* to." She paused, remembering her promise to Lars Trimble. "In your place, I would let them stay."

Then there was silence. Thul traded glances with Gezor and Zamorh. He must have found agreement there, for a few moments later he nodded to the ambassadors. "How can we say no? To any of it? Your decision is eminently fair. And more generous, perhaps, than we deserve."

"We also have a suggestion as to how your new government may be set up," added Gregach, "though, once again, you may do as you like. It seems logical that Thul be named governor, with Zamorh as minister of internal affairs and Gezor as minister of external affairs. Ambassador Stephaleh and I have had much time and opportunity to observe our former aides; we feel that their respective strengths can best be put to use in these positions."

Thul and Zamorh appeared to accept the recommendation. Gezor, on the other hand, looked a little skeptical—as Gregach had anticipated. But he didn't refuse, and Stephaleh took that as a sign that the meeting could be brought to a close.

Now all I have to do, she told herself, *is inform the Ariantu. . . .*

Her aides—the non-Sullurh ones, of course—had set it all up for her. An eight-screen monitor system, through which she could speak with each Ariantu pretender to paac leadership and at the same time maintain a separate tie to Picard on the *Enterprise.*

Gregach had understood when she asked him not to

attend this session. Without question, his presence would only have made a bad situation worse.

However, Thul stood on her right, representing the Sullurh. After all, if they were going to accept responsibility for Kirlos, their leadership had to start here and now.

And in the background, there were the three Starfleet officers. For "moral support," as La Forge had put it.

"Ariantu," she began. "We have weighed your claim against that of your on-planet brethren. And we have decided that the Sullurh have a greater right to govern here."

"No," said the one called Matat, her features twisting savagely on the viewscreen. "They are *nothing*—certainly not *Ariantu*."

"Nonetheless," said Stephaleh, "they are *here,* and they have *been* here for millennia. You can't just come back and shove them aside."

"We will not stand for this," said another—Keriat, if she recalled correctly. "We reject your decision."

"We?" echoed the ambassador. "Then which of you will rule Kirlos?"

The question was followed by a flurry of answers—one from each of the seven screens devoted to the Ariantu. She waited until the commotion died down.

"You see?" she said at last. "If there is no *we,* how can you make a claim, legitimate or otherwise? I suggest that you all go home and reconcile your own differences. Then perhaps you will someday want to return to Kirlos and file a more peaceful claim—with the Sullurh government.

"But be certain that your return is *peaceful,* my friends. Because the Federation and the K'Vin Hegemony will both be watching over this world. And we

265

have more ships at our disposal than the two you see before you now."

That set off another spate of curses and threats. But the threats were empty ones. Obviously each ship's leader knew the weakness of his or her position. Without a single leader, they couldn't hope to accomplish anything.

The only contingency Kirlos had to fear was irrational behavior. If one of the Ariantu decided to launch a suicide attack just for the hell of it . . .

One by one, they broke communication, until only a single visage remained. It belonged to the one called Lektor.

He looked at Thul. "I will be back," he said. And somehow it seemed more of a promise than a threat.

Then he vanished like the rest of them.

"Well executed, Ambassador," said Picard. He paused, turned to someone offscreen for a moment. When he turned back, he was smiling a restrained but satisfied smile. "I am told that the Ariantu are retreating. It seems that we need not worry about them—at least for a while."

She shrugged. "I have a feeling they won't come back, peacefully or otherwise. Kirlos was important to them for its mystery, its allure. I think those qualities have been stripped from it by now."

"Yes," agreed Picard. "And good riddance."

Finally they were alone. The Sullurh had gone back to their homes; the *Enterprise* officers had remained in conference with their captain.

Gregach sat and stared into his drink. Somehow, Stephaleh decided, he seemed younger than her image of him. More vital.

Had some good come of all this after all? she wondered.

"You know," he said, "my government will no longer allow me to stay on Kirlos."

She nodded. "I know. Not enough for a full-time ambassador to do here, now that the Sullurh will be taking over the administrative duties. And where do you think you'll go next?"

He shrugged. "I'm not sure. I would like to think this has worked out well enough for me to be allowed to *pick* my world. If so, it will be the frontier for me." He paused. "And you?"

She smiled. "Back to Andor. Oh, I suppose I'll stay here for a little while to make sure all the pieces fit right. Then I'll retire—go home and see my family again. Discover if my children will still talk to the mother who abandoned them for a career among the stars."

"It was a *good* career," said Gregach. "And it ended on a high note."

Her smile broadened. "Thank you, Ambassador. I hope they see it that way as well."

"You Andorians are an odd lot, I will say that." He snorted and took a sip from his glass, then ran his tongue over his tusk to lap up a stray drop.

"No odder than you K'Vin." She rubbed her hands together to work out some kinks that had forced them to curl up. "Will our societies ever see eye to eye, do you think?"

"No, my dear. And I will tell you why. The K'Vin believe in taking action; Federation members think too much. We'll just have to be satisfied with agreeing *not* to see eye to eye—and hope that we'll never come to blows over it."

"Well said, my friend." Stephaleh regarded him. "I will miss you, Ambassador."

He leaned a bit closer. "And I *you*, Ambassador."

A comfortable silence.

267

"I have but one request," said the K'Vin.

"Which is?"

"In what little time we have left, allow me the chance to win at least *one* game of dyson."

She laughed. "You may try, Gregach. You may try."

Chapter Twenty-three

BURKE LOOKED UP from his tactical console. "Commander, we are being hailed by the K'Vin embassy."

"Already? That's a pleasant change." Will Riker rose from the captain's chair and stepped to the center of the bridge. He had resigned himself to a wait of several hours before receiving a response from Kirlos, but less than an hour had passed since Ensign Burke had sent his message to the Sullurh embassy.

When the familiar features of Gezor appeared on the main viewscreen, Riker bowed politely. "Minister, I am honored by your attention to—"

"Don't call me that!" snapped Gezor, raising his gruff voice to be heard above the chorus of insistent beeps that issued from his desk monitor.

The Sullurh's curly mop of hair appeared somewhat damp and bedraggled, reminding Riker of Data's report on the malfunctioning air coolant systems. The entire infrastructure of Kirlosia had been badly shaken by the wormhole's creation; shock waves had produced the effect of a substantial earthquake, resulting in widespread mechanical breakdowns throughout the underground city.

Gezor shook a fistful of computer printouts at the first officer. "What is all this?"

"I'm simply following the established procedure for arranging the departure of our away team from Kirlos—a Petition for Personnel Departure, a Transfer of Accessory Equipment, a—"

"Yes, yes, I know what they are. I created the damned forms in the first place." Gezor scattered the papers in an attempt to wipe a trickle of sweat from his forehead. "But I don't want them. Contact the K'Vin embassy directly about these matters."

Riker shook his head. "But both the K'Vin and Federation embassy staff insist that the Sullurh embassy is now responsible for all departures from—"

"Oh, go away!" Gezor waved off an aide who edged close to his elbow and plucked anxiously at his sleeve. The administrator turned back to address Riker. "And as for you, Commander, never mind any of the petitions. I'm far too busy to fool with all that nonsense. If you'll just leave me alone, you can take the team off-planet whenever you please."

"Thank you," said Riker, bowing to show his appreciation of the gesture. "And many cool days to you and yours, Minister Gezor."

The viewscreen went black.

"Sorry, sir," said Burke as he examined the readout from the communications console. Was that a note of satisfaction in his voice? "We seem to have lost contact with the embassy. I will try to reestablish the link."

"That won't be necessary, Lieutenant," said Riker. "I wouldn't want to distract the minister from his new duties. He's a busy man." His grin grew wider and wider as he contemplated the blank viewscreen. "Oh, yes, a *very* busy man."

"And one final item," said Beverly Crusher as she ran a finger down the list on the data padd. She kept her eyes focused on the medical report as she spoke. "The last quake casualty—one Lars Trimble—was discharged from sickbay's critical care unit this morning. Since the medical facilities in Kirlosia received first reconstruction priority, the staff can handle a new influx of patients. Mr. Riker has already arranged to transport all Kirlosian patients back to the planet."

"Excellent," said Picard.

At the sound of his voice, Crusher glanced up, but the movement of the fish in the aquarium of the ready room drew her attention away from the captain's face.

"As soon as the away team has been beamed aboard, the *Enterprise* will break orbit. We should reach Tehuán in just a few days."

"Counselor Troi will be pleased to hear that," said the doctor, quickly rising from her chair. "Evidently the colonists are most anxious to return to their homes now . . . now that the threat from the Ariantu fleet has been neutralized."

Crusher was already halfway to the door of the ready room when she spun around and added, "Oh, I have a message for you from Wesley."

"Yes?"

Her brow wrinkled in thought. Finally she shook her head. "It was something about graves and a pillar of state?"

Picard looked blank for a moment, then nodded. He quickly keyed in instructions to the computer and a book appeared on the screen. Picard scrolled through the pages until he found his place. He read the passage aloud.

>"With grave aspect he rose, and in his
> rising seem'd
> A pillar of state; deep on his front engraven
> Deliberation sat and public care;
> And princely counsel in his face yet shone,
> Majestic though in ruin: sage he stood,
> With Atlantean shoulders, fit to bear
> The weight of mightiest monarchies.

"From Book Two of Milton's *Paradise Lost.*" Picard stared at the page. "It seems Ensign Crusher has not neglected his classical studies after all. But . . ."

Looking up at the doctor, he cocked one eyebrow in silent enquiry.

This time Crusher did not avert her eyes. In a quiet voice she said, "I suspect it's a sort of . . . apology. For doubting the wisdom of a starship captain."

"I see." He held her gaze for a moment longer, then cleared the computer screen. "Apology accepted."

Data never paused for breath. Once settled in a chair in the ready room, he delivered his mission report in stupefying detail without the slightest break that would provide an opportunity for a tactful interruption.

However, Picard was so pleased by the return of the away team that he listened to the narration of events on Kirlos without revealing any sign of impatience. Geordi interjected an occasional comment, but he also seemed willing to indulge the android. Worf's concession to the team leader was less enthusiastic but properly stoic for a Klingon; he stood unmoving in the background.

"Many Sullurh have already assumed key posts in the administration of the planet," concluded Data at last. "Given the large numbers of their race who were employed by the K'Vin and Federation embassies, the transfer of authority should proceed smoothly."

"Apparently Minister Gezor is not so optimistic," said Picard. He rushed on before Data could inquire further; there were limits to the captain's patience. "However, Kirlos is no longer our concern. It is time for us to move on."

"Agreed," rumbled Worf. His eyes drifted toward the doors of the ready room, then snapped back to Picard. "Sir."

The captain rose from his chair, formally signaling the end of the debriefing. "Commander Data, Lieutenant Commander La Forge, Lieutenant Worf. Well done."

Any pleasure Worf might have felt in the commendation was masked by his swift exit from the room, but the captain's praise brought smiles to the faces of the other two officers.

"Commander La Forge," called out Picard to keep the chief engineer from leaving with the android. "Geordi."

The captain walked out from behind his desk; he carried the arizite statue of the Ariantu warrior.

He held it out to Geordi. "I thought you might want to keep this, as a memento of Nassa Coleridge."

Geordi reached out slowly to touch the smooth surface. He drew back his fingers as if burned.

"Thank you, Captain. But it's . . . too cold." Picard was afraid his offering had only hurt Geordi more, reminding him of the professor's death rather than her life, but then the young man smiled. "You keep it, sir. Nassa will get a kick out of knowing it's with someone who'll appreciate it."

"Er, yes," said Picard. "I'm sure she . . . will."

He smiled back until the engineer had left the room, but once alone, Picard made a mental note to tell

Deanna Troi about Geordi's strange manner of speaking about the professor in the present tense.

In any event, he had to admit to some relief at La Forge's refusal of the gift. Despite his offer, and it had been sincere, Picard had been loath to give up the statue. It might not hold any welcome associations for Geordi; for Picard, however, it was closely linked with the passage from the arizite quarries of Tehuán to the wormhole of Kirlos. Throughout that troubled journey the marble carving had been his talisman, solid to the touch while he struggled with intangibles.

The captain walked to the far end of his couch and placed the figure on an empty side table, then stepped back to judge the effect.

Just as he had suspected: the statue fit very neatly in that spot, centered in a soft circle of light that accentuated the veins of color running through the marble. Yet, despite its polished beauty, Picard pitied the unknown Ariantu warrior frozen in eternal combat, forever leaping forward to grapple with an unseen enemy.

Picard had fought his own private battle during the last few days—and won.

Epilogue

FOR THE MOMENT, things were quiet again. Thul was alone in his house, sitting in a chair that had been undamaged by the tremors.

If he closed his eyes, if he ignored the cracked and broken things on his floor, he could almost imagine that none of it had happened. He could almost believe that Lektor had never come. That the explosions and the other incidents of terrorism had never taken place. That the Howling God mechanism had never threatened to hurl Kirlos into oblivion.

But he couldn't keep his eyes closed forever. And when he opened them, he knew it *had* happened. All of it. There was no escaping the facts—or the Sullurh's culpability for them.

They had created havoc. They had killed. They had caused misery and pain.

These things could not be erased. Maybe Federation law could not hold the Sullurh responsible for what they had done, but each individual could hold *himself* responsible.

And they *would*. He would see to that.

What had happened in this age of the Return would not be hidden behind the curtains of history. It would be remembered, passed on from generation to generation; and with each telling, the Sullurh would be redeemed a little—would grow a little wiser, perhaps.

For something like this must never happen again, he resolved. *Not in our lifetime or any lifetime to come.*

They had been given a second chance. He prayed they would use it wisely.